Trepidatio books may be ordered through booksellers or by contacting:

Trepidatio

www.trepidatio.com

or

JournalStone

www.journalstone.com

The views expressed in this work are solely those of the authors and do not necessarily reflect the views of the publisher, and the publisher hereby disclaims any responsibility for them.

ISBN: 978-1-947654-44-0 (sc)
ISBN: 978-1-947654-45-7 (ebook)

Trepidatio rev. date: November 16, 2018

Library of Congress Control Number: 2018908118

Printed in the United States of America

Cover Artwork: Daniele Serra
Interior Layout + Cover Design: Jess Landry

Edited by Jess Landry
Proofread by Scarlett R. Algee

THE
RUST
MAIDENS

To Bill, for inspiring the words

&

To Jess, for polishing the words

ONE

Pray for the Rust Maidens.
Even after all these years, those words suck the breath right out of my chest.

I shiver in the street near the old steel mill, reading and re-reading those graffiti letters on the crumbling asphalt. The red spray paint is faded now, but time hasn't erased it the way it should have.

Instead, here are my memories, waiting to greet me.

There's a rusted-out chain link fence in front of me, and past that, the industrial stacks that graze the sky. But I don't look there. My eyes won't move past these words.

Pray for the Rust Maidens.

As though all the blessings in the world would have done those girls any good.

My breath fogs around me as the December chill settles deep in my bones. Cleveland. It's the same as I left it: cold as a broken promise, and just as cruel. This is a city that remembers everything, even what's best forgotten.

I shiver in the dark, clutching my entire life in one duffel bag. I could have called my mother from the Chester Avenue Greyhound station across town when I got in, half an hour ago. But I didn't. I wanted to come here first, and I wanted to come alone. Somehow, I thought seeing this place after all these years would change something, but now that I'm here, I feel worse than before.

I turn away from the graffiti and look to what's left of the skyline. The mill is almost a mile from my parents' house. That'll be a long mile too, especially with the wind whispering its dark lies over the lake.

I pull up my jacket collar. If I stay out in the cold much longer, I'll risk pneumonia, and that won't do at all. Cleveland couldn't kill me before. I'll be damned if it murders me on my first night back.

It's not quite midnight yet, and my mother would still pick me up if I called her. I grimace at the thought. Here I stand, forty-six years old, and still needing a lift. Nothing's gotten better for me since I left. I've grown older, but no wiser.

So I start walking alone, past all the places I once knew.

The Presbyterian Church, with its pockmarked walls and missing shingles and stained glass window with a crack down the middle. I can't help but smile. After everything that congregation did to us, the decay is exactly what this church deserves.

The corner store, once open twenty-four hours, with coffee always on the burner and a little gold bell over the door to announce everyone as they came and went. The whole place is boarded up now, though you can still see the old advertisements peeking out of half-broken windows. The prices are all wrong. It's 2008, and smokes are at least a dollar more than what's advertised. This place must have closed ten years ago, but the prices in the window remain the same. It's trapped in-between. Trapped like me.

Past the shell of an old Bell Atlantic phone booth. The receiver is long gone, but I'm almost sure I hear a giggle crackling from the end of the severed cord. I shake my head and tell myself it's the wind.

$$\mathcal{D}\mathfrak{C}$$

I'm on the last block now, which means there's no way to avoid it. Denton Street dead-ends in a cul-de-sac, so the only way to my parents' is past the one place I don't want to see.

The house where my cousin Jacqueline grew up.

I tip my face to the sidewalk, my boots shifting between the jagged cracks in the cement. As I draw nearer, these are the things I promise myself:

I won't look at her split-level up ahead.

I won't think of her inside, waltzing barefoot down the hallway, her steps softer than a ghost's.

I won't listen for her laugh, crystalline and sweet as a summer day.

I won't, I won't, I won't.

It doesn't matter, though. By the time I climb the front steps to my parents' house, I've broken all three promises.

At the door of my own home, I knock, and my mother answers.

"Why didn't you call me?" She sighs at me. "I would have picked you up, Phoebe."

Hearing my own name—especially back in this place—gives me a start, like a spider crawling up my spine. "It's fine," I mumble. "It wasn't very far."

That's not true, and we both know it, but my mother doesn't argue. She doesn't do anything. She doesn't move to hug me, and she doesn't invite me in. We linger on either side of the threshold, studying each other. Her face hasn't changed as much as it should have. It's been so long, yet she still looks like my mother. I wonder if I still look like her daughter.

Inside, the phone rings, an old-fashioned jacked-into-the-wall kind, and she goes to answer it, leaving the door open in her wake. I stand here, not certain what to do. I shouldn't have expected any more than this. My mother and I were never ones for affection. That's a good thing. Right now, the thought of anybody touching me—here, in this city, on this street—makes me almost too queasy to stand.

With a deep breath, I slip into the house and latch the door behind me.

"Thank you," she says from the kitchen. "Please tell him I love him."

The phone clunks back into its cradle, and she returns to the room, her face more lined than before.

I don't ask her who it was. It's easy to guess. Someone from the Sweet Evergreen Nursing Home, no doubt. I've always loved those chipper names for places where people go to die. Like calling my father's last home and testament something upbeat will stop his mind from shrinking into itself. No matter where he goes or what the doctors there do, his past will still crash further away from him every day, like driftwood in the lost recesses of Lake Erie. The last time I spoke to him on the phone, he couldn't even fathom me, the voice of his only child. In the background, my mother was sobbing so hard that she couldn't take the phone from him, which left me to hear the endless loop of his questions.

"Who is this? Do I know you? Where are you from? Who is this?"

I was too numb to answer. The next week, my mother took him on the long ride to Sweet Evergreen on Cleveland's East Side, and now here I am in his stead, back to help her clean up what's left of their lives. So much for my parents' golden years.

"It's too late to order takeout," she says. "But there's pizza in the fridge."

I shake my head. "I'm not hungry."

I might as well have not bothered to answer, because my mother returns to the kitchen, where she reheats two slimy slices of yesterday's dinner and delivers them to me on a yellowed paper plate. I sit at the flimsy card table in the corner and don't complain. The dining room furniture has already retreated to storage, along with the couch where I sprawled out every summer growing up, and the Montgomery Ward stereo I cranked so loud that Bob Seger nearly blew out the speakers. There's an echo in this house where my childhood used to be.

After I've choked down stringy cheese and grease, we linger together in silence. There's plenty for us to discuss, but no way for us to cut through the marrow of years to get to it. We certainly don't want to talk about *them*. Those five girls. The so-called Rust Maidens. As my mother tosses my plate in the trash, I sneak upstairs to my bedroom. I expect it to be empty too, but I'm wrong. Everything is as I left it when I was eighteen, not a single knick-knack out of place. Along the far wall, a *Jaws* poster stares back at me, tape peeling at the edges but somehow intact. When I was thirteen, I spent a month's allowance to bribe the usher at the old theater at Kamms Plaza to save this poster for me when the film's run was over.

"Worth every penny," I'd told Jacqueline when we were walking home afterward. She just laughed.

That sweet clear laugh I can still hear.

My mother materializes next to me in the doorway. "I thought it would be rude to move your things," she says, as though I asked for an explanation. I didn't. I'd rather not have anything about this place explained to me.

"I'll sleep downstairs," I say, and close the door.

But before I can move toward the steps, my mother catches my hand.

"Phoebe," she says, and pulls me into her arms. The weight of the time we've lost is suddenly heavier than I ever imagined it. The weight of twenty-eight years. That's how long it's been: twenty-eight years, four months, and eight days. I always remember the exact number, adding another tally mark each morning over my coffee and creamer, like I'm a bored prisoner tracking the incarceration of my own life.

"I missed you." She holds me a little closer. "Thank you for coming back."

"Thank you for having me," I say, and don't know whether or

not I mean it.

We stand a long time this way, pretending we're a proper mother and daughter. It's a passable lie.

"I should go to bed," she says, and disappears across the hall without another word.

)O(

All night, I wander up and down the stairs and through hollow rooms, a specter in my own life—or what used to be my life. Now it doesn't belong to anyone.

Last month, my mother sold the house to an investment firm. They're tearing down the whole street and converting it to condos. Or they were, until the recession got the best of them. But since they've already got the permits and paid the construction crew, they're still tearing it down. Just for the fun of it, I guess.

In the kitchen, I tiptoe through the darkness and open the door to the attached garage. My breath lodges in my chest.

My Chevy Impala, split-pea green and somehow in pristine condition. My father, his calloused machinist's hands always eager to tinker, must have kept it this way for when I came home and we could work on the car together. No matter how many times I told them otherwise, my parents always thought I would be back.

"Maybe this Christmas," they'd say on the phone, but every December came and went without a visit, until this one. Now here I am, but my father's gone. Everything I do always feels a moment too late.

I shut off the garage light and close the door behind me.

Outside, I sneak through the backyard, overgrown and gray, already knowing where I'm going. A place I'm astounded still exists. In the dark, it's no more than a shadow high up in the elm tree, but I could close my eyes and see it clearly any time of day.

When I was a kid, other girls had vanities and oversized makeup kits and closets bulging with flared jeans and culottes and bow blouses. I had a bug house. For my thirteenth birthday, my father and I converted a treehouse into a summer sanctuary for butterflies and lightning bugs and annual cicadas. This was my past, and it was supposed to be my future. A girl obsessed with insects, who would go to school to learn about insects, who would raise and study and love insects. Now all that's left of that dream is rotting in an old tree that stands alone in my parents' yard, surrounded by empty lots where houses used to be.

My feet unsteady, I start climbing the rope ladder. It's frayed and shaky, and I'm half-convinced it won't hold my weight, but I manage to get to the top, where I stand at the threshold of what used to be mine. Then I step inside, the ceiling just high enough that I don't have to hunch. The place smells musty, a heady blend of rotten leaves and earth and a past best left forgotten.

Here, in the gloom, I should be alone, but I'm not. There's something curled against the far wall, something that seems to be moving. The night whirls around me, and I wheeze out a gasp, convinced I've cornered a ghost.

But the figure shifts, and I see it's only a sleeping teenage girl. She's smaller than a shadow and nearly as insubstantial. Her eyes open and flick up at me.

"I'm sorry," she says, and scrambles to her feet.

I stare at her shape, still half-obscured in darkness. "What are you doing here?"

"I don't know," she says, and shrugs. "I just come up here sometimes. To think."

"Does Mrs. Shaw know?" I ask, and the question sounds all wrong to me. It's always weird to call your mother by a formal name. Even weirder when you don't know your mother anymore.

The girl shakes her head. "Nobody really knows," she says. "Nobody really cares, either. Have you seen this neighborhood lately?"

I exhale a laugh in spite of myself.

The girl hesitates, studying me in the moonlight. "You're Phoebe, aren't you?"

I don't say anything, but she knows she's right. She's in my backyard, after all.

The girl keeps watching me, her face bright and hopeful. Given that starry-eyed look of hers, she's liable at any moment to pull out an autograph book and a red pen. A gruesome and obscure celebrity—that's what I've become.

"I'm Quinn," the girl says, as though I asked her. I realize I should have—that would have been the polite thing to do, the thing anyone with even the most elementary manners would have done—but these days, I interact with so few people that I don't remember what's normal anymore. I'm a woman with almost half a century of life experience, who still can't do a convincing impression of a human being.

"I'm Phoebe," I say, not because she doesn't know my name, but because I feel like I don't. I tell myself it's good to keep practicing it, to keep reminding myself what's what. Quinn moves out of the shadow and sits cross-legged next to me. I expect her to ask me about the girls, about what happened to them, but instead, she does the opposite. She talks about herself. Her whole life story pours out of her in an instant—she's eighteen and aimless and desperate to escape this town—and from the way her voice keeps rising higher, I wonder if I'm the first person she's ever had to listen to her, to really listen.

I sit with her, not saying a word, and I suddenly feel bad for no reason. It's probably because I don't even care about myself these days. That means this girl certainly can't rely on me to care about her.

"I can't believe it's you," she says, breathless from spinning the yarn of her life. "We thought you were never coming back."

I almost ask who *we* are, but then I'm not sure I'll like the answer, so I just sit back on my heels and stare at the floor, saying nothing while my fingers follow a shape etched into the floorboards. A triple moon. It's a beautiful sign: two crescents on either side of a full moon.

"I didn't carve that," Quinn says, as though I accused her. "It's always been here. At least since I was a kid."

I nod. I know it isn't her work. That's because I remember who did this, whose hand made this mark that can never be erased.

"I should go." I withdraw my fingers from the etching and move toward the doorway. "You should go home, too."

"Home?" Quinn scoffs and gazes out into the haze of the city. "Nobody on this street has that anymore."

I climb back down the fraying rope ladder, but that doesn't stop her. She follows behind me, chattering the whole way, though I do my best not to listen. I've got enough problems of my own. I don't need hers.

I get to the back step, desperate to be free of her, but the door's locked. Of course it is. This latch always caught. My dad never did fix it like he said he would.

I shift into the space between houses and move for the front door. I'll have to knock again. This is becoming a strange habit: requesting to be let into my own home. Quinn keeps pace behind me.

At the end of the cul-de-sac, the bulldozers are ready to start their work for the day. Next to the rubble-filled lot where the old mansion used to be, an abandoned house is being prepped for demolition. Glass and wood and plaster and all those other things that gave shape to our lives will be crushed to dust in an instant.

"Phoebe." Quinn puts a hand on my arm and I turn toward her.

Please just leave me alone, I want to say. *Go away, go away, go away.*

But out here, the sun is starting to rise, and in the vague glow of daylight, her face is clear to me for the first time. She looks like someone I used to know. The way her copper hair falls across her eyes, how she chews her bottom lip, the quiet movement of her steps, like she's dancing just above the pavement.

I don't know this girl. Her family didn't move to this street until after I left. But that doesn't change how much she reminds me of *her*. In a way, she reminds me of all of those girls. How out of place she seems, even at home.

"Can I show you something?" she asks, and I can't stop myself. I say yes.

I follow her now, down the sidewalk, past a row of hollow houses.

"It looks like most people have left already," I say.

Quinn nods. "They've been leaving for years. Now we've only got a week until we have to be out, too."

Halfway down the street, she stops in front of a home, quiet and abandoned and familiar.

"This was where Doctor Ross and his family lived." She glances at me. "Violet was his daughter."

I swallow hard. "I know," I say, and wish I didn't.

Quinn starts toward the front door, but I hesitate in the yard. She looks back at me.

"Nobody cares if we go in." She starts up the porch steps. "Like I said, nobody cares about much here."

Once they're empty, houses never look the way you remember them. But the Ross family left pieces of themselves behind, enough to put a bit of them back together. An end table tipped over against a wall. A red sectional sofa left moldering in the corner, the velvet upholstery puckered at the edges. A dingy leather bag with a rusted stethoscope inside.

"I explore here sometimes," Quinn says. "That's how I found this."

She leads us down a hall and into a narrow bedroom. Violet's room.

"You recognized that symbol in the treehouse," Quinn whispers, and I wonder who she doesn't want to disturb. "I think you'll recognize this too."

She points to a spot on the exposed plaster. My throat goes dry, and I creep closer to it. It's a crude mark, not elegantly etched like the other one, but it's uncanny how similar it is. A pair of crescents flanking a circle. A triple moon.

I reach out and touch the symbol. It doesn't appear to be drawn on the wall. It looks like it's coming from beneath. Something scratched this from behind the plaster.

Quinn watches me quietly. "It's related to the girls, isn't it?"

she asks. "To the Rust Maidens?"

But I won't listen. I shake my head and inch away. "You're imagining things where there aren't any," I say. "And you're bothering me. Please stop bothering me."

"But Phoebe—"

I don't wait to hear another word. I just put my head down and charge out of the room.

Quinn calls after me again, but I'm already running down the hall, out the front door, and along the sidewalk, the melody of the construction crew punctuating my every step. This isn't real. Nothing in this place is real, Quinn least of all. She's a nobody, the same as me. A silly, superstitious little girl. That's all. I can't read into what she's saying or showing me as being any more than that.

The front door of my parents' house is unlocked now, and I go inside.

"Mom?" In the emptiness, there's an echo. "Where are you?"

I want to talk to her. I don't want to be here by myself.

But the living room is quiet. No furniture, no parents, only an old Bible left in the corner to collect dust. My mother is gone, maybe for a minute, maybe for the day, and she went without saying goodbye. Now I'm alone in a place I don't want to be.

I think again of that house Quinn showed me, and the symbol on the wall. Who drew it? And why? It can't be them. They can't be back here. Not now. Not after all these years.

I breathe in. This is ridiculous. I'm a grown woman, spooking myself with the past. I need to start packing. I need to do something. That's why I came back, to put these ghosts to rest. That's what I'll do.

I turn toward the steps leading up to my bedroom, just as a shadow moves past the window and across the floor.

You're back, I almost say, relief threading through me, but when I look to the front window, dread clogs my throat. The figure outside isn't my mother. It's not Quinn, either. There's someone else on the porch. Someone lithe and sprightly, as familiar as a resurrected nightmare.

And oh God, I think I know who it is.

TWO

The morning of our high school graduation, I crept outside at dawn to feed my bugs.

With the sunrise dancing in my hair and a Tupperware canister tucked under my arm, I climbed the rope ladder to the elm tree. The industrial skyline hung over me, hazy as always, its veil of smog like an eternal omen. Below, Denton Street was quiet, but the calm wouldn't last. My parents would be up soon. Everyone would be up. This was a big day for us, the morning another crop of drifting neighborhood kids pretended to matriculate to adulthood. The Class of 1980. I couldn't wait to see how spectacularly we'd all fail.

At the top of the ladder, I peeled back the plastic that draped over my treehouse, and slipped inside. The place was a mishmash of accoutrements. A clear tarp over the windows kept in the heat, though a keyhole-shaped incision in the plastic ensured the bugs were no prisoners of mine. Trays of larvae were stacked in corners, and a row of plants along the far wall flourished, ideal for the insect in search of a midnight snack.

But I had their favorite food. In the center of the treehouse, I slid off the starburst lid on the harvest-gold Tupperware, revealing slices of navel oranges and Gala apples, all bathed in honey water. An exquisite feast, and one that the butterflies devoured with ravenous glee.

With their breakfast delivered, I reclined on the floor, arms folded over my chest, as I listened to the tiny flapping of a hundred eager wings.

Nobody in the neighborhood understood this place. None of them understood me, either. They didn't see these little creatures lapping at sugar and giving thanks with every twitch of their antennae. And it wasn't just butterflies here. Lightning bugs, cicadas, grasshoppers, praying mantises: almost anything that wasn't human was welcome.

"Who keeps bugs in a hovel?" my mother had asked when I'd first requested to convert the treehouse. My father, who'd always been on my side, told me to find something to convince her, so I eschewed issues of *Tiger Beat* and *Seventeen* and scoured every *Reader's Digest* and *National Geographic* until I found an article about just such a house in England. The full-color pictures were apparently enough for her to give me a trial run. After the first year, when the insects didn't perish wholesale, she allowed me to keep the experiment going indefinitely.

"As long as you keep your grades up," my mother said, not realizing that these bugs were better than grades. They were my dreams, fluttering to life in the plastic-draped hothouse. This was the only future I could imagine: raising insects in quiet places. Their lives made more sense to me than people's did. They never quarreled needlessly, and they never excluded someone just for fun. They were decent and gentle and the closest to kind that anything could be, and they followed comforting patterns—sometimes to the day, sometimes even to the hour. Eating, sleeping, reproducing: their lives were all mapped out for them.

I followed patterns of my own. Behind the potted milkweed, I rummaged around blindly until I pried my treasure free: a red tartan thermos. I unscrewed the yellow cap and took a long sip, not certain what I'd stored inside. It took only a moment for the smooth molasses flavor to settle in before I could identify it.

Myers's Rum, mixed with a bottle of Coke, now flat as the Cleveland shoreline. It didn't matter. I smiled and quaffed another drink. It seemed only fair. There was nectar for the butterflies, and a different kind of nectar for me. Anything to chase away the infinite drone of living in this dead-end city on this dead-end street.

My head buzzing, I bid farewell to my bugs and climbed back down into the world. There was someone I needed to meet before graduation.

Out front on the street, the neighborhood was just waking. Or what was left of the neighborhood. After the last layoff at the steel mill, we'd lost almost a third of the families on the street, and the empty houses with no curtains and no souls reminded us every day of their absence. Even a Frank Lloyd Wright-style mansion sat silently at the end of the cul-de-sac, a bleak reminder of what was to come, no matter who you were or how well you'd planned for the future.

The June morning was chillier than it had any right to be, and I wrapped my arms around my body to keep from shivering. On the sidewalk, my feet tracked through something. I stopped on the crumbling cement and stared down at what I'd walked through.

It was a trail of footprints. The water was dark and strange, like a quagmire. I followed the path as far as I could, but it ended abruptly at the curb. I turned, ready to retrace it, to understand what this was, when a voice floated down from a nearby porch.

"Hello, Phoebe."

I smiled even before I saw her. Jacqueline. Younger than me by three months, she was my cousin, but more like my twin. We'd done everything together—cut our first teeth, spoken our first words, smoked our first cigarettes. We were practically two halves of one girl.

She was already dressed in her cap and gown, looking eager to get this whole thing over with.

"You ready?" I asked.

"I am." Jacqueline took an uncertain step toward me, gazing backward at her front door.

"Forget about her," I said, and laughed.

"If only that would solve things." Jacqueline flashed me a smile I didn't believe. She was the only person I knew who could sometimes look like she was crying, even when her face was still.

And, in a flurry of curlers and scowls, here was a big reason why: Aunt Betty, shoving her way out of the house to get to me.

"Out of here," she said. It was no secret what she thought of me. I wore the wrong clothes, and said the wrong things, and drank entirely too much. Whatever a nice girl would do, I did the opposite. That meant I was bad news. A bad influence. Nothing but trouble for Jacqueline.

I fled to the sidewalk, the neutral zone where Aunt Betty couldn't chase me off, even if she wanted to. From there, we stood in a stalemate, her on the rim of the porch and me two steps from the street.

"You know the rules, Phoebe." She grabbed Jacqueline's arm. "She doesn't go anywhere alone with you."

Together they vanished back into the house, and I sighed. This was how it always went. Her appearing out of nowhere to admonish me, and me running away, but not staying away.

I waited, loitering on the edge of the lawn, and counted slowly to myself. When I reached the number ten, Jacqueline appeared at her upstairs window and waved down.

"See you soon," she mouthed through the glass, and I smiled back at her.

Back home, my mother was waiting for me in the living room, a Virginia Slim dangling between her pursed lips. "Did Betty bother you again?"

"Always," I said, and fumbled with the record player.

My mother hesitated, carefully weighing her next words. "Do you want me to talk to her?"

I grunted and dropped the needle in the groove. "Do you honestly think it would matter?" The only person Aunt Betty hated more than me was my mother.

She started to say something else, but Tom Petty cut her off first. His nasally voice poured out of the speakers, and I murmured along to "American Girl."

Heavy footsteps plodded overhead, and our eyes shifted upward.

"He's coming down soon," my mother said. "Don't say anything about tomorrow."

"I won't." I wasn't a fool. We all knew not to talk about it until it happened, though of course, it *would* happen. Every few years, it was the same: the steel union voted in solidarity to go on strike, and the picket lines formed in earnest for weeks. Yet no matter how well they bargained, each time when it was over, there were fewer jobs to go around.

But you couldn't talk about it. That was another rule of the neighborhood: never bother the men about work. They went to the mill five days a week and did their time like a chain gang, and we should be grateful to them. Grateful, not questioning.

My father came downstairs, as my mother gulped the rest of her drink and set the empty glass on the edge of the turntable.

"Are you ready?" he asked us.

"Ready enough," I said with a shrug. "But I want to take my own car."

My father raised an eyebrow at me. "That hunk of junk? I'm not sure it'll make it to the corner store."

"That car can go anywhere," I said. "It could make it to the stars."

He grinned. Ever since I'd turned sixteen and bought the Impala with saved-up allowances and lunch money, this had been our game. My father would smirk and disparage the automobile we'd fixed up together, and I'd brag back about it.

"Naw," he said with a wave of his hand. "It couldn't even make it to church on time."

"You're wrong." I folded my arms. "It could make it to Jupiter."

My mother poured herself another drink, downed it, and rolled her eyes. "Are we done now?"

My father's grin didn't falter. "Let's leave the Impala at home this time, Phoebe," he said, "and go together."

"I guess that's okay." I smiled back, and we departed as a family for my graduation.

☽○☾

At the football stadium, amidst a sea of black satin monotony, Jacqueline and I found each other.

"Your mother." I shook my head. "She never lets up, does she?"

"Never," Jacqueline said with a sigh.

We swapped seats in the last row so we could sit together. It would throw off the order for roll call, but we didn't care. What could they do to us now? We were almost free.

As the commencement speaker droned on, I scanned the faces around us, memorizing some of them for what might be the last time. The preacher's daughter. The doctor's daughter. The millworkers' sons. The guy who would become a lawyer because his daddy was. The girl who would be lonely because her mother was.

None of them noticed me watching, except for one—a girl with bandages wound tightly as a roll of barbed wire around her arms. Lisa Carter. Her father worked on the same line as my dad. Not that that made us friends or anything, but the way she looked at me seemed strangely intimate. From two rows away, she stared until I felt split open, her gaze severing me in half. My flesh tightened on my bones, and I couldn't stop myself from shivering.

"You okay?" Jacqueline whispered, and I nodded absently.

A few seats over, someone took a picture, and the camera flash glistened off Lisa's body. With both her sleeves rolled up, the exposed flesh on her arms was almost dewy, and the hem of her graduation gown was damp too. It hadn't rained today, so there was no reason for it, no reason she would be here in such a state.

I inhaled to steady myself. This was a hot day, so maybe she'd run through the sprinklers before leaving Denton Street. That seemed like the bizarre sort of thing that Lisa would do, drenching herself and not bothering to towel off afterward. Or maybe she'd walked through those same inexplicable footprints as I had.

Or maybe she'd made the footprints.

She scratched her bandages and grinned at me, and I gave her a half-hearted smile. My stomach in spasms, I turned away and searched for anything else to look at, anything to keep me from thinking about that odd girl staring at me.

I found something to look at, all right. In the next row ahead, a couple huddled together. But no, they weren't huddling. The girl cowered into the guy, her shoulders hunched, while he just sat back, as unengaged as a neutral country. Thanks to the crowd, I couldn't quite see their faces, but I didn't need to. It had to be Clint and Dawn. No other pair in the school could sit side by side, hand in hand, without ever really touching each other. I sucked in a breath as someone's head bobbed out of the way, and I could see Clint clearly. He was watching me, and when he saw me gazing back, he raised one hand tenuously in a kind of listless greeting.

Jacqueline, the seer of everything, snapped her tongue. "Did he just *wave* at you?" she whispered, the notion so anathema to her she practically spat the words like tiny fireballs.

I nodded. After everything, he still liked to pretend we were friends. And part of me—the part I hated most—wanted to wave back, wanted to be friends, wanted to forget.

But there was Dawn right next to him, with her swollen belly, to remind me why that couldn't happen.

Clint of the chiseled jaw and broken promises.

You're my one and only, Phoebe.

I've never felt this way before.

I'll love you forever.

Of course, I didn't think forever would end with a backseat tryst when my parents took Jacqueline and me out of town for a weekend on the lake.

"We went to Put-In-Bay," Jacqueline said later. "I guess, in his way, Clint did too."

I didn't hear about the rendezvous until after the results came back from the test purchased covertly at the Leader Drug Store downtown. I imagined Dawn struggling with the eye-dropper and vial from the e.p.t. kit, and Clint standing over her, frowning and barking orders, as if he knew what he was doing.

Two hours later, when the bull's eye in the test tube confirmed it was everything they feared, he abandoned Dawn to cry alone in her parents' wood-paneled bathroom and materialized at my front door, all swollen eyes and snot-dripping nose and "I'm so sorry, it was just one time, won't you forgive me?" Like my compassion was the salve that could reverse that one misbegotten night.

I slapped him so hard across the face that his class ring ricocheted off my finger and landed somewhere in the privet shrubs. It's probably there still, interred in the dirt with the future I'd never have.

The news spread like a biblical plague down Denton Street, and once everyone found out about Dawn's "condition"—that was how they described it, as though the thing coiled up in her belly was a malignant tumor, not a baby—the mothers held an emergency Saturday morning meeting, complete with stale digestive biscuits, Lipton tea, and a flock of knit brows. Since the father in question was now the son-in-law she'd never have, my mother asked to recuse herself ("conflict of interest," she claimed), but she was conscripted nonetheless. Neighborhood housewives valued nothing if not conformity.

The meeting lasted exactly forty-three minutes.

"They were playing rock-paper-scissors with that girl's life," my mother told me when she returned home. Only in this game, the choices were "clinic," "adoption," or "let her keep it, we guess."

The mothers on Denton Street had always been like that. With their housewife-boredom and their so-called good intentions, they took it upon themselves to make decisions for everyone, especially the girls, and we tended to do whatever it was they wanted. After all, our own mothers were usually in the room when the vote was taken.

Indeed, Dawn's mom was there that day, though she didn't say much, instead cowering back in the corner, head down and eyes damp. You didn't get a say when your child caused this much of a scandal for the neighborhood.

The meeting ended when the iced tea ran low, and the mothers oh-so-charitably resigned to letting Dawn finish high school and deciding what to do *after* the baby was born, as though all the options would still be on the table then.

Dawn wasn't in the house for this discussion. She wasn't even in the city. A well-meaning aunt from Akron had arrived on Denton Street that morning and spirited her away to the Towpath Trail, twenty-five miles out of Cleveland, to ensure there was no chance the girl might overhear the discussion. Like the gossip was as potent as Cleveland smog and the wind might carry a toxic whiff of it to her if she were too close. Nobody thought to consult the one person whose opinion mattered most. Dawn had caused enough trouble, the mothers reasoned; she was lucky anybody was still speaking to her at all.

Up at the graduation podium, the whining voice announced my name, and I turned away from the past to retrieve my diploma.

After the ceremony, Denton Street brimmed with barbeque and good tidings. Today was a banner day.

"Biggest graduating class this neighborhood's ever seen," the adults marveled.

That meant no dropouts, no suicides, no tragic accidents.

We'd all made it. Plenty of people in this city couldn't say the same.

To celebrate, we opened hastily-wrapped presents purchased on sale at Higbee's and listened to promises that "we'd all go great places," even though we knew there were so few places to go and far too many of us to fit into what was available. Us girls knew this better than most. If there was limited space in the world, then we were the first ones on the team to get cut. No room for us at the steel mills, the boardrooms, the operating rooms. No room for us anywhere. We'd become wives and mothers, and only if we were lucky—and smart enough to do it in that order. Dawn had learned that lesson the hard way.

She didn't get a graduation party. Sequestered at home, she paced back and forth behind her parlor window. Clint, however, had no problem enjoying himself, flitting from one cooler to another until the beer ran out and he saw no need to stay.

After an hour of Kraft cheese-slathered burgers on flimsy paper plates, I saw no need to stay either. It was always the same at these Denton Street celebrations. Parents imbibing until their eyes filmed over, kids sneaking whatever booze was left. The preacher stopped by to remind us what sinners we all were, his only daughter at his side. Helena. She was a walking baby doll, with her rosy cheeks and pretty pink dresses her mother sewed at home on a treadle. Almost the same age as Jacqueline and me, Helena was a summer baby, so she was a year behind us in school. She acted older, though, always telling us how to be, always for our own good. Just like her dear old dad.

Jacqueline shook her head. "I bet she'll head over here in a minute."

I shrugged. "Maybe we'll get lucky today," I said, but I already knew we wouldn't.

When Helena got close to us, Jacqueline and I turned our backs to her, trying to hide in plain sight. It did us no good. She stopped at the picnic table where we were sitting, and nodded at the outline of the flask in my pocket.

"Do you really need to drink that, Phoebe?"

I grinned. "If you're around, I sure do."

At this, Helena crinkled up her nose and scowled. Jacqueline inched closer to me, not saying a word, both of us waiting to see what she did next. If she'd tell on us to my parents. Or worse, to Aunt Betty.

With a smug smile, Helena started to say something, but a camera flashed a searing white light in our faces, and we shielded our eyes, half-blinded.

When my vision returned, Violet, the doctor's daughter, was standing next to us. Of course it was her. She was probably the one who'd taken Lisa's picture at the ceremony today, too. Ever since freshman year, Violet had been omnipresent with that camera, cataloging the whole neighborhood. Why you'd want to remember this place was anybody's guess.

"For you," she said and handed over the Polaroid.

I stared at it, two faces emerging from nothing. No Helena in this one, just me and Jacqueline. I was clear enough, my eyes wide, but not her. She'd turned away at the last instant. Now it was a picture of me with a blur at my side.

"Thanks, I guess," I said.

"Come on, Violet," her mother called across the lawn. "Stop bothering people with your pictures."

I grimaced. *She's not a bother*, I wanted to say, but Violet was already gone.

Helena was gone too. She'd moved on to a couple of younger girls lounging nearby in lawn chairs.

"Shouldn't you be crossing your legs at the ankles?" she asked them.

"Let's get out of here before they come back," Jacqueline whispered, and she and I huddled together at the picnic table, waiting until Aunt Betty turned her back for a second helping of corn on the cob. This was our chance. With the picture shoved in my pocket, we broke from the crowd and sneaked like river rats to my Impala.

We weren't even off Denton Street before Jacqueline twisted the silver dial on the radio to WDOK. "Top of the World" blared across the stereo. I shuddered. Easy listening. It was the worst.

"But I like the Carpenters." She laughed. "What's so bad about that?"

"Everything," I said, grinning, but it didn't matter. I never changed the station when Jacqueline was with me. I couldn't bear to see a moment of her joy fade away. We drove the rest of the way across town, the windows down, breeze in our hair, and Jacqueline singing syrupy sweet songs at the top of her lungs.

$$)O($$

Bayton Beach was empty when we got there. Not a shock these days; no self-respecting parent would take a child anywhere within a square mile of this place. Jacqueline and I had come here years ago as kids, before everything fell apart. Before the mills all across town started the layoffs. Before the Cuyahoga River swallowed so much poison that it couldn't extinguish itself anymore. Before the people started moving away to the sterile, open arms of the suburbs.

We shouldn't be here now. We should know better. We certainly shouldn't go into that water, as dark and wicked as heartbreak.

Our shoes landed in the dirty sand as we dove in, headfirst and fully clothed. The water rose up into my mouth, and I swallowed the tang of earth and brine.

We were alone in a way we so rarely were. Girls were babysitters, but we were also babysat, constantly watched and never trusted on our own. It was nice to be here. Though we were isolated, it felt safer somehow.

Jacqueline did a backstroke in circles around me. "Are you excited about the fall?"

I watched her dizzying movements, my breath coiling in my chest. She never talked about the future. I was the one that had everything worked out. A soon-to-be biology major at Case Western Reserve, the best school in the state. I was the bad girl with the good grades. An enigma to everyone, sometimes even myself.

"It'll be great," I said, and doggy-paddled near her. "I'll only be across town. I'll visit every weekend."

She smiled. "Sure you will."

Back on the shore, we cleared out a clean space and settled into the secret places we used to burrow and play.

Jacqueline dug her wet feet deep into the sand. "The union votes tomorrow," she said, and her voice quivered. Unions and mills and strikes made all our voices quiver.

"Don't worry," I said. "It'll work out."

Jacqueline peered up at me. "How can you be sure?"

"Because it has to."

We watched the sun dip in the sky, and sorrow fizzled in my chest. This was a day I didn't want to let go of, not yet. It was the last day, and the first too, a marker that bisected our lives.

I wanted to tell Jacqueline that we should stay here in this moment, never stirring from the sand. Become mermaids, perhaps, or some other gorgeous yet gruesome beasts.

But as the day faded away from us, I said something else instead.

"I'll race you to the sun."

Jacqueline glanced up at me. Grinning, she scrambled to her feet and started running.

For an instant, I watched her go, her thin body gliding across the sand like a pale stone, her feet barely touching the ground. Then I squealed and ran after her. Across the divots in the trash-laden shore and over broken Miller Lite bottles, all to see which of us could reach the edge of the world first. With the shore stretching out to what might as well have been infinity, we both lost, but together, we won.

)O(

It was night by the time my Impala lurched down Denton Street, creeping back into the neighborhood under the thin veil of the never-fully-dark evening. We always had light here, thanks to the flame over the mill. Less than a mile away, it burned bright and tireless in the sky, all day and all night. Our sentry, our beacon everywhere we went. No matter how far Jacqueline and I strayed—out past the Flats, or skipping along the lake, gin and laughter brimming in our bellies—we could always find our way by the wink of that fire. It was the North Star that guided us home.

We pulled into my driveway. All the charcoal grills had gone cold, and there was no one left on the street. As she climbed out of the car, Jacqueline cradled herself and shivered.

"Where is everyone?" she asked.

I shook my head. It was unnervingly quiet, as if we were the only people left in the world. That was what the neighborhood was slowly becoming: abandoned. There were nineteen houses on Denton Street, and the bank owned eight of them. To keep our lives intact, we were all holding on with both hands, not that we honestly believed that could help us if our number was called.

"Let's not go home yet," I said, and Jacqueline nodded.

Hand in hand, we moved through the shadows of the neighborhood. The two of us always took the long way: down my side of the street, around the end of the cul-de-sac, and back up the opposite side. As we went, we indulged our superstitions, avoiding all the many cracks in the crumbling sidewalk, our fingers tapping the fire hydrant at the end of the street, holding our breath past the abandoned Frank Lloyd Wright-style mansion.

We ended, as we always did, at the empty house next to Jacqueline's. Three winters ago, the bank had seized the property, apparently with the sole intention of letting it rot away. A warning for what would happen if you were foolish enough to lose your job.

What they hadn't seized was the spare basement key the former owners had kept hidden outside. Next to a piece of half-rotten lattice in the untilled garden, I uncovered the toothed

34

silver, and we let ourselves in to a house that belonged to no one.

Downstairs, everything was as we'd left it. Two crooked lawn chairs we'd salvaged from a long-ago Wednesday garbage pickup, a dusty bottle of Old Crow bourbon, and a Coleman lantern that was liable to gas us to death if we weren't careful.

"Don't turn it up too high," Jacqueline said.

"I won't." If we were lucky, we could get the fuel to last us the whole summer.

She and I sat together in the lawn chairs, giggling and celebrating and tossing back shots quick so we didn't have to taste them.

"I'll miss this," she said, and I almost corrected her, almost reminded her that there would be nothing to miss. That I'd be back every weekend, just like I promised.

But then she looked past me, and something shifted in her face.

"Phoebe," she whispered, nearly gagging on my name.

My throat closed up as I followed her gaze. The lantern glow flickered over a shape at the bottom of the stairs. Someone was standing there, watching us for longer than we cared to imagine.

With a guttural moan, Jacqueline fumbled for my hand, anything for us to be closer to each other and farther from this thing gawking at us.

"Who is it?" she asked. "Who's there?"

Her arms still bandaged and damp, Lisa emerged as if from nothing. "The moonlight's singing to us tonight," she said, and her fingernails dragged across the crumbling walls. This set my guts churning. Something about the sound made me think of a corpse digging its way out of a shallow grave.

I braced against the crooked lawn chair, and it lurched under my weight. What was she doing, hiding here in the dark?

"Lisa?" I said, but she didn't look at me. Instead, she moved into the center of the room and settled on the floor, stretching her long legs out across the cold concrete.

Our hands still locked, Jacqueline's gaze shifted from Lisa to me and back again.

I sniffed in a heavy breath, and the scents of mildew and faded Lysol filled my lungs. Stay calm, I told myself. After all, this wasn't a specter or even a stranger. It was Lisa. We'd known her since grade school. An odd one, to be sure, but she was only a girl, just like us. Besides, this wasn't so odd. We'd left the door at the side of the house unlocked. She must have slipped in after us. Still, neither Jacqueline nor I had heard her come down the stairs. How could she move without making a sound?

I shrank back in my chair, desperate to pretend this was normal. "Congratulations on graduating today," I said. "How's everything with your family? How's your sister, Kathleen?"

Jacqueline attempted a smile. "Yes, how is Kathleen? Is she still at the *Chicago Tribune*?"

Her eyes vacant, Lisa stared at the wall, not seeing us, maybe not seeing anything.

"Things change," she whispered at last. "Sometimes it's for the better, and sometimes it's not."

Jacqueline tightened her fingers around mine, squeezing my hand until it throbbed. I knew what she was thinking. We should run. Tethered together, we could sprint for those stairs and get out of here before something happened.

But there was Lisa, right in front of us. The one who'd always been forgotten. I didn't want to be the same as everyone else. I didn't want to abandon her if something was wrong, and by the looks of her, something was most definitely wrong.

I tried to steady myself, but my voice trembled anyhow. "Do you need us to call someone, Lisa?"

At this, she looked up, and her eyes flashed before going dark again.

"Who would you call?" she asked. "My father? Because I don't think he can help me now. I don't think he could ever help me."

Lisa rose to her feet, somehow taller than only a moment ago. Shadows danced about the room. Maybe hers. Maybe not.

We watched, dumbfounded, as she fiddled with the gauze on her arms, carefully at first, until a strange look twitched across her face. Then with her gaze on me, she smiled and ripped off the damp bandages. They peeled away from her body like dead flesh. Instantly, water gushed out of her, as though someone were wringing out a sponge.

I sat there, my insides twisted up and useless. I couldn't move. I couldn't breathe. But Jacqueline was quicker than me, and smarter too, like she practically knew it was coming. Her hand on mine, she yanked me backward out of the chair and pulled us toward the wall, but nowhere in the room was safe. The gray liquid kept coming, kept seeping down Lisa's body, spilling on the concrete in thick rivers, coating the toes of our shoes.

"Don't worry," Lisa said and wandered back toward the stairs, her leaking body making plink-plunk sounds as she went. "I'm fine. Everything is fine."

For a bottomless moment, Jacqueline and I didn't move. The quiet footsteps retreated out into the night, and the basement went still again. Everything was almost as it had been—the Coleman lantern still flickering, the dust-caked bourbon bottle in the corner, the broken lawn chairs at our feet. But there, in the center of the room, was the trail of Lisa, of who she was and what she left behind.

Fear unraveled from Jacqueline's wide eyes, and we stared at each other, hoping that one of us could utter the words to reverse what we'd just witnessed. But there was no magic spell to undo it, so with our hands clasped tighter than ever, we took the long stairs back up into the night.

Outside, Lisa was halfway down the block. Heading home, I guessed. I wanted to run after her. I wanted to find out what was wrong and ask her how to fix it. But something else was happening out here. In her wake were red lights, so bright they were almost blinding. An ambulance. At first, I stood there stock-still, dumbly assuming that someone thought to call a doctor for Lisa, as if anyone but us knew what had happened. Then I heard Jacqueline exhale at my side.

"Dawn," she whispered, and I realized she was right. The paramedics were gathering up someone, and though the lights obscured all the faces, a sliver of moonlight glistened off that belly, as round as the world.

That pint-sized beast must have finally torn its way out of Dawn's womb. Something in my chest twisted, and for the first time, I felt so very sorry for her. For where she'd been and where she was going. At least it waited until after graduation. A small mercy.

"Why the ambulance, do you think?" I asked.

Jacqueline shook her head. "Maybe there were complications."

Complications. That was a nice word for it, for this entire night.

Down the street, the last paramedic on the sidewalk hollered something indistinct to the man in the driver's seat before he secured the stretcher and closed all the ambulance doors. As the engine roared to life, I held a superstitious breath, convinced if I exhaled too soon, the world might cascade away from me, and I'd suddenly be like Lisa, dripping dark water and heartache.

But I didn't exhale in this moment, and the world stayed put, at least for now. With Dawn tucked safely inside, the ambulance wailed on its way, and Jacqueline and I stood shivering on the street as we listened to the sirens fade into the night.

We couldn't linger here for very long. After everything, it didn't feel safe out in the open.

"Come on," I said, and we hurried away from tonight. But we only made it halfway down the block before we saw them. Another set of footprints, gray and uneven and leading toward the abandoned mansion at the end of the lane.

I shuddered. "Lisa really marked up the whole neighborhood, didn't she?"

"Phoebe," Jacqueline whispered, "Lisa lives in the opposite direction."

She was right. We'd seen Lisa departing the other way, toward her home. These colorless prints couldn't be hers.

Jacqueline shivered again, her slight form fragile and uncertain. "What's happening?"

I wished I knew. But I was certain of this: we shouldn't go home. Not tonight, not without each other. So we went to the only place we knew.

Up in the elm tree, the butterflies and cicadas and lightning bugs were waiting to greet us. This wasn't the greatest hiding place—anybody could discover us here if they wanted, but we already knew they wouldn't. My parents had stopped bothering to worry about my whereabouts sophomore year when I'd disappeared for three days to attend a Dead concert in Pittsburgh, and Aunt Betty would rather let Jacqueline be wicked and stay out all night with me so she could dangle something over her later like a rotten carrot, a punishment in the making.

Jacqueline sat back in the corner, her face obscured in shadow. "What's wrong with Lisa?" she asked. "What would cause that?"

I shook my head. "Maybe some weird injury or accident?"

All I could do was guess. Nothing they taught us about in health class looked anything like Lisa Carter did tonight.

In the dark, Jacqueline exhaled a wheeze. "Do you think she'll be okay?"

I hesitated. "No, I don't," I said. "But did you really think Lisa would be okay before today?"

This was perhaps the unkindest thing I could say. It was also the truest.

Jacqueline buried her finger in a knothole on the wall and didn't say anything else about it. We should have kept talking about Lisa, but after everything, we were so tired. Side-by-side, we curled up on the bare floor, watching the butterflies sleep beneath the milkweed leaves.

"Do you know all of them?" she asked, and I nodded. I even had names for some of them. Lyssa. Atropos. Maia. But in the dark and sometimes in the light, I couldn't be entirely sure which was which, so try as I might, I occasionally called them by the wrong name. They never seemed to mind, though.

But they were resting now, and we didn't disturb them. Instead, Jacqueline and I closed our eyes too, and the night slinked away from us.

THREE

At dawn, the world resurfaced with all its usual patterns. The paperboy went on his route, the news thudding against front steps. On the street, a car radio surged and then cut out, the driver too courteous to let Gary Numan play so loudly. A mile away, the flame above the mill burned brightly, reminding our fathers where they were due. Like it or not, Denton Street slowly awakened around us.

The treehouse was awakening, too. In the morning light, monarchs glimmered and nested in Jacqueline's red hair. I smiled and watched her quietly. My sweet cousin, always looking like a fairy-tale princess in exile.

She opened her eyes, and all the butterflies scattered.

"We have to go now," I whispered, and she stretched out and yawned before nodding at me.

"It was nice to escape for a while," she said, and together we climbed down the rope ladder and back into the dusty world.

On the sidewalk in front of Jacqueline's house, I held her hand tightly, not wanting to let go. We knew what was to come. She'd sneak in through the door, and Aunt Betty would be there, waiting in her work smock, a single foot tapping in dismay. She might have stayed up all night just to savor this moment. She'd chastise Jacqueline for skipping out on the graduation parties yesterday, and for staying out all night without calling, and for picking a friend so feisty and thoughtless as me.

"Do you think everything will be all right?" Jacqueline asked, and at first, I thought she meant with her mother. Then the memory of Lisa washed over me, and I realized it wasn't all just a bad dream. Last night had happened. Lisa murmuring about the moon and oozing gray water. Dawn being rushed off to give birth at midnight. It was all real.

I swallowed hard, my mouth dry. Part of me wanted to scream, but I couldn't upset Jacqueline, not moments before she had to return to her mother.

"Everything will be fine," I said. "I'm sure we'll see Lisa today and she'll have some silly explanation for it."

Not that I could imagine any explanation that would set me at ease.

A shadow passed by the front window of Jacqueline's house. Aunt Betty knew we were outside.

"I should go," Jacqueline said, and squeezed my hand before disappearing inside. After she was gone, I waited for her to come to the window to wave goodbye. I counted to ten, and then to twenty, but the curtains never fluttered.

Alone, I walked the quarter-block back to my house. Somehow, despite the same routine of the street, nothing looked quite the way we'd left it yesterday. The houses were there, of course, just like they should be. But the draped windows stared out at me, drowsing eyes that never rested, and a scent of rotten earth and restlessness breezed through the neighborhood. Maybe it was the possibility of the strike that did it. Or maybe it was because this was tomorrow, the first morning of adulthood, of not belonging to anyone or anything. Maybe I was imagining things that weren't there.

At home, my father had already left for the mill, so I slipped upstairs and into the shower to avoid my mother's silent judgment. She would chastise me soon enough for sneaking off from the parties. I'd rather have a moment to myself first.

But as the water cascaded over me, I wasn't alone. Lisa's face shuffled in and out of my mind like the visage of Death in a tarot deck. There and gone, something to try to decipher but never to understand, not truly. Maybe there was nothing to understand. What we saw last night could have been nothing more than a prank. Lisa had always been a strange, superstitious girl, babbling under her breath about things the rest of us couldn't imagine. Maybe she'd perfected this arcane magic trick just to terrorize the local girls.

That had to be it. A joke. She was probably at home right now, giggling over her caper.

The water cut out in the shower and I shivered, wishing I could invent better lies to tell myself.

With my hair wrapped in a towel, I gathered yesterday's clothes from the floor. Violet's Polaroid of Jacqueline and me crinkled in my back pocket. I'd forgotten it was there. I was already forgetting so much of yesterday. I practiced remembering all of it: the commencement, the lackluster barbeque, the beach with Jacqueline. That was the last day, and today was the first. Something new. Something unknown.

In my bedroom, I placed the picture in a dresser drawer with the others, dozens of them. Thanks to Violet, I had snapshots from choir recitals and Fourth of July parties and birthdays I'd rather have forgotten. Some of the images weren't half-bad. It was something Violet loved, I guessed. Junior year, she'd brought home college brochures from the Art Institute in Pittsburgh, desperate to convince her parents to let her attend. No dice.

"No girl of mine will waste her time at some silly art school," her father had said, and put the brochures in the fireplace for kindling. The next day, I found Violet sobbing under the bleachers, where I'd sneaked off during study hall. Without a word, I'd passed her my flask, and she downed the rest of the vodka. Four shots' worth. I didn't complain.

This dresser was stuffed with other things, too: mood rings that never worked and a Pet Rock I never wanted, and all our notes and diaries, the ones Jacqueline and I kept when we were girls. When she was done with a journal, she would pass it to me.

"I don't want my mother to discover my secrets," she'd told me, and gave them to me instead.

With a heavy sigh, I closed the drawer and got dressed.

Downstairs, I tiptoed to a corner of the living room and tucked myself next to the bookshelf brimming with my mother's favorites. *Madame Bovary* and *Wuthering Heights* and *Anna Karenina*, and all the other classics where women succumbed to fates not their own. There was a Bible too, as uplifting as all the other tragedies, but in this house, we rarely read that one. Sunday sermons were more than enough for us.

"You shouldn't have left early yesterday," my mother said from the kitchen. "Betty was livid."

"So what?" I tossed my wet hair out of my face, moving out of the corner and toward the oak cabinet filled with vinyl. Anything to occupy my nervous hands. "It doesn't matter what I do. She'd find something to complain about."

"You don't have to help her along." My mother peered at me through the doorway, and one eyebrow twitched up. "That's some dress."

"Thanks," I said, and smiled. In my bedroom, I'd wiggled into a red velvet sheath, the micro mini one that always made my homeroom teacher frown. But now I was an adult with no homeroom and no teachers until fall, so I could wear whatever I wanted, Mother's modesty be damned.

On the kitchen table, the portable radio crackled with the day's news, but I didn't want to listen, so I dropped the needle on *Stranger in Town*. Bob Seger rushed through the speakers. There was something about that voice, gruff and working class and just like us. That was what I wanted to hear today.

Perched at the sink, my mother didn't flick off the radio. Instead, "Hollywood Nights" competed in a stalemate with a drone of staticky updates. Today's temperature a high of 79 with a chance of precipitation. The Indians lost a game to Seattle last night, and they'd probably lose to Oakland tonight. The DJ shouldn't even have to announce that. With the season the team had been having, defeat was practically implied.

My mother scrubbed a Corelle dish, and I swayed in the doorway, trapped between two rooms, unsure what to do with myself.

And then, the words that stopped our hearts.

"This just in: the Steelworkers Union Local 13232 has gone on strike."

In an instant, the whole house seized up, and I couldn't hear a thing. No creaks of a floorboard, no rotation of the record. Just a blank din where the possibilities of the day had been only a moment ago. Our breathing, our lives, everything suspended in those syllables.

Gone on strike.

We knew it was coming. Nothing about this was unexpected. But that didn't make it any less agonizing.

Slowly, the world seeped back in, one piece at a time. The rush of the kitchen faucet. The crackle on the turntable. The DJ moved on to a story about Ronald Reagan and how yesterday would have been Marilyn Monroe's 54th birthday. A thousand miles away, in the living room, Bob Seger was still singing about California coasts, but here in this place, we couldn't be further from Beverly Hills and sunshine and freedom.

My body surged forward a step, feet slipping out of my woven sandals, and I wanted to run, to flee this feeling of helplessness and pointlessness, of a future that was worse than a mirage. A future that was nothing at all.

My mother was more practical.

"Go down to the corner store, Phoebe." Her hands shaking, she opened her purse on the counter and removed a five from her wallet.

On the nearby wall, the phone rang, and she and I both froze. We already knew who it was: one of the Denton Street housewives, eager to call an emergency meeting.

My body went numb. I refused to stay in this house and be anywhere close to that conversation as our mothers pretended their talk could fix what had happened. With my head down, I took the cash and disappeared out the back door. My mother and I didn't discuss a grocery list. She trusted I already knew what we needed. Barbeque sauce, a pound of ground beef, and a bright yellow box of Velveeta for Sloppy Joes, my father's favorite. My mother couldn't soothe his soul, but she could soothe his stomach.

This journey was a familiar one, and I could make it with my eyes closed. Past the religious knickknack shop and a row of abandoned houses to McMillan's Corner Nook. The bell dinged over me as I scurried inside. I detested it for announcing me. My mother wouldn't come to this place for the same reason I didn't want to be here: the woman working behind the counter.

Aunt Betty turned toward the door. "Phoebe," she said, and for once, my name wasn't blasphemy on her lips. "I just heard on the radio."

I nodded solemnly at her before ducking down the condiments aisle. The world was inside out today: I was a graduate with nowhere to be who had a father with no job, and an aunt who liked me. By the time I reached the counter with the rest of dinner, Betty already had the ground beef taped up in heavy white paper spotted with blood. It was almost worse when she didn't loathe everything about me. This made me wish things were different every day.

She rang me up and took the five-dollar bill like it was a sacrament. "Tell your father I'm sorry," she said, and meant it.

"I will." I gathered up the brown paper bag in my arms, doing my best to hide the quiver deep in my muscles. The only thing that outweighed Aunt Betty's disdain for my mother and me was her adulation of her brother, my father. It was also why she detested us so much in the first place: my mother, the woman who stole him, and me, the child who kept him away. But moments like this made me see her for what she always was: a little sister too dependent on her big brother. So dependent that years ago, she'd insisted on moving to Denton Street with her new husband and newborn Jacqueline, just because we'd bought a house there. Part of me hated her for that, for continuing to torment my mother from down the block. But part of me was grateful, because I got to have Jacqueline so close to me.

With the grocery bag heavy in my arms, I headed back out to the street. Only a couple miles away, a thick breeze pirouetted off the lake. It caught the bottom of my dress, and in a whirlwind, red velvet tented up around my body.

Breathless, I stopped in front of the window of the Holy Heart Curio Shop and used the reflection to adjust my wayward sheath. Even unfolded and smoothed around my hips, the hem hit only a smidge above mid-thigh. Far too short for the Holy Ghost's approval, but just right for me. Probably just right for Marilyn, too.

My gaze shifted past my own reflection and into the store, where a purse-lipped shop lady stared back at me, clutching her crucifix and glaring at my scanty attire. I recognized her. It was the preacher's wife, Helena's mother. I smiled at her before scurrying off.

I took the long way home, not realizing where I was going until I'd already stopped in front of Lisa's house.

From the sidewalk, I tilted my head and squeezed one eye closed. That was the only way this place looked straight and durable. Otherwise, the house was just an epitaph. The once-baby blue siding had grayed and peeled from every corner, and there hadn't been gutters on the roof since the last time the Browns made the playoffs. Half the slate shingles lay sullenly in dead rows where flowers once grew, and the whole foundation was crooked, as if it longed to escape itself.

No one on Denton Street wanted to visit here, but today, I knew I should. After last night, somebody had to check on her.

47

At the front door, I knocked and held my breath, praying silently that Lisa would answer. She didn't.

Her father appeared, hunched over and almost growling, more shadow than man.

My stomach somersaulted, and I gripped the paper bag tighter in my arms. I hated speaking to him. I hated the very idea of him. He always looked one minor slight away from a barroom brawl.

In place of hello, he grunted, looked me up and down, and showed his teeth.

"Whatever you're selling, girl, I'm not buying," he said, and I almost laughed aloud and spat in his face, because if I was selling what he was really thinking about, he'd purchase it in a heartbeat.

"How's Lisa?" I asked, my gaze locked on him, not faltering, not flashing my fear for him to see.

"Get out of here," he said. "Now."

Not a terrible idea—this wasn't my fight, after all. But if he didn't care about her, then whose fight was it?

A car backfired on the street behind me, the discordant noise punctuating the silence between us. He puffed on a Marlboro Light and blew the smoke in my face. I didn't blink. I didn't slink off the way he thought a woman should. I just stared at him.

"Where is she?" I asked.

"Nowhere that's your business."

With the bag still pressed into my chest, I tightened my hands into fists. "I'll call the police."

He shot me an ugly grin. "They wouldn't come if you did."

Defeat fizzled in my blood. He was right. The Denton Street housewives, nosy ones and genuine ones alike, had placed a bevy of anonymous calls about this house, but it never did any good. Mr. Carter went to the mill and always clocked in on time, and how could a man who was a good worker ever be a terrible father?

But he wasn't there today, of all days. A day of solidarity,

when the men would walk out together and form their picket line in front of the mill's chain-link fence. That meant he'd
stayed home for a reason. My breath heaved, and I knew for
sure it was worse than I thought. Lisa was in serious trouble,
and maybe dead already. I envisioned her body leaking and
twisted and limp on her mattress upstairs, her father draping
her with a stained Raggedy Ann bedsheet and calling it a day.

I needed to get into the house. I needed to check on her. So
I kept talking, anything to fill the space.

"Shouldn't you be at the mill?" I gritted my teeth to keep
them from clattering. "Or did the other men not want you
there? Sent home early, huh?"

For a moment, I was certain he would strike me. Instead, he
reached into his back pocket—slowly, as if to frighten me, as if
he was about to show me a magic trick with a switchblade—
but he only pulled out another cigarette. He made me watch
while he lit it and took a long drag.

"You think you're so clever," he said finally. "But everybody
in this neighborhood talks about you. The little troublemaker.
Drunk half the time, and hanging out with bugs the other half."

I scoffed. "You mean like right now?"

With a snarl, he took a step out the door.

"Nobody wants you around, Phoebe. Not me. Not your Aunt
Betty." He paused, savoring his next remark before he'd spoken
it. "Sometimes not even your own mother."

A low blow, and a well-placed one, but no way I'd let him
know that.

"It's okay." I smiled and wished him dead. "If I waited until
I felt invited, I'd never go anywhere at all."

My hands quivered with rage, and I let the brown paper bag
slip from my grasp. It landed with a thud on the splintered
porch boards. Now I was the one who advanced. A single step
toward him, and then another. His face went ashen, but he
didn't fall back.

"How is she?" I demanded.

"She's fine." His shoulders broadened, blocking the doorway.

"There's nothing wrong with my girl."

"He's right." A figure swathed in a moth-eaten afghan appeared behind him. Lisa, smaller than I remembered her. "I told you last night, Phoebe. I'm fine."

But nothing about her looked fine. Her face wan, she was withering away right in front of me. I wanted to move toward her, to rescue her from this place, to wrap her in a blanket that didn't stink of nicotine and regret, but I hesitated for just a moment, and that moment was precisely what her father was waiting on.

"Now get," he said, and the door slammed in my face.

I stood defeated on the slanted porch before picking up the bag of groceries and trudging back down the steps. Again, I told myself this wasn't my fight. Lisa wasn't even my friend. She never had been. But then, she'd never been anyone's friend, and maybe that was the problem. Besides those anonymous calls, nobody ever cared enough to bother with her.

But there was someone who did care. Kathleen would want to know if her sister was in trouble.

At the end of Denton Street, I dropped a handful of coins in the payphone and stood baking in the sun beneath the white bell logo on the blue booth. The operator transferred me to Chicago, and the newspaper transferred my call to the proper extension.

It only rang once before she answered.

"This is Kathleen Carter, *Chicago Tribune*." I could barely hear her over the hubbub of the office. The rustling of papers, the click-clacking of a typewriter, the silent calculation of her beats and sources and word counts brimming beneath the thrum of her voice. Just because she answered a call didn't mean she stopped working. I imagined her holding the rotary phone in one hand, and the whole world in the other.

"Hello," I said, still stunned that she'd picked up.

"Yes, who is this?"

"This is Phoebe Shaw, and I'm—"

"Phoebe Shaw." She repeated my name like a curse. "You know my sister."

In an instant, the background noise of the office fell quiet, and everything about her shifted, her voice now strange and sharp and afraid.

"Is she okay? Is Lisa okay?"

"I don't... I'm not sure." I expected more lead-up than this, more time to formulate what to say. Now I was cornered by my own doing. "Something happened."

A long, anguished pause. "Something with my father, right?"

"Maybe." My heart twisted, as I wondered if I'd terribly miscalculated, if I should have left Kathleen out of it, at least until I knew more. "Honestly, I don't know."

There was a single exhale on the other end of the line, before she said, composed as before, "Thank you for calling, Ms. Shaw. I'll be there tonight."

The phone clicked, and the drone of the dial tone filled my ears until they ached.

I hung up, not expecting Kathleen to make good on her promise. Plane rides were expensive, and always a hassle to book. It would probably be a week before she finally managed to get back here, if she came back at all. Denton Street was filled with nothing if not good intentions.

))((

When I got back to my house, the brown paper bag heavier than before, Jacqueline was already there, rocking back and forth on the porch swing.

"Hey, you," she said.

"Hello." I climbed the stairs, grateful to see a friendly face. "What are you doing in enemy territory?"

"Mom's working late tonight." She hopped off the swing and started toward me. "She said I could come over for dinner."

This wasn't so unusual. Anytime Aunt Betty had a swing shift at the store, she permitted her daughter to dine at our house, so long as my father was there to monitor us and keep my bad influence in check.

I grinned. "But dinner's not for, like, seven hours."

Jacqueline shrugged. "I guess I'm here early, then. Also," she said, and all the light left her face, "I thought maybe we could talk."

About last night, no doubt. About Lisa.

"How do you think she's feeling?" Jacqueline asked, the two of us sitting together on my bedroom floor.

"I wish I knew," I said.

We wouldn't look at each other. We just stared at our laps, quietly inventing reasons why Lisa was unraveling.

Outside the window, a kid shouted in the street, and a chorus of children giggled in refrain.

"This could get bad," Jacqueline said, and her eyes flicked up at me. "What happens when the housewives find out about her?"

The thought of this chilled me. All of our mothers had been itching to send Lisa away for years. That was why they made all those anonymous calls. Always for her own good, they claimed. Maybe it would have been good for her to be away from her father, but that wasn't the only reason people worried. They also fretted and gossiped about how strange she was, always babbling nonsense and wandering the neighborhood at all hours. Now they had the perfect excuse. With her body oozing gray, they might send her to a hospital, and we'd never see her again.

"We should get out of here," I said. "Just for a little while. Just to avoid problems."

Problems like watching them put Lisa in an ambulance, the same as Dawn. Problems like waiting around and fearing if we stepped out of line, if we were strange like Lisa, then we could be next.

Jacqueline interlaced her fingers and leaned against the green Berber carpet. "That would be nice," she said. "But how, Phoebe? We don't have anywhere to go, and we don't have any money."

I smiled suddenly to myself. "That's not true."

Somewhere, hidden in this house, was a government bond

that was supposed to go to my college fund.

Or Jacqueline and I could use it for something else. To get out before it was too late.

In my parents' bedroom, we rummaged through dresser drawers and dusty cabinets and under-the-bed shoeboxes filled with 1975's tax receipts. Though my mother was just down-stairs in the kitchen, back already from the housewives' point-less meeting, the radio was turned up loud with the afternoon's latest news, dismal as always, so she couldn't hear us, not even when an old cardboard box toppled from the top shelf of the closet and landed at my feet.

"Be careful," Jacqueline said, as a hundred nothing notes floated to earth like cherry blossoms.

I stacked them back in the box, one by one, checking each, and cursing every time it wasn't what we wanted.

Next to me, Jacqueline searched through a stack of my life. Birth certificate, Social Security card, immunization records. All the proof you'd ever need of my existence.

She shook her head. "I'm glad I don't have to worry about things like this."

"Like what?" I asked, shoving a bundle of IRS papers back into the closet.

"Colleges and bonds and a future."

My head snapped toward her. "Don't say that. You have a future."

"Yes, one where I end up like my mom," she said, and sat back, her hands suddenly idle. "That's what always happens, isn't it? We turn out the same as our parents."

I shuddered. "It isn't always like that," I said, and hoped I was right.

Jacqueline turned away from me and looked around the room. "Is there anywhere else your mother hides things?"

"I'm not sure," I said.

I realized how little I knew about my own mother. Who she was, what she wanted, what she did when she wasn't cooking and cleaning and playing the good homemaker. If I was going to turn out like her—which I obviously wasn't—I didn't even know exactly who I'd be.

Then her voice carried up the stairs to me, as if I conjured her.

"Phoebe," she called. "I need your help with dinner."

"We'll look for the bond later," Jacqueline whispered, and I grabbed her hand as we headed down the stairs to the kitchen.

)O(

A quarter after five, my father came home, years older than when he left, and we circled the dinner table. All of us together, my parents and me and Jacqueline, munching on the Sloppy Joes that were supposed to fix everything. But with silence clotting thick in the air, nothing here was fixed. Instead, it felt as if everything had only just started to break.

"Phoebe," my father said, and I perked up at his voice. "Will you have time this weekend to help me change the oil on the Impala? It's past due."

"Of course." I smiled, waiting for him to say something else, about how that car couldn't make it out of the driveway. Then I would say it could reach the stars. Any star in the galaxy.

But my father just stared down at his plate, mouthing empty words to himself and shaking his head, as if arguing with his stuffed cabbage.

I wanted to keep talking. I wanted to do anything.

The doorbell rang, and nobody moved to answer it.

"I'll get it," I said at last, not really thinking it would be for me. But I was wrong.

Kathleen was standing outside, not looking at all how I remembered her. The day she left Denton Street eight years ago, she was wearing a pressed blue suit, her posture finishing-school perfect, her hair slicked back in a tight bun. No doubt then that she was headed for anywhere but here.

Now, in the yellow cast of the frosted porchlight, her face streaked with tears and her hair wild, she looked like one of us all over again.

"Hello, Phoebe," she said, sniffling. "Thank you for calling me today."

I inched onto the porch, and the humid June air twisted between us. I wanted to tell her how impressed I was that she got back to Cleveland so quickly, but she cut me off first.

"There's something I need to show you."

I inhaled a heavy breath and started to say something, but behind me, the screen door creaked open.

Jacqueline glided onto the porch, her footsteps quiet, floating everywhere she went. "Phoebe? Is everything okay?"

"You're Jacqueline, right?" Kathleen stared at her and, not waiting for a response, added, "Good. Let's go."

"Wait." I reached for Kathleen's arm, as she turned away. "What do you want to show us?"

"Please come on," Kathleen said, her eyes dark. "Lisa's asking to see both of you."

She was already down the steps and to the sidewalk before I could argue.

"Why us?" Jacqueline whispered.

"I have no idea," I said. But I knew we couldn't ignore her.

☽○☾

Breaching the Carters' front door wasn't a dare any of us in the neighborhood would accept eagerly. You might toy with a Ouija board or taunt Bloody Mary in a mirror, but nobody was foolish enough to enter that house, especially not at night. Especially not a few hours after you'd already confronted the patriarch of the property.

Fortunately, their father wasn't a problem at the moment. Sprawled and snoring on the couch in front of the TV, he'd rather leave his baby girl to rot in her room than interrupt his routine of self-pity and endless fifths of Mad Dog 20/20.

"Come on," Kathleen whispered. She guided us along the drab shag carpet, past ancient stains and her luggage dropped haphazardly on the floor. Pens and loose-leaf paper and a Canon

55

camera, along with bottles of darkroom chemicals, peeked out through the open zipper. She'd come back planning to stay for as long as she needed, as long as it took to rescue her baby sister.

Lisa's bedroom was at the end of the hall, light seeping out the bottom of the closed door. You could smell it before you were inside. It reeked of stagnant water and earth and something unknown, something that seemed to have passed a threshold and returned. Something not alive.

Inside, Lisa was sitting cross-legged on her mattress, waiting for us.

"Hello again," she said, her shoulders back, still draped in that same afghan. Though she appeared even smaller than earlier today, she wasn't as tragic as I expected. The transformation had imbued her with an air of obscure royalty. For the first time, she possessed something so secret, so exalted, that none of us could understand it. A dubious queen of the unknown.

Kathleen exhaled, long and slow, to steady herself. "Will you show them?"

Lisa shrugged. "If they'd like to see." She regarded both Jacqueline and me. "Would you like to see?"

My lips parted, but I didn't have a chance to answer.

"Yes," Jacqueline said, and the sharp edge in her voice chilled me.

Lisa smiled and tossed her hair, withered and strange and not her own, out of her eyes. "Okay then."

She took her time. Later, I thought how she had all the moments in the world to waste, how we were the ones who needed to see, not her. She already knew what was there. Snapping her tongue, she gathered herself up and perched on the edge of the bed. Then, with steady fingers, she rolled up one sleeve. I was expecting more gray water to pour from her like a mysterious fountain.

But it was so much worse than that. There was a deep gash, carved into the entire length of her arm. Not carved, though. This wasn't done with a cruel hand. The skin had peeled on its own, withering away like she no longer needed flesh. Her body did this to itself, and it was worse than just a wound. Beneath the skin, in the place where her bones should have been, there was something long and corrugated and oxidized.

Rusted metal. Lisa's body was built of rusted metal.

I stumbled backward, and Jacqueline nearly went with me.

"A doctor." I choked on the words. "We need to get her to a doctor."

"That's the problem." Kathleen's jaw set, and she took a long time before she spoke again. "Doctor Ross was already here. I called him first thing. He said not to worry, that he was figuring something out. Like he already knew."

Jacqueline squinted in the dim of the exposed bulb. "Knew about Lisa?"

Kathleen shook her head. "About the others."

I swallowed hard, and the room twisted around me for an instant before everything came into sharp, nauseating focus. The footprints leading away from the abandoned house last night. The footprints before graduation yesterday morning. And those were just the ones I knew about. For the first time in her life, Lisa wasn't alone.

"Who else?" I asked.

Kathleen crossed her arms over her chest. "He wouldn't say. He just told us to sit tight and wait."

As if Lisa could wait much longer.

"What happened?" Jacqueline was kneeling in front of Lisa now. "How did it start?"

"It was funny," Lisa whispered in a sing-song. "You feel it inside your belly, twitching like a little worm. That's the first sign. Do you have a worm inside you, Jacqueline?" Then she looked at me. "Or maybe you have one instead."

Eyes wide, I shook my head and backed away from the bed, toward the wall. Still kneeling, Jacqueline's hand grasped blindly behind her, and I reached out and pulled her up off the floor. We stood together, staring at Lisa, not entirely certain what we saw.

Then a voice cut through the silence, sharp and cruel.

"Girls?" A guttural howl wailed down the hall. "Where are you?"

At once, my whole body went cold. Not right now. Why did he have to wake up right now? I couldn't do this again. I'd been willing to confront Mr. Carter on the front porch in the daylight, but coming face to face with him at night and inside his own house seemed like the stuff of nightmares.

Kathleen, however, knew exactly what to do. She must have been planning for this possibility. In an instant, she was across Lisa's bedroom, prying open the window.

"Go," she whispered to us. "Now."

His footsteps were just outside the door, and we didn't have to time to think about it. Hand in hand, Jacqueline and I climbed through and dropped to the ground. We didn't stop, not until we were halfway down the block.

"Are you okay?" I asked her when we were finally on the sidewalk in front of her house. Breathless, she nodded at me and tightened her hand around mine.

But even then, we weren't free. There wasn't much time left. Dinner was done, Aunt Betty's shift was over, and already I could see her dim figure coming down the sidewalk from the direction of the corner store. I'd have to leave Jacqueline soon. After everything we'd seen, I couldn't stay with her.

"If there are others," Jacqueline said, "where are they? And what if there'll be even more coming?"

"We can't worry about that," I said, shaking my head. "We have to get out. Before it's too late."

Aunt Betty's silhouette was closer now, only six or seven houses away.

"And go where?" A sob lodged in Jacqueline's throat.

The figure was right there, two houses down, almost close enough to touch. Almost close enough to swat me away.

I looked once more at Jacqueline. "We'll figure out something." I clasped both my hands around hers. "I promise."

"Goodnight, Phoebe," Aunt Betty said, and her hot breath prickled the back of my neck.

"Goodnight," I said, not to her, but to Jacqueline, who was already vanishing into the house. Aunt Betty slammed the door behind them and latched the deadbolt emphatically, just so I could hear it from the outside.

Alone again on this terrible street, I blinked in the moonlight, my eyes burning. I counted to ten. This time, Jacqueline came to the window and waved goodbye. I smiled and waved back.

But I couldn't go home. Not yet. I looked back toward the Carter house. There was a figure standing there on the crooked porch. Kathleen. I walked toward her, and she came down the sidewalk to meet me.

Beneath a garish streetlight, we stood together in silence. After a moment, I glanced down at her nervous hands, shaking in the chill of the night. A constellation of tiny scars dotted her arms, each mark the shape of a lit Marlboro Light.

"It's why I left," she said when she noticed me staring. "It's why I told her to leave too. To drop out of school and come to Chicago. Come to *me*." Her face twisted in recollection. "*But someone needs to be here for him*, she'd said. Like he was ever there for us."

I peered across the street toward Dawn's house. All the lights were off.

Kathleen wiped a clump of tear-soaked hair from her cheek. "I should do something." Her eyes, those dark eyes just like Lisa's, just like their father's, gazed into me. "Right?"

"Whatever you want," I said, fidgeting. "She's your sister."

I didn't think of what this plan would be. Not for the rest of the night, when I couldn't sleep, and not the next day when an ambulance, now quiet and brooding, brought Dawn home, the reverse of that night after graduation. From the top of the treehouse, I tried to catch a glimpse of the mewling infant that had stolen her freedom, but all I managed to see was a flash of Dawn's stringy blonde hair before someone ushered her into the house and yanked the blinds closed.

)O(

It wasn't until two days later, when the afternoon edition of the *Cleveland Press* thumped against the front door, that I knew what Kathleen was scheming.

There it was in a back section, printed in bold, dark letters.

BEWARE THE RUST MAIDENS: MYSTERIOUS ILLNESS STRIKES DENTON STREET NEIGHBORHOOD

I should have guessed. She was a writer, so naturally, her solution was to write about it. How she could betray her own sister with such a kitschy headline was inconceivable to me, but that wasn't the worst part. It was where they filed the article: in the News of the Weird section. Our neighborhood had become a punchline, a throwaway joke, and now everyone knew. Doctors, and strangers, and those who wouldn't care about what happened to them. Invaders, reading these words with their late-day coffee and secretly planning their own trip to Denton Street to get a look for themselves.

And I'd been the one to encourage Kathleen to make this happen. I was the one who called her, the one who helped to turn their suffering into this. I'd tried my best to fix things, and like always, I'd only made it so much worse. I was exactly what Mr. Carter accused me of being: the girl who was nothing but a troublemaker.

Me. My fault.

FOUR

They arrived at dusk. Some came by car, others on foot, and one group—invasive as kudzu vines—even chartered a bus. Polaroid cameras tucked in fanny packs, they stalked along the road, those who wanted a glimpse of our neighborhood's unmentionables, pretending to be long-lost relatives searching for an address, all the while snapping pictures and whispering with one another.

We gathered on the porch after dinner and watched them violate the neighborhood.

"They're only nuisances," my father said, puffing absently on a billiard pipe, as though girls on Denton Street had always changed into monsters and out-of-town interlopers had always sought them out.

Jacqueline sat with my mother, and the two of them played a game of checkers. I tucked myself in the corner behind the swing and tried not to sob.

None of us talked about the strike. My father's picket duty was finished for the evening, and that was that. When he came home, you could practically hear him slap the dust off his hands and call it a day.

This was the great lie we invented, that we could actually escape ourselves. I'd learned at a young age how outsiders saw us during strikes. Labor union members with cardboard signs, arms looped solidly together, the faces of our fathers and brothers and uncles creased and contorted in cries of righteousness. These were the front-line moments that won photographers national awards and made the covers of *Time* and *Newsweek*.

But these weren't our usual moments during strikes. Our usual moments were all monotony, all waiting. Families unmoored and silent, the rhythm of our days stolen from us. The long hours between, as the weight of our predicament settled heavy on our shoulders and our futures became enormous, accusing question marks. Nobody wanted to photograph us like this, the four of us on the porch, smoking a pipe or playing checkers or screaming as loud as we could without making a sound.

In this way, perhaps the Rust Maidens were an almost welcome relief in early June, a distraction from our own very real problems.

Within an hour of the newspaper arriving on our porches, all the housewives had invited each other over for tea so they could take turns reading the article aloud. The story confirmed that only girls were affected. Nothing else was quite so clear. What was causing it, or the identity of the other Rust Maidens, was unknown. Kathleen had managed to bribe a nurse at the local hospital and learned that a total of three patients had been cataloged away under special case files. None of the girls were named in the article, but I knew that meant Lisa plus two Jane Does. Or, at least, Jane Does to me. A girl was never a Jane Doe, not really. She always knew her own name, even if the world didn't.

"And anyhow," my mother said, apparently continuing a conversation she was having with herself, the first half of which the rest of us weren't privy to, "it's just a weird illness. That's all those girls have. Stitch them up and let's move on."

I rolled my eyes. "Yes, because whenever I come down with a cold, my bones always rust away."

"An exaggeration, I'm sure." My mother hopped a black token over three of Jacqueline's red ones. "Those girls are just playing it up for the attention."

I buried my head in my hands and said nothing else.

At eleven o'clock, as my parents watched the nightly news, I walked Jacqueline home. We stood outside her house without speaking.

"It isn't your fault, you know," she said finally.

I shook my head. "I was the one who called Kathleen."

"It would have happened anyhow," Jacqueline said. "People eventually would have found out."

"Maybe." I hesitated. "How about Monday morning?"

Jacqueline squinted at me. "For what?"

"For leaving," I said. "I haven't found the college bond yet, but I've got a few hundred dollars saved up. That'll last us a little while."

Her eyes went dark. "Phoebe, I don't know."

"If you don't want to leave—"

"I want to," she said. "I'm just not sure. What if it doesn't work?"

"What if staying is worse?"

She nodded. "We'll see what happens," she said, before squeezing my hand and disappearing inside her house. I counted and waited until the lights went on upstairs in her bedroom. She waved at me behind the curtains, and I waved back. There was a comfort in that light, in knowing she was there. I would sometimes glance out my own window in the middle of the night and see that light glinting down the street, and I would feel the tug of home, of happiness aching inside me. Nothing in the world could hurt me as long as we were both here.

I turned and started back down Denton Street when a figure swam into the edge of my vision.

"Hey," someone in the shadows said.

Part of me was certain it was a Rust Maiden, or all of the Rust Maidens, here to wave their long bandaged arms at me like the accusing fingers of Death. To claim me as their own. I held my breath as the figure came into focus.

Clint loitered on the porch of the abandoned house next door, steadying himself against the railing with one hand and holding a half-empty bottle of Jim Beam in the other. He didn't know about the hidden key. We never told him. Anytime he wanted to get away from his parents, he came here, but he couldn't get inside. Just like he deserved.

With a smirk, he plodded unevenly down the steps and came nearer to me. Up close, he looked the same as he always did, a little ragged but mostly none the worse for wear. I wondered for an instant if anyone had bothered to tell him about the Rust Maidens, or if he had bothered to care when they did.

"How's Dawn?" My voice wavered, not entirely certain I wanted the answer.

Clint shrugged. "She's doing her best to recover, I guess."

He guessed. Fury surged inside me. What did I ever see in him? I should have always known I could do better than this careless boy next door. Poor Dawn. If only she'd known that too.

"And the baby?" I asked.

"My responsibility," he said and chugged from the bottle. "Dawn's on bed rest, doctor's orders, so her parents expect me to take care of Eleanor." He let out a rueful laugh like a cat puking. "As if I know how to breastfeed and change diapers."

I shifted on the sidewalk, and Clint studied my face before he leaned in closer. Maybe it was on purpose, or just an artless swaying of the body, the embarrassing result of too much whiskey. I shivered and inched away from him. I should run, but I wanted to know more about Dawn and what had happened at the hospital. About why they'd taken her away.

But as I stood there, the words didn't come. How could I form the question that needed to be asked? *Is the mother of your child a monster?*

"That's a pretty name," I said finally.

Clint threw back another shot of whiskey before smearing his hand over his wet mouth. "What is?"

"Eleanor." I stared at him. "You just said your daughter's name is Eleanor, didn't you?"

"Oh, that," he said and rolled his eyes. "Not my first pick. I wanted to go with Linda. You know, after Linda Ronstadt." He hesitated, waiting for me to agree with him, but when I said nothing, he added, half under his breath, "Dawn thought Eleanor sounded more timeless or something."

I backed away. Nearer to the street. Nearer to home.

But Clint wouldn't let me go that easy. He swayed again, this time closing the distance between us.

"Maybe you can come over to my house later," he said. "We could hang out."

His hand was on my arm before I could stop him. Not a gruff touch, but light and inviting. Like a memory. Like the first time. Now I remembered what I saw in him: the possibilities, the thought of a night not ending alone, here in a neighborhood that knew loneliness all too well. That almost made it worse, the reminder of what a fool I'd been to want Clint, to ever consider him as a way out.

"Your girlfriend's in trouble." I yanked my arm away from him. "Don't try to get me in trouble too."

"Don't worry," he said, as I turned back to the street. "I doubt you'll ever get yourself into the kind of trouble she's in right now."

In the dark, I walked home alone, thinking of what Clint's words meant for Dawn. For what she'd become, or was becoming.

What any of us girls could become.

))C((

The rest of the week, I stayed awake every night, packing what I could and silently making plans. Calculating tolls and gas prices and mileage. The Impala could take Jacqueline and me anywhere. To the moon. To the stars. To safety. By Sunday, I was almost ready. That was when the worst of them arrived.

Government men.

We weren't sure if the three of them were CDC or FBI or some other arcane three-letter acronym that stood for "Not Your Business," but here they were, in the hideous flesh, the men of the dark suits and darker glasses. You couldn't see their eyes behind those tinted lenses, and sitting on the lawn out in front of the church, my pale dress smeared with grass, I almost wondered if they had eyes at all. Or if they had souls, either.

We knew what they wanted: to study the girls. Maybe to take samples from them, or just steal them away to a lab somewhere. All of this done on behalf of the people, even though they'd somehow forgotten that girls were people too.

Earlier that morning, the men had come to the corner store immediately upon arriving in Cleveland, so Aunt Betty made her round-robin calls to everyone on Denton Street, including my mother, warning us of the impending invasion. She also learned the men's names, which she shared liberally, as if calling them by their proper monikers would bind their power, the DC Rumpelstiltskins. Not that it helped us any. We couldn't keep the older two straight.

"I think the taller one's Jeffers," I said as we watched him stalk across the lawn.

Jacqueline shook her head. "No, that's definitely Godfrey. The shorter one with the blond hair is Jeffers."

She and I went back and forth like that for a while, less because we cared which was which, and more because it gave us something to do. Anything that made us forget why they were here.

None of us, however, had trouble remembering the third.

"Adrian," Aunt Betty had told us. No last name, not that he even needed one, not with that ridiculous wannabe Cary Grant face of his to buoy him through the formalities of life. You could almost hear the collective sigh of the neighborhood girls as he smiled and introduced himself to everyone. His dark glasses off now, eyes bright, knowing his power but pretending not to.

"The young dumb one," I said, scoffing.

Jacqueline laughed. "You would say that."

I scowled as the church bell rang and he scurried across the lawn. "What does that mean?"

"It means he's your type, Phoebe." She grinned. "He looks like a good time and trouble."

I turned away, a flush burning my cheeks. "It doesn't matter," I said. "We won't be here much longer."

Jacqueline nodded, all the brightness gone from her eyes. "Do you have it all worked out, then?"

"Close enough," I said. "Even if we don't know every detail, that's okay. We can make it up as we go along."

After the service, I walked Jacqueline home, and somehow, the government men beat us there. Out of all the places for them to stay, they opted to rent the abandoned house next to hers. That might have been the worst of it. They'd stolen our party spot. Now if Jacqueline and I wanted to sneak a drink, we'd have to do it in my treehouse or on a late-night drive in my Impala.

Not that it made any difference. We'd soon be gone from here. Then we could drink anywhere we wanted.

Fresh off a shift at the corner store, Aunt Betty appeared at the front door and hauled Jacqueline inside, threatening me with a broom if I didn't "shoo." I rolled my eyes and started toward home.

As I passed the house next to Jacqueline's, Adrian emerged from the side door. When he saw me, he flashed a smile. "Phoebe Shaw, yes?"

I hesitated, caught off-guard by the greeting. Then the truth settled over me, and I sneered.

"You memorized all our names?" I envisioned him on the plane ride from Washington, poring over DMV photographs of everyone on Denton Street, learning our mothers' maiden names and our heights and weights and anticipated majors in college. "That's creepy."

He shrugged. "That's my job."

"Some occupational requirements," I said. "Must wear a suit. Must sort through mountains of useless papers. Must be a creep."

I expected him to snarl or insult me back, but he only smiled again. "It's a living."

That grin of his lingered a moment longer, and I liked it more than I should. I hurried off without another word. Jacqueline was wrong. He was not a good time. Or if he was, I'd never know it.

Trudging home alone, I made myself a list of promises.

I would avoid him.

I would avoid all of them—the government men and the tourists and the doctors with their stethoscopes and thermometers and scalpels they didn't even know how to use, at least not on patients like the Rust Maidens.

I would get out of here. We only had to survive another night, Jacqueline and me. Maybe I'd come back for school in the fall, if the Rust Maidens were fixed by then, but if not, then we'd figure something else out. Maybe we'd build a bug house in Alaska and study what kind of creatures could live in the permafrost. That would be a welcome change from this place. And not much colder than a winter spent on Lake Erie.

This would all be okay.

The next morning, I gassed up the Impala and put my pittance of luggage in the trunk. My mother was down the block at one of the communal housewife meetings, and Aunt Betty was there too, already dressed in her smock for her next shift at work.

I waited for twenty minutes after my mother left. By then, the tea and gossip would be flowing, and she wouldn't double back. Now was my chance. This was when Jacqueline and I could finally escape. I crept down the block to Jacqueline's house and knocked on the front door, almost as familiar as my own. I held my breath until she opened it.

"Are you ready?" I asked, smiling, but instantly, I knew she wasn't.

There on the other side, Jacqueline stood with her shoulders slumped, still in her pajamas.

"Today's the day," I said, the hopefulness waning in my voice.

"I know," she whispered.

I gaped at her. "Do you need help getting ready?"

She shook her head.

My throat tightened, and I inched toward her. "What's wrong?"

"Nothing," she said, but when I asked her to come out, she said she couldn't. And she wouldn't let me in, either.

"I'm sorry," was all she'd say.

Then she slammed the door and vanished from my life. Just like that.

FIVE

The figure is still standing on the front porch. This is no mirage, no matter how many times I blink and wish it away. I close my eyes and try my best to remember where I am.

Back home in Cleveland, in my parents' almost-empty house.

I open my eyes and look again. I tell myself I was wrong. It turns out I don't know who this visitor on the porch is. She's not one of the Rust Maidens, that's for sure. She can't be. It's been too long, and they wouldn't look the same. But my fingers shake anyhow, and I loop the chain across the door, pretending that little gold link will be enough to keep out the past.

"Hello?" the voice calls out brightly. "I can see you. What's wrong in there?"

Though the curtains on the windows are pulled shut, they're too gauzy, old floral-printed linen that was never nice, not even when it was new. That means while my figure is blurred too, I'm still visible. Of course I am. Fabulous scheme, Phoebe. Hiding in plain sight.

This is ridiculous.

My hands still shaking, I drift forward and creak open the door, but I leave the chain on. Just in case.

On the other side is a face I don't recognize. It's a girl, older than any of the Rust Maidens were, but probably fifteen years younger than me. I don't know her, haven't ever seen her before, though she looks strangely familiar. Everything on Denton Street is an echo of itself, the past repeating into the present, like mirrors set up to reflect one another into eternity.

She smiles at me. "Is Mrs. Shaw here?"

"Who are you?" I blurt out the question and immediately regret it. This is no way to start. I'm trying to be someone better than myself. Better than a middle-aged woman who fears ghosts who don't fear her. I swallow hard and try again. "What is it that you need?"

This somehow doesn't seem much politer, but the girl's smile only broadens before she answers both my questions.

"I'm Nora," she says. "Mrs. Shaw and I have tea every Thursday at eleven."

This whirls around my brain for a second. Is it Thursday? Is it eleven? Does my mother even drink tea?

A long moment passes as I recalibrate myself to a reality in which my mother still hosts regular social occasions like a regular woman.

Nora purses her lips, a shadow crossing her face. "But if she's not here—"

"No, she's not."

I want to send her away. I want to be alone in this place, where I can fold up my bedroom and wallow in whatever self-pity is the order of the day. Poor Phoebe, too lonely for friends and family. Poor Phoebe, too old for hopes and dreams. Poor Phoebe, too haunted to even close her eyes and rest.

On the other side of the door, Nora fidgets and looks ready to turn away on her own. That would make this easier, if she had the decency to leave me in peace. But no, that's not the way this should go. Again, I'm trying to be a better version of me.

"My mother should be back soon." I hesitate before sliding

the chain off the door. "If you want to come in and wait."

This last part isn't exactly an invitation. More like an incomplete thought. But Nora takes it as an offer anyhow, and crosses the threshold.

There's a stranger in my house. But she's only a stranger to me, not a stranger to the house itself, or to my mother, or to probably anyone else in the neighborhood. That makes me wonder if after all these years, I'm the stranger here.

"You said Mrs. Shaw is your mother?" Nora inspects my face, cataloging my features, as though she were expecting to discover me here. "That means you're Phoebe, right?"

I nod, but say nothing else. It's not surprising she knows my name. My mother used to have pictures of me arraying the living room. Newborn me above the mantle. Me on the first day of kindergarten, cluttering a corner. Me at graduation over the turntable, though why she'd want to remember that day, so close to when everything disintegrated, I'll never know.

The pictures are gone now, packed away with the rest of our lives, but the outlines of their frames remain on the walls. Over one of their dubious teas, my mother probably mentioned me too, mentioned that once upon a time, she had a daughter. I'm a cautionary tale in the neighborhood, a "what not to do" if you'd like half a chance at a good life.

We linger in silence as I try to remember how to act in a situation like this. Nora smiles again, and I start to wonder if her friendliness in odd circumstances is almost a strange kind of nervous tic.

"Do you want me to get the tea?" she asks.

I shake my head. Pretend to be a good hostess, Phoebe.

My nervous hands clasped in front of me, I wander into the empty kitchen and stand disoriented for a moment. Tea. I didn't know my mother liked tea. She always drank cordials and amaretto and whiskey straight from the bottle when things got bad. But then, who isn't a fan of tea? I suppose everybody enjoys a cup of Earl Gray or chamomile now and then. .

I can't imagine my mother having a weekly meeting with

this girl, either. It seems like something she would have told me about, an offhand snippet to punctuate the end of another stifled phone conversation.

"Oh, darling, I have to go now. Nora's here, and I can't keep her waiting for her Twinings."

But nothing like that was ever mentioned, not even once. Of course, I don't know my mother these days. I haven't known her for years. And maybe it's a new habit, one she's picked up since my father went into care. Someone to keep her company one day a week, because her only daughter wasn't good enough to do the job.

The cupboards are dusty, and I wipe away a handful of cobwebs as I search through them. In the last one over the stove, I strain on my tiptoes and peek inside. A yellowed box of Lipton sits sullenly in the corner. I swear it looks like the same box that was here when I was a kid.

At the sink, I fill the kettle and pretend everything is normal.

When I bring in the pot and two mugs to the dining room, Nora's already seated at the card table in the corner, a bright smile on her face. But somehow, I get an odd sense of movement about the room, the air churning and restless, as though she were searching the corners and crevices, and only rushed to the chair when she heard me lumbering in with the teapot.

"Almost all packed up," she says, her hands patting her thighs in a strange kind of rhythm. "I can't believe your mom's really leaving."

"I can't believe it myself."

The Lipton over-steeps and ends up bitter, but Nora doesn't complain. She has plenty else to talk about. Her words ring in my ears like the fallout of a too-loud rock concert.

"This was a beautiful house in its day. I hear it's got quite a history."

"This whole neighborhood has history, they say. But it was before my time."

"It has to be hard for you to be back here, Phoebe. After all these years. After everything."

I fidget in the folded chair. She's asking things without ever saying them. It's a clever skill, one I almost admire.

She stirs sugar in her tea. "That summer had to be awful for you."

"Yes," I say, and my mouth aches with confessions I've needed to make for almost thirty years, "but I imagine it was worse for them."

The spoon stops turning in the mug. "For whom? For the girls?"

"Yes, for them."

I breathe in, ready to say something, ready to tell this stranger, this peculiar girl everything. All the things I've been hiding for almost three decades. But when I look up, my mother is standing there in front of us, her jaw slack, her fiery gaze fixed squarely on Nora.

"You," she says.

Slowly, Nora stands from her chair, her face twisted somewhere between agony and quiet rage. "I told you I'd get in here someday, Mrs. Shaw."

My chest tightens, and I look frantically between them. My mother moves toward Nora, hands curling into fists.

"You waited until I left, didn't you?" she asks. "You'd do anything to get into this house. Wouldn't you, Eleanor?"

I can't move. I can't breathe. That name steals my breath away. Eleanor.

"You're Dawn's daughter," I whisper, and the words taste of ash.

A harsh smirk twitches across her lips. "I would've thought you'd call me Clint's daughter."

I should be wounded by this, a slight against my past romances, but I'm not. Eleanor's probably accumulated a lifetime of stories about me and how I was more than acquainted with her father.

"You were about to say something." Eleanor moves toward me. "Tell me what it was."

"Enough." My mother cuts between us. "You weren't invited in, my dear."

"But I was, Mrs. Shaw." Eleanor grins. "Your daughter invited me."

Her jaw set, my mother seizes Eleanor by the shoulders. With one strong arm in her back, she hustles the invader to the door and shoves her through it. "Try it again," she says, "and I'll call the police."

The door slams, and the figure on the porch vanishes almost as quickly as it appeared.

But that doesn't mean she's gone. I close my eyes and see her there.

Eleanor, all grown up. The girl I thought was a stranger is instead someone I know. I wish I could respool this day and try again. Not let her in at all, or have her be someone else. Someone I truly don't know and never will.

"It seems unreal," I say.

For some reason, it never occurred to me that it would happen, that the baby from that long-ago summer would ever be anything but that same woebegone infant.

"That girl." My mother snaps her tongue. "Sneaking into places she doesn't belong."

I try to catch a steady breath. "She's done this before?" I ask.

"Too many times to count." My mother rolls her eyes. "She's like a cockroach, always trying to find a way in."

I hesitate. "What does she want?"

"The truth, I guess." My mother chirps up a laugh. "Like any of us know that."

I swallow hard, and wish I didn't know.

My mother tells me of Eleanor, of her series of dead-end jobs at places that always folded up almost as quickly. First at the corner store when she was a teenager, probably working under Aunt Betty, poor kid. Then a small clothing factory on the outskirts of Lakewood that didn't stay open more than a couple years. Now she's at a gas station a few blocks away, where she trades cigarettes for spare change under a plastic window, but that's not likely to stick around either. Management's already talking about making cuts due to "the economy," that favorite Rust Belt excuse for conscripting people to the unemployment line.

I listen quietly to the checklist of Eleanor's life, all of it so painfully banal that it makes me want to cry.

"Don't feel bad, Phoebe." My mother watches me, her gaze almost pitying. "It's not your fault. How can she expect anything better? She's nothing but a troublemaker. Just like—"

Her voice cuts out abruptly, and I stare at her.

"What were you going to say?" I ask.

She waves one hand at me and turns to the place where the liquor cabinet used to be. "Nothing, dear."

"It wasn't nothing." I take one step toward her. "You were going to say 'just like her mother.' Right?"

"Yes, it happens that I was." She purses her lips and brushes past me toward the card table. "But I didn't say it."

That's what she meant, though, and that's all that matters.

She clears the kettle and the mugs and takes them to the sink, where she eagerly rinses away every trace of Eleanor from the house.

I watch her from the doorway. "Does she live with Clint?"

My mother scoffs. "No," she says, half-lashing the word. "Clint doesn't really live anywhere these days. Not unless you count a barstool as an apartment."

This revelation should tug at something deep inside me, my lost first love, but instead it's neither jarring nor interesting to think of him that way. If anything, it's the most obvious and boring punctuation on the end of a most obvious and boring life.

"So where does Eleanor stay?"

"With her grandmother." My mother hesitates before clarifying. "Clint's mother. They're almost moved out already, from what I hear."

I nod absently. Naturally, Eleanor would be with Clint's parents. Dawn's family moved away that fall after everything that happened. Moved away and never looked back.

"Eleanor's not a child anymore." My mother turns from the sink to face me. "She's an adult, Phoebe. She could leave here or stay or do whatever she pleases."

"I guess," I say, but I wonder how much leaving would help

her. Look at how much it helped me.

The dishes scrubbed clean of Eleanor, my mother dries her hands on the only dishcloth left in the house, a fusty thing dotted with faded strawberries pouring out of a pitcher.

"By the way," she says, her eyes going dark, "where were you this morning?"

"Just outside," I mumble, and motion for the door. I can't think of anything better to say. I didn't expect her to be awake and gone so early. I certainly didn't expect her to ask me about it.

My mother shakes her head. "I get up and you're gone, and you know, for a minute, I thought—"

Everything goes suddenly still in the house, and she doesn't finish this sentence. She doesn't have to. We both know what she thought, how she was sure I'd joined them at last, those girls we can't forget.

"I didn't go far," I say. "I was just down the block. You could have come looking for me."

She lets out a strident laugh that sets my blood buzzing. "Did looking for you help me before? When you left without saying goodbye?"

She leans over the sink to steady herself.

"Where did *you* go?" I ask, desperate to change the subject.

"To see your father." She glances up at me. "I'd hoped you would come with me."

I shake my head. I don't know that I'm ready yet to see him like that. My strong father, now thin and frail and gone. At least, gone in all the ways that count.

"Maybe tomorrow," I say, and hope the day never comes.

$$)O($$

For dinner, we order takeout and eat at the little card table. My mother wipes it down twice before she sets out the Styrofoam containers of linguini, and though she says it's just because of dust, I know it's to ensure we get no trace of Eleanor in our pasta.

Afterward, she turns in early, but I stay downstairs. I won't go into my bedroom. I haven't been back there since last night, when things were different somehow. Before I met Eleanor. Before Quinn showed me what's in that house.

I'm not ready to take apart my room yet, to dig through boxes of keepsakes and secrets. But I am ready to take apart something else.

In the backyard, winter blisters in my lungs. I always forget how cruel Decembers in Cleveland are. What an unrelenting thief the weather can be.

But I have something to do now. Something that matters. The treehouse hangs over me, a reminder of that summer. I don't care what the investors do with this strip of land. They can leave it to rot, for all that it matters. But these memories are mine, and it's time for me to dissect them. To leave the treehouse in pieces, so nobody else can inherit my mistakes.

I climb up, armed only with sheer will and a hammer I found in the garage. That's enough to do this job.

Piece by piece, I dismember my life. It feels better than it should.

Rusted nails and shards of wood slough off to the yard below. Over and over, I remove these fragments of the past, remembering everything in spite of myself.

Here's the plank where the potted milkweed sat.

Here's where I used to hide my flask.

Here's the triple moon sign etched in the heat of that summer.

Here's where Jacqueline and I curled up side by side and pretended we could outlast forever.

Specters swirl around me as I pry up a board in the corner. The water damage is extensive here, and there's a rotted-out section in the middle of an old knothole, just enough for my fingers to slip through. Just enough to find what's waiting there for me. Wood and decay, and what feels like bone.

For the longest moment of my life, something inside the decay is holding my hand.

I exhale what must be a scream, or the closest thing to it, as my body lurches against what's left of one wall. The board tumbles to the ground below, and my hands quiver in front of me. They're mine, they're mine, they're mine. What was there isn't touching me now, if it was anything at all. It's hard to tell in this place. Even when I'm really alone, I might imagine someone is here in the darkness. I might imagine that I know who it is, and that's why those fingers felt cold and damp and withered, yet strangely familiar too.

I clutch the hammer to my chest and decide to call it a night. It's not even midnight yet, and the treehouse isn't entirely dismantled. It's half here and half gone, an appropriate relic for Denton Street. I might just leave it that way. I might not be brave enough to risk another rotted board.

My coat bundled tight, I climb down. Quinn is waiting there to greet me.

"I found something else," she says. "Something new."

I shouldn't go with her. I just spent the last hour obliterating the past. But I can't help myself. If she's discovered another sign, then I have to know.

I don't even agree. She just starts walking, and I follow. We travel past Jacqueline's house. There's a notice on the door about the demolition that no one's bothered to remove or read. All the lights are out inside, but that doesn't mean the place is abandoned. The same upstairs curtains remain across Jacqueline's bedroom window, and I turn away, terrified if I count to ten, they might flutter and reveal someone I once knew.

"This way," Quinn whispers, and leads me through the open back door of the preacher's house. Like Violet's, it's empty now, and ready to crumble, maybe as early as tomorrow.

I've never been in here before, even though I'd been invited to Helena's birthday party every year. My mother had begged me to go, just to keep the peace, but I always refused, leaving her to invent a new excuse each August. It wasn't Helena's fault, really. It was just that I spent enough time in her father's other house on Sundays, and that was bad enough. No way was I spending my Saturday with the family too.

Now, standing in what's left of their lives, I regret not RS-VPing. It wouldn't have hurt me, not like it ultimately hurt her, anyhow.

I run my hands through my hair. "Why are we here, Quinn?"

She paces down the hall and into the center of the living room. "There," she says, and points to the air. "Can you hear it?"

I strain to listen. A strange echo lilts all around us, faraway, yet whispering in my ear.

"It sounds like someone singing," she says. "Don't you think so?"

That's exactly what it sounds like, but I shake my head. "It's only the wind whistling through."

It's not them. I tell myself it can't be them.

"This isn't wind, I promise you," Quinn says, and something moves behind her. The muscles across my back constrict, and everything around us comes into sharp focus.

Quinn shivering before me, unaware of what comes next.

The winter air sparkling with ice and regret.

My breath fogging in front of me, letting me know I'm still breathing, even though I can't feel it.

Then she's here with us, a wraith as much as her mother. Eleanor, materializing from the shadow. I wonder if this is the only way she knows how to appear: swiftly and inexplicably, like she has to surprise people if she has any chance of them not exiling her. She must have seen us come in and followed.

"So you hear it too?" she asks.

Quinn whirls around and glares at her. "Of course we do," she says. "And anyhow, what do you want, Eleanor?"

I exhale a sigh. It's no surprise these two know each other. They live in the same neighborhood. They've probably argued on this street a hundred times before. But Eleanor wants nothing to do with Quinn. She's here for me.

"You think it's for you, don't you?" Eleanor moves toward me. "But what if it's for me? What if it's my mother?"

I shrug and push back the moldering curtains on the window, anything to keep my hands occupied. "You can think whatever you'd like."

"You were going to tell me something today." Eleanor keeps inching forward, nearer to me each moment. I can feel her eyes accusing me. Of what, even she doesn't know. "What were you going to say?"

I turn to stare at her. She's blocking the doorway and I can't get out. All I want to do is run. All I ever want to do is run.

"It was nothing," I say, and almost believe myself.

Quinn glances between us. "Why are you so sure Phoebe knows anything?"

"Because she was closer to them than anyone," Eleanor says. "She was there with them that last night. I'm sure of it. That's why she left."

She's right. Maybe now it's time to admit it. To say what I saw. What happened that summer, that final evening when I ran. Maybe I should confess it in front of Eleanor and Quinn, and all of the ghosts on Denton Street we've tried to forget.

But I can't. Because the moon's pouring in through the window now, and I see what wasn't clear before.

There's a tiny gash on Quinn's arm. It's deep and red and glinting with something. I don't have to look close to know what it is.

"Phoebe?" Quinn stares at me. "What's wrong?"

I swallow a sob. "Nothing," I say, and wish it were true.

SIX

For the next three days, I called Jacqueline. She wouldn't pick up. I went to the house when Aunt Betty was at work. No answer. Every time I knocked, I would see her shape flutter past her bedroom window, but she wouldn't look down at me. Not so much as a twitch of the pale lace curtains. I wasn't worth the trouble.

This was my fault. I'd invited the tourists in, and I'd pushed Jacqueline to leave when she wasn't ready. It was almost as if I couldn't help myself. If there was a bad decision to be made, you could be damned sure I'd run toward it at full speed.

That night, the women of Denton Street gathered in our kitchen, where they sucked down cigarette smoke and discussed the Fourth of July block party. I huddled in the doorway and listened.

My mother sat at the table, notes sprawled out in front of her. She was the secretary, and had been for long as I could remember. "Next item of business: shall we secure a permit from the city to close off the road like we did last year?"

They all voted yes, and my skin buzzed with unease. This event was the cornerstone of our summer, and we were going to pretend that this was indeed like every other year. Though so far, very little about 1980 looked like anything I could even call life.

"I bet the strike will be over by next week," Clint's mother said, apropos of nothing. "Then things can get back to normal."

My mother scribbled something to keep her hands busy. "Of course," she said. "Remember when they fixed up the mill equipment last year? Why bother doing that if you're going to lay off your whole workforce?"

All the mothers nodded and gave each other tight, miserable smiles. Nobody wanted to point out the truth: that other than a few gears on the conveyor belt and a new door for the blast furnace that the state inspectors demanded the mill replace or else, there had been no major repairs to the place in almost a decade. The owners were letting our lives rot out from underneath us.

One of the women at the table hesitated, a pack of Lucky Strikes quivering in her hand. "Do you think it's our fault?" she asked. "I mean, what's happening to the girls?"

The others didn't say anything. They crossed their arms and smoked the last of their cigarettes and pretended the green and orange geometric shapes on the linoleum were too fascinating to look away.

"It's not our fault," Clint's mother said finally. "Girls are always trouble."

"But what if it's something in the water?" a voice in the back asked.

"Or something in the air? The smog's gotten thick this year," the preacher's wife said.

My mother's fingers tightened around her highball glass. "Or maybe it's something at the mill."

Everyone went instantly quiet, and I knew, without a doubt, they'd all been thinking the same thing.

"Don't say that." From the corner, Aunt Betty moved toward my mother, and I wondered if she intended to slap her for the mere suggestion. "Don't blame the men. They didn't do this."

I exhaled a sharp laugh. "Of course not," I said. "We wouldn't want to hold them accountable for anything."

At this, Aunt Betty turned away from my mother, and glared right through me. "Do you have something to add, Phoebe?"

"No," I said, and smiled. "I think I already did."

I was out the door before anybody could say another word.

I went walking. Around and around the neighborhood, part of me convinced if I made enough loops on this street, I could set the world straight, and Jacqueline would come with me. Or better yet, maybe if I could take the right number of steps in precisely the proper order, everything would balance out and the Rust Maidens wouldn't exist at all. They'd simply be normal girls in a normal neighborhood.

Not that anything on Denton Street—or in Cleveland, for that matter—was normal anymore.

)O(

The doctors arrived in the neighborhood on a Thursday afternoon. I was standing in front of Jacqueline's house when they poured out of a black Cadillac across the street, looking like mourners decked out for a funeral.

Adrian came out of his rented house and joined me on the sidewalk as the whitecoats took their bags of tricks into Dawn's. There were too many of them for a routine checkup. My stomach lurched as the realization sank deep into me.

Clint had meant what he said. She was one of them. Dawn was a Rust Maiden.

"Will they take the girls away?" I blurted the question before I could stop myself.

Adrian glanced at me, gauging his next words carefully.

"That was the initial plan," he said. "But too many had been exposed by the time we got here. We'd have to quarantine half the city now. It would cause a panic." He hesitated. "And we'd rather not do that."

Rather not. That meant they still might.

"And in the meantime?" I asked.

"We'll keep them under observation," he said, "and wait to see what happens."

He was standing right next to me now, close enough that I could reach out and touch him. Not that I would reach out, or did reach out. Just that I could have.

A good time and trouble. I'd practically replaced his name in my mind with that phrase. With Jacqueline's phrase. Her voice echoed everywhere I went.

She was lost to me, and I had to know why. That meant going to the last person in the world I wanted to see.

$$)O($$

At the corner store, next to a news rack filled with warnings about the Soviets and Dorothy Stratten's plastic-sealed face on the cover of *Playboy*, I ordered coffee and stared across the counter at Aunt Betty. She stared back, looking bored at my very existence.

"What's wrong with Jacqueline?" I asked, doing my best to steady my voice.

She popped her pink gum in my face and shrugged. "Nothing, so far as I know."

"Something *is* wrong." I took a big gulp of hot coffee, and the skin on the insides of my cheeks peeled away from the heat. I only half noticed. "She won't talk to me. She won't answer my calls."

"Then I'd say something finally went right with that girl." Aunt Betty shot me a smug grin.

My fingers tightened around the Styrofoam cup, and I imagined tossing the contents into her face. Not that it would do any good. If Jacqueline didn't want to talk to me now, I doubted maiming her mother would help my chances.

The bell chimed again and again, and tourists poured into the store, their cameras slung around their necks.

Aunt Betty glided off to service their every need. "All in a day's work," she mumbled, and I loathed everything about her. But I didn't leave. I hoped to glean something about Jacqueline yet.

Another ding of the bell over the door. I turned in time to see Kathleen and Lisa skitter down the farthest aisle. The two of them must have sneaked out. No way had the doctors approved this errand.

I took another sip of coffee and steadied myself. Now was as good a time as any for a confrontation.

At a rack of prepackaged fruit pies, I cut Kathleen off. "How could you?"

Lisa scurried off to the corner to buy smokes, her leaky arms wrapped up tighter than a sarcophagus.

Kathleen didn't say anything for a long while. She just glared at me, as if anticipating this. "I didn't do anything," she said, and took a heavy step forward. For an instant, a dark glimmer of her father danced behind her eyes. I inched away from her, my stomach cramping, but before I could say a word, she caught herself and retreated, cheeks pink with shame.

"I wouldn't do that to Lisa," she said, quieter now. "What I submitted was a real piece of investigative journalism. The editors gutted it."

I inspected her face and realized she wasn't lying. Though perhaps it wasn't the editors' fault. Maybe it was, at least in part, the fault of the writer. How could Kathleen possibly manage an iota of objectivity when she was writing about her own sister? More than likely, she submitted a piece that was more heartbreak than it was facts and figures. The paper might have just done the best with what she'd given them.

"Why draw attention at all?" I asked.

"Because," Kathleen said, her voice heaving, "nobody here cared. Not the doctors or our parents or anyone. I thought if other people knew, they might help us. They might do something. Instead, they came to our street to gawk." She exhaled a soft moan. "We're alone in this, Phoebe."

A thorn twisted in my heart. She was right. I started to say something else, to question her about all of this, but in the next aisle, Lisa cried out. In the moment she'd been separated from Kathleen, the tourists had circled her near the neon Marlboro sign. With their laughter echoing off the ceiling, they moved in on her, pulling at her bandages and snapping pictures so close to her face that the negatives were sure to come out blurry. But that wasn't the point. As long as they had some kind of proof, that was what mattered. Lisa screamed out and tried to flee, but there was nowhere to run. Every direction she turned, another hand was grasping at her, eager to pinch off a piece of her skin as a macabre keepsake.

All the air escaped my lungs, and I stood paralyzed for an instant as something deep inside me shifted. Then, I was weightless and moving across the store. With rage poisoning my blood, I reached into the circle of invaders and pulled Lisa back toward Kathleen. She cried out and tucked herself against her big sister.

But I wasn't done. Freeing her wasn't enough. I was suddenly the one in the middle of the tourists, my arms flailing, ripping their cameras off them, once or twice even snapping the thick, canvas straps against the backs of their necks. My arms overflowed with the wretched devices, but I didn't hesitate, my fingers nimble and ready. I yanked open the backs of their cameras, exposing the film and spoiling their hard work. They wouldn't take another image here, not today. The ribbons of film unspooled like viscera from a slit belly. Yards and yards of it, one camera after another, until they were all empty. Then I dropped them to the floor with a clank and stomped on the carcasses of the Polaroids and the Minoltas and the Pentaxes just for good measure. Just to make sure they couldn't do this again.

By the time I was finished, Kathleen and Lisa were already gone, though I hadn't heard the bell ding to signal their exit. Maybe they went out the back. Maybe it didn't even matter. They were away from here and safe from these tourists, who no longer looked so formidable. One of the older ladies started to weep, quiet little mewling sounds, while the rest of them gaped at me with those same useless expressions. They were only any good to themselves if they were together as a group, tittering cruelly as they tormented the girls. But stun them even a little, and they were as worthless as the film now limp and sullied beneath my feet.

"Get out," Aunt Betty said, sneering as she rounded the counter. She pointed at the door like I didn't know the way. "Now, Phoebe."

I didn't stay to argue. There was no point. She would only call the police if I did.

At the counter, the pastor's wife clucked her tongue at me as I passed. To her, I'd proved what the locals had always believed about me.

"She's a danger," they'd said since I was a barefoot five-year-old, squealing and chasing wasps down Denton Street. And they were right. I was a danger. I would always be a danger to people like them.

)O(

Back home, my mother was waiting at the front door to greet me. "What were you thinking?"

I stopped halfway up the porch stairs, my heart tugged tight. How did she already know?

Aunt Betty. She must have called the house as soon as that bell dinged over my head. She hated talking to my mother, but would always make an exception to break bad news. Especially bad news involving me.

I shrugged and pushed past my mother into the house. "I didn't do anything."

"Really?" She followed me inside, still waiting for a proper answer or apology or something else resembling contrition. When I said nothing, she rolled her eyes and went to the liquor cabinet to pour herself a drink, as though the only way to deal with her wayward daughter was to imbibe heavily first.

"You can't keep doing this." She swirled the amaretto in her glass. "You make yourself too visible to people."

My head heavy, I leaned into the corner and tried to make my body smaller, tried to fold into myself, so miniscule and friable that I wasn't there at all. "Would you rather I just disappear?"

She pretended not to hear me. "Things are hard enough right now," she said. "We don't need this kind of trouble."

"And you think the girls need it?" I moved forward, broadening on instinct. "You think they asked for it?"

She shook her head, not looking at me. "This isn't about them, Phoebe. This is about us. Our family's barely hanging on here, and you're just causing problems." She pursed her lips, measuring her next words and then saying them anyhow. "Sometimes I think that's all you're good at."

The words kicked me in my chest.

All I'm good at.

The skin on my face tightened, a precursor to the tears I knew would come. I had a choice. I could have said anything to her, or nothing at all. I could have taken the high road. But the rage rose up the back of my throat—rage at her, at the tourists, at the mill, even at the Rust Maidens themselves for daring to exist—and within myself, I reached for whatever could injure the worst.

"At least I'm good at something." I flashed a cruel grin at her. "What are you good at, mother? Raising a pretty little family? Because from where I'm standing, it looks rather ugly right now."

My mother stiffened, and I hesitated. Her fingers quivered around the stem of her cordial glass, and I was sure she wanted to strike me. Open-handed across the face, as hard as I deserved.

But she didn't. She simply set her glass down on the mantle and retreated to the kitchen.

"Dinner will be ready in an hour," she said, tossing the remark over her shoulder as an afterthought.

I settled back in the corner and hated myself a little. I didn't need to say that to her. It did no good. She had hopes, once, for a life that was more than what this town could ever offer, but she took the obvious way out. Become a wife, a mother, and nothing else. All her dreams turned to cinders, crushed like a cigarette butt beneath a high-heeled shoe.

After a supper of roast beef and thin conversation, I sneaked out back to my treehouse. I wasn't alone. Midges, those nasty little flies with no sense of propriety, had started their annual invasion, and if I didn't do my best to keep them out, they might chase away the other bugs.

With my bare hands, I cleared them from the milkweed and the walls and even plucked one or two from the wings of the butterflies. It was nasty work, but necessary, I told myself. This wasn't a place for them. If I didn't protect my sanctuary from invaders, then nobody would.

"That doesn't look very fun," someone said behind me. I whirled around to see her standing there, an invader all her own. Helena, the preacher's daughter. Her pale eyes flickered at me, and she almost smiled, but then apparently thought better of it.

I froze in the corner, bug guts still dangling from my fingers. Out of all the neighbors on Denton Street to be up here in my treehouse, she was one of the last I expected. I barely knew Helena. Did she think my butterflies and I wanted an impromptu sermon?

I stared at her, waiting for her to start lecturing me, but she just settled down and sat cross-legged in the doorway, like a Girl Scout about to break into a verse of *Kumbaya*.

"Is there something you need?" I asked.

She inhaled deeply. "Are you still planning to run away?"

This question tightened around my heart. No one should know about my plan. No one except Jacqueline and me. I wouldn't look at Helena now. I just kept clearing away the midges. "Who said I was ever planning that?"

She giggled. "It's a small neighborhood, Phoebe. People know things, even if you don't tell them."

I wiped my hands on the hem of my dress. "What does it matter to you?"

"If you want to go," she said, "then I think you should leave. But you should do it alone. No one else needs to be bothered with your schemes."

My gaze flicked up at her. "My schemes?"

"You can't save everyone," Helena continued, her words echoing in the preachy cadence of her no-good, do-gooder father. "It might be difficult for you to accept that, but in the end, it's best for all of us."

My fingers twitched into fists. "What are you talking about? Why are you even here?"

I glared at her, but it didn't matter. There she sat, an uninvited sentry in the doorway, and I suddenly got the sense I was trapped inside my own sanctuary.

I shifted against the wall, pretending I didn't care, that I didn't feel oddly afraid for no reason. "Isn't it almost past your curfew? You wouldn't want to scandalize the congregation."

She shrugged. "I'm not so worried about that anymore."

"Really?" I scoffed. "You, of all people, not concerned about fire and brimstone?"

She smiled. "Things change. Sometimes it's for the better, and sometimes it's not."

A midge landed on my cheek, and I tried to shoo it away. "That's odd," I said. "Lisa said the same thing the other night."

Dread seized up inside me as I realized it. Just to be sure I knew, she shifted, and the collar of her cardigan drooped, revealing a patch of leaking bandages wrapped around one shoulder.

Helena, a Rust Maiden.

With a wide grin, she stood up and took a step toward me. And another step, and another, until I was backed against the shadows of the far wall, where I couldn't see anything in the dark but her.

"Don't look so afraid, Phoebe," she whispered, and her breath tasted of salt and ash. "It's only me."

My lips parted to scream, but I didn't have a chance. Behind her, a new shadow emerged. And a soft voice, at once alien and familiar.

"Leave her alone, Helena."

The figure in the doorway moved toward the window, where the moonlight drenched her face. Jacqueline. After all these days apart, she was here, like she'd never left.

For a moment, Helena didn't budge. She steadied herself, almost expecting this. "We were only talking. What's so wrong with talking?"

"Just go," Jacqueline said. "Now."

Helena snapped her tongue. "You're no fun," she said, retreating. Before climbing back down, she looked once at Jacqueline and grinned. "See you later."

I exhaled a breath I didn't know I was holding. And then we were alone. Just the two of us, just like it had always been. I stared at Jacqueline, half-convinced she wasn't real, that this was only a wishful vision conjured in the moonlight.

"Hey, you," I whispered, and inched closer, fearful she'd dissipate into smoke right in front of me if I wasn't careful.

But she didn't vanish. She kept watching me. "Hello, Phoebe," she said.

I reached out for her hands, but she pulled away. "Let's get out of here, please." Panic split my voice in two. "I can get the car. We can leave tonight."

The cold evening air coiled around me as I waited for her to say something, to tell me she was ready.

She only shook her head. "I can't."

I felt my face twist in pain. "Everyone's going crazy here, Jacqueline. We can't stick around this place anymore."

"I don't have a choice," she said.

Everything in the world slowed, and I couldn't hear a sound, not the whir of the steel mill a mile away or the cicadas crooning outside the window or even my own breathing. It was so simple, what came next. Her movements almost random, almost meaningless. Face heavy with shame, tipped to the earth, not looking at me. One hand, trembling on the hem of her denim shorts. That hem peeled up, only an inch or two.

But even in the dark, it was enough to see what Jacqueline was hiding.

A gash in her thigh, wide as the palm of my hand, weeping tears the color of smog.

SEVEN

In the dark, I walked Jacqueline home, asking her an endless series of questions.

"What's happening?"

"How do you feel?"

"What's it like?"

But every time, she shook her head. "I don't know, Phoebe," she said. "I can't describe it. I don't know any more about this than you do."

We lingered on the sidewalk in front of her house. This wasn't the best place for her, but she insisted it was where she needed to go.

"I need some time," she said.

Desperation swelled through my voice. "Why come to me at all, then?"

"I had to." Jacqueline gnawed the dead flesh from her bottom lip. "I couldn't let Helena bother you like that."

I stared at her. "But how did you know she was with me?"

A gray expression crossed her face, as if she'd been caught in a lie. "Because," she said, "I could hear her."

My throat constricted. "You heard her halfway down the street in my treehouse?"

"Yes," she said, and turned toward the porch. "I have to go."

I wanted to argue with her. I wanted to tell her it wasn't too late. We could still get out of this place. In fact, that might be the only thing to do under the circumstances. But she wouldn't listen.

"I need time," she kept repeating.

"Jacqueline, please." I surged toward her, catching her fingers. Her hand felt strange and rough against my palm. "Don't leave me."

She gazed back at me, flashing that same look of sadness she'd always had, ever since we were kids. "Come by tomorrow," she whispered. "We'll talk then."

And with that, she was gone. Into the house, out of my reach. I stood there silently on the sidewalk. All I ever seemed to do now was watch her walk away from me.

I counted to ten, but she didn't come to the window.

Back in the treehouse, I curled in the corner. This was the place I used to feel safe, but nowhere could protect me now.

The world was simpler. Uglier too, but simpler. My life was no longer about tolls and highways and easy escapes. Everything had winnowed down to one thing only: how to protect Jacqueline.

Maybe that was all that had ever mattered to me. Maybe that was why I'd been so set on getting us out of Cleveland in the first place. She was the one I worried about. Jacqueline, my cousin, my best friend, the girl I considered my sister. I could still save her from whatever was happening. From whatever came next.

The treehouse seemed smaller that night, as if the ceiling dropped a few inches each hour. I would doze for a bit and then open my eyes, convinced this would be the time that the butterflies and cicadas would have fled, abandoning me to suffocate beneath the wooden planks. A coffin of my own making.

Morning arrived, however, hot and cruel as it was, and I was still here, the same Phoebe.

If only Jacqueline was the same, too.

There was only one way we could do this. No government men, no doctors, and most of all, no Aunt Betty. None of them could know about her. I had to make sure of that.

But I didn't have to be alone. Some things I could do on my own. Not this, though.

I needed to talk to my father. To tell him what was happening. He'd always understood everything when I was young: the treehouse and the Impala and the strange restlessness in me. We were the same, in our own way. This was something we could figure out together.

He was in the kitchen with the other men when I found him. They didn't see me in the doorway at first. That was the only reason they said the things they did.

"Those girls couldn't have picked a worse time for this."

"This isn't making the company want to sign a contract and call us back to work any quicker."

"They're probably doing it on purpose. For the attention."

These were men who should know better. The good dads, the good providers. And there my father was. He didn't participate, but he didn't disagree either, and he'd given them the forum— our kitchen—to do this. That was almost worse: him not having enough conviction to choose one side or the other.

Then the last of the conversation, a final remark to punctuate the rest, this one from Lisa and Kathleen's father, his gaunt body gnarled in the corner.

"We should just let the doctors have what they want."

What they want. At this, I choked down a breath. My father's gaze shifted across the room, and he saw me there.

"Phoebe," he said, my name on his lips as empty as an apology.

I stared at him, unblinking, until the edges of my vision wobbled. Then I gathered what was left of me and said in a voice steadier than I could believe, "Mom wanted me to tell you that dinner will be late tonight."

This was a lie, an off-the-cuff fabrication, and we both knew it. But the other men didn't. They smiled and thought I was just being a good daughter, here to relay a message. I suppose, in a way, I was. I wanted my father to know that I'd seen him in his complicity, that I knew who he'd become. How he'd toss the girls aside for making a mess, and would probably toss me aside the same way, given the chance.

The men resumed their conversation, lobbing useless theories about the girls back and forth as I watched my father, who was different in every way now. With our gazes locked on each other, he opened his mouth to say something, but I wouldn't listen. Whether he was about to speak to me or to the others, it didn't matter anymore. I vanished through the back door and headed to Jacqueline's house. All the way there, I thought about what Mr. Carter had said.

What they want. What the doctors wanted. What our parents wanted. Never what the girls wanted.

I knocked on Jacqueline's door, but she didn't answer, so I retreated to the sidewalk, hoping to spot her in her window. No luck.

I glanced around me and spotted someone else instead. Toward the end of the cul-de-sac, Dawn waited behind the sheer curtains of her parlor. A prisoner behind a white picket fence, her Farah Fawcett haircut all grown out and limp around her shoulders. Nobody had taken her to a beauty salon in months. It was one of an infinite number of punishments for all the trouble she'd caused.

She stared out into the daylight she couldn't penetrate, and at first, I thought perhaps she was watching me. But no, she was looking at something behind me, on the other side of the street. I followed her gaze to Clint's house.

I turned back at her. "There?" I pointed, and Dawn broadened as if she hadn't expected me to speak to her or even see her. Maybe she didn't believe she was visible at all anymore.

She nodded and pointed in the same direction, her finger thin and crooked and not her own. It was the first time I'd seen evidence of her transformation, but I didn't stare. She was motioning so ferociously that I couldn't ignore her. After all, she couldn't go there herself. But I could.

My steps heavy, I crept onto the front porch. No one was there. All I saw was an old milk crate in the far corner, stuffed with blankets.

My gaze shifted back to Dawn's window, and I turned up my palms in confusion. But she nodded again, like I was in the right place, like I just had to keep going.

Then, at my feet, something babbled inside the crate. I hesitated, unable to look, even though I knew what I'd find. Another babble, and another after that, and finally, I peered into the tangle of blankets.

Eleanor, all pink cheeks and bundled-up fists.

It was the first time I'd seen the baby. I was expecting something odd or remarkable about her, something to reveal what a problem she'd been. A giant scarlet B for *burden* on her forehead. How terrible to be a nuisance just by being born, but that was what she was. A burden to Dawn, to Clint, to all of Denton Street.

I looked down at her, tucked inside the makeshift bassinet. She cooed back. The sound trilled right through me, and something about it made me want to weep.

Behind me, the screen door flung open. Clint was standing there, a pitcher of tea in his hand. The Long Island variety, no doubt, almost certainly left over from his mother's morning meeting with the other Denton Street housewives. As the gossip and heat indexes ticked higher in the neighborhood, so did the alcohol content of the before-noon drinks.

Clint motioned at Eleanor. "You can take her for a while if you want."

My urge to cry suddenly washed away from me, replaced instead with the overwhelming desire to wrap my hands tight around his throat and not let go.

"She's not an automobile, Clint," I said, half growling. "You don't just let people take her out for a spin. You don't leave her alone on the porch in a crate, either."

The pitcher shook accusingly in his hand. I glanced back to Dawn's parlor window, but she was gone.

Clint moved to the opposite side of the porch, as far from Eleanor as he could get. "What do you know, Phoebe? You don't have a kid."

You don't get to judge was what he meant. Poor Clint, having to suddenly take responsibility for his own actions. What a terrible inconvenience that must be.

He set the pitcher on the chrome Formica table and dropped into a wicker chair.

"You know, my parents will babysit her if I need them to," he said. "Maybe you and I could catch up a little."

At first, I didn't know what he meant. Then as he grinned, his intention clear, I stared back at him, remembering everything. Us together, us as close to happy as you could get on this street. Clint hadn't changed. He was the same aimless boy he'd always been. The same boy I'd once loved.

I inched toward him. "Can I have a drink too?"

One eyebrow arched. "Sure," he said, "if you'd like."

I moved across the porch, one careful step at a time. He watched me approach, shifting in his chair, more eager than he had a right to be.

When I was in front of him, the table at my knees, I smiled, and he smiled back. A tremble ran straight though him, a kind of primal anticipation. I looked down at him and kept smiling. Then I reached out, and with a single swipe, my hand glided across the table, sending the plastic pitcher tumbling to the concrete floor. As the sticky sweetness pooled at our feet, Clint exhaled a pitiful little moan, and he might as well have been mortally wounded.

"Things aren't the same anymore," I said. "You're a father now. Start acting like it."

I turned and trudged down the steps. I didn't want to hear

his response. I didn't want to hear anything from him. By the time I reached the sidewalk, he'd already disappeared inside the house again, probably in pursuit of more refreshments. Eleanor fussed inside the crate, alone in ways no child should ever be. The urge to rush back and rescue the baby from her own father nearly overwhelmed me. But what would I do with her? Take her home and rear her myself? The kid would be better off raised by wolves than by me.

I wished from the pit of my soul that Jacqueline and I had gotten out of here when we'd had a chance.

Halfway home, I passed Doctor Ross's house, where Kathleen was crouching outside in the bushes. I stared at her a while, thinking how this was one of the most normal sights I'd seen all day.

When she noticed me standing there, she looked back for a moment, before rolling her eyes and sprinting out of her so-called hiding spot.

"Come with me," she whispered, and before I could argue, she seized my arm and pulled me into the shrubs.

Frowning, I regarded her through the stalks of overgrown chickweed, waiting for an explanation.

"They're interviewing the families," she said, half-defensive, and motioned to the window over us. With a sigh, I poked my head up and peered inside.

In the family den, Godfrey and Jeffers loitered against the walls while Adrian was front and center, seated on a red sectional with Violet. He kept talking at her, but all Violet did was gaze at the carpet, her eyes so far downcast she might as well have been sleeping.

I squinted harder. The edges of the cushions were dripping and stained. Violet's inadvertent doing.

Another Rust Maiden. That made five of them: Lisa, Dawn, Helena, Violet, and Jacqueline. We were losing girls quicker than we could keep track.

As Adrian kept droning on, Violet shifted in her seat and held back tears, even as her body did more than enough weeping for her. In a way, she looked the same as Lisa had in her bedroom that night. The gray water, the withering hair, the soft skin that peeled away, no longer needed. It was an unfolding set of symptoms, but as the girls changed, you could still see each of them hidden there behind the decay. Somehow, nothing about them was ugly. They were just different. Simple as that.

At the next window over, two shadows passed by, and Kathleen pulled me down by the waist to keep us from being spotted.

Voices seeped through the glass.

"What are they doing here, John?" Violet's mother. "Can't you ask them to leave?"

"I'm sorry," Doctor Ross said, and honestly sounded like he meant it. "You know I can't."

"I hate this." His wife was sobbing openly now. "I hate those men being in there with her. I want them out of our house."

"We have to play nice, Sarah," he said. "We're already in trouble. The hospital's saying I didn't act in the best interest of public health."

I inhaled a sharp breath. That was why he didn't push to quarantine Lisa. He didn't want them to steal Violet too. Now he was going to pay for that.

His wife sniffled. "Will they take your medical license?"

A pause. "I don't know."

Another sob, throaty and desperate. "I just want her to be okay. I want everything to be okay."

"I know," he said. "So do I."

This felt wrong, eavesdropping on their sorrow. Kathleen and I should go. We should be anywhere but here.

I glanced one more time through the window at Violet. Her father shuffled back into the den, and with Adrian next to him, he huddled close to Violet on the sectional, collecting vital signs, scribbling notes, whispering apologies to which she only shrugged.

"What are we going to do?" Kathleen asked.

A prickle of hope bloomed in my chest. The doctors and

government men were keeping track of this. They had answers. That meant that maybe I could solve this on my own. The government men would help me, even if they didn't know it.

)〇(

That night, I waited until their rented car vanished down Denton Street. Suppertime. That meant they'd be gone for an hour, maybe more.

The spare key was where we'd always left it. It was more valuable to me now than before, all those lost nights spent partying in this basement.

I scoured the house for the case files until I found them upstairs, in Adrian's bedroom. I recognized his jacket and tie crumpled on the mattress. Naturally, what I wanted was in his bedroom. My gaze avoided as much else as I could, convinced I'd find some unmentionable that would make me blush. Me, the invader, intrepid but easily embarrassed.

Besides, I had work to do. A stack of documents was piled in front of the nightstand. File after file, a thousand statistics and measurements and ridiculous anecdotes that didn't mean anything to anyone. A story about when Lisa got mono in the fifth grade, or how Dawn had worse-than-usual morning sickness.

The door creaked open behind me.

"Find anything you like?" Adrian was standing in the doorway.

I hiccupped a strangled moan. I should have heard the downstairs lock or the creak of the steps or something, but I didn't, and instead, here I was, caught by the worst person possible.

"I thought you'd gone to dinner," I said.

He smiled. "Jeffers and Godfrey took the car downtown. I just went to the corner store for a sandwich. Saw your aunt heading home."

"Lucky you." I glared at him, waiting for the handcuffs. These types always had handcuffs.

But tonight, there was no arrest. He just motioned at the files.

"Go ahead," he said. "You know the girls better than we do. You might be able to make sense of it all."

At first, I thought it was a trick, but when he said nothing else, I went back to rummaging through the files. Not that it did me any good. There was nothing here. They didn't have any good theories. After everything, they knew no more than we did.

"I'm sorry," Adrian said, sensing the disappointment in my face.

"It's not your fault." My lips pursed and relaxed. "I just thought you'd know something by now."

He exhaled a strained laugh. "So did we."

I closed up the last manila folder and thought about what Lisa's father said today. "You said before you weren't going to take the girls away. Have the doctors changed their minds?"

Adrian whistled through his teeth. "We don't know yet," he said. "That's why they keep monitoring them. To see what we find."

I stepped toward him, fear coursing through me. "I don't think it's contagious. Honestly, I don't."

It was the wrong thing to say, an obvious ploy on my part to protect someone. Pathetic and dumb and dangerous to Jacqueline. Way to go, Phoebe.

Adrian inspected me. "Why do you believe that?"

A shiver cut through my body, and I shrugged. "It's a theory I have, that's all."

It was a theory, to be fair, and a good one. Since Jacqueline had whatever *it* was, then I should have it too. Heck, I'd been around all the girls and hadn't caught anything. No sign of transformation anywhere on my body. I was proof there was no contagion, but I couldn't tell him that. I couldn't have him asking questions about me, and especially not about Jacqueline.

Adrian leaned against the wall. "So what other theories do you have, Miss Shaw?"

I almost laughed in his face at this. *Miss Shaw.* Like I was some Girl Friday in an old black-and-white movie. Or, better yet, the femme fatale. They always had more fun. They also died sooner, but it seemed better to live it up in the moment than to never live at all.

"I don't know anything," I said, and handed the snarl of folders back to him. "Nobody does."

He put the files back where I'd found them. "So now I've helped you," he said. "Maybe you could help us."

I scoffed. "How's that?"

"Nobody on Denton Street likes us very much." He stacked and rearranged some scattered papers. "It would be good to have someone who knows this neighborhood."

"An inside man." I glared at him. "I don't think so."

"That's a shame." Adrian stepped forward, and we were suddenly face to face, closer than we'd ever been. "Because it would help the girls more than it would help us."

That wasn't true, and I knew it, but it would haunt me anyhow. I would lie awake tonight, wondering if he was right, if helping him meant helping Jacqueline.

My skin buzzing, I trudged downstairs, and Adrian followed. At first, I assumed he was testing to see how I got in, but he never asked.

As I moved through the empty living room—these government men were nothing if not spartan—I closed my fist up around the key and decided not to put it back in the garden. Better to have a way in, just in case I needed it again.

He crossed in front of me and opened the front door, pretending to be a gentleman or something. I skittered onto the porch.

Chuckling, Adrian lingered at the door. "Next time," he said, "just knock, Phoebe. I'll answer."

I glanced at him over my shoulder, and Jacqueline's words echoed again in my head. *A good time and trouble.*

On the street, I hesitated, the humidity of June wrapped like heavy lace around my shoulders. I should go home. I should talk to my father and tell him how he and the other men were wrong about the Rust Maidens, how it wasn't their fault and never would be. How I needed his help. How Jacqueline need-ed his help.

But then I glanced up at her house right next door, to her window looming over me. Those familiar curtains fluttered, and there she was, motioning me upstairs.

Me. I could protect her. I could stop this. We didn't need anyone else. We just needed us.

The front door was unlocked. Not Aunt Betty's carelessness, but Jacqueline's careful plan. She knew I'd come.

I moved without sound up the stairs and past Aunt Betty's room. Inside, she was asleep between swing shifts, murmuring in the dark.

"Charles." Her voice rose up like a dead thing from the past. "Charles, where are you?"

This stopped me cold. Charles, my uncle, Jacqueline's father. Gone for almost ten years, but still here in his own way, in the nightmares that wouldn't end. A heart attack that had shattered my aunt's heart too. Shattered everything for her and turned her into what she'd become, thorny and resentful and disgusted with the idea of my mother and me. She hated us more the moment she had less.

But her pain didn't matter tonight. Jacqueline was all that mattered.

I reached the end of the hallway and opened the door.

"Hi, Phoebe," she whispered.

She sat inside, cross-legged on the floor, beneath the glow of the brass swing lamp. Since this morning, everything about her had changed.

The skin on her arms and legs looked thick and strange, like puckered leather, and her hair had wilted around her face. The same as Dawn's. The same as Lisa's. As though it wasn't hair at all anymore, but something thin and stringy, the consistency of seaweed. She was soaking wet, too, but that seemed so minor, so silly, compared to everything else, to a body that had turned so irrevocably against her.

On instinct, I reached out to her, and she reached back, but she withdrew just as quickly. She didn't want to touch me, not with those hands, jagged at the edges. Not with those fingernails that had turned to broken glass.

I tried not to tremble. "Has your mother seen you like this?"

She shook her head. "Not yet. I've been avoiding her all day."

That meant Jacqueline had been alone. I should have been here with her. I shouldn't have left her to transform in the quiet, all by herself.

Everything in me turned inside out, and I dropped to the floor next to her and took her hands in mine. The glass skated across my palms and sliced me open, again and again, but I wouldn't let go. Red dripped onto the shag carpet, and a sour, faded gray dripped there too. Jacqueline and me, mixing together. Blood sisters of sorts.

I touched the sharp edges on the ends of her fingers. "I could get tweezers. Maybe if we can extract it from you. Maybe that will help."

Jacqueline nodded. "Okay," she said, quivering.

But I was pushing her again, trying to make her do what I thought was best, and that hadn't helped us so far.

"Are you sure?" I asked.

"I'm not sure of anything, Phoebe," she said, her eyes whirlpooling with desperation. "I don't know if it's better to leave it or to remove it. I don't know if anything will help." Then, with a sob, "I don't know who I am anymore."

Half stunned, I sat back, our fingers still entwined, my hands still bleeding. "We'll wait," I said. "It's fine. It'll all be fine."

But the moonlight crept into her bedroom and glistened off the glass, and we both knew, both thought the same thing. This wasn't something you could just wait out.

"No," Jacqueline said, suddenly resolved. "Let's try to get it out of me now."

At her vanity table, I dug through cuticle scissors and emery boards and pots of broken Coty eyeshadow until I found a pair of tweezers. It seemed like such a good idea, like if I could just

remove these pieces, then she'd be herself again. Then everything would be okay.

"Are you ready?" I asked as I kneeled in front of her, and she
nodded.

My fingers slick with blood, I did the best I could, which
wasn't nearly good enough. The tips of the metal tweezers
prodded at Jacqueline, and the glass slipped this way and that
inside of her.

She winced, and tears the color of bile streaked both cheeks.

"Do you want me to stop?" I asked, my voice rasping, but she
shook her head.

It didn't matter, though. The glass wasn't an extraneous part
of her. It was all of her. Each time I dug the tweezers deeper
into her fingers to remove a jagged shard, I might as well have
been ripping out her bones. Even when I extracted a piece, another one would surface. Over and over, her never-ending sup-
ply of decay.

She set her jaw. "Keep going," she whispered, and I hated
myself for listening.

I tried again, but this time, I excavated too deep. The metal
slipped in between her skin and what was left of the marrow,
and I lost the tweezers inside her. Everything about her was
peeling away, or oozing, or filled with pockets too deep to fathom.

"It's stuck," I said, fear rising in my voice. The tips of my fingernails groped inside her, and I twisted the edge of the tweezers, desperate to free them. But it was too much. The pain
she'd been swallowing finally overwhelmed her, and with her
mouth slack, her head drooped back.

And she cried out.

It was like nothing I'd ever heard. That scream so other-
worldly but almost familiar too, like the lullaby of a factory.
Like a thousand rusted nails dragged against a plate of steel.
The sound shuddered through me, and I wanted to scream
too. But I couldn't. Jacqueline doubled over into my arms, and
I held her as we quivered together. Then we pulled back and

stared into each other's eyes, knowing what we'd done, knowing it was too late, and having to wait until it happened.

It took almost no time at all.

"Baby?" A voice, that hideous voice, in the bedroom on the other side of the house. "Baby, what's wrong?"

There was no stopping it now. It played out in my mind before it happened, as inexorable as the tides.

The footsteps down the hall, heavy and determined.

The slow twisting of the doorknob, as if by a spectral hand.

Aunt Betty, emerging from the darkness, from a sleep that shouldn't have been disturbed.

Her startled face, as she saw me, but more importantly, as she saw Jacqueline, and the truth drifted behind her eyes, like a bad dream that couldn't be undone.

And then, in an instant, everything that had ever mattered was gone.

EIGHT

Aunt Betty's mouth slipped open, and the cry that followed echoed to the slate roof and beyond. It didn't sound like Jacqueline's, though it was almost worse. It was the wail of a mother who'd just lost what was left of her life.

"What have you done?" Aunt Betty's voice was guttural and strained, and when she spoke, she wasn't looking at Jacqueline.

She was looking at me.

"I didn't do anything." I stared back at her. "Do you think I'd ever hurt Jacqueline? That I could do this to her?"

"Yes," Aunt Betty said, kneeling right in front of me now. "I do."

With an open hand, she slapped me hard across the mouth. I fell backward to the carpet, more stunned than hurt. The tang of blood filled my mouth.

She started at me again, but I lunged and caught her arm midair. Taking hold of both her wrists, I held her convulsing body away from mine, and I thought of waltzing her right to

Jacqueline's bedroom window and tossing her out of it. If I didn't, it would only be a matter of time before she tried the same thing with me. In a way, this would only be self-defense.

But Jacqueline knew me too well. She knew the look on my face, dark and not worth trusting, and she couldn't let me hurt her mother or let her mother hurt me again. Her head tipped back, Jacqueline parted her lips and screamed again. Only louder this time, and different. Gone was the sound of a factory. Now everything about her was sharp like glass breaking, or like a cathedral bell crashing down from a turret.

The noise sent shockwaves through my body, turning me to porridge inside. It must have done the same to Aunt Betty, because she collapsed in my arms. Even once the moment passed and we could both stand again, we were too shaky to pick up our fight where we'd left off. For once, Jacqueline got what she wanted.

I curled in the corner as Aunt Betty went to the phone in her room and called my father. He arrived a minute later to claim me, like I was a misdelivered package.

"Please get her out of here." Aunt Betty was openly weeping to him as his footsteps fell heavy in the hallway.

"I won't go," I said, and clung to Jacqueline, my hands wet and stained with rust and blood. "Don't make me leave."

But my father, the turncoat in my own family, took me by the arm and dragged me out of the bedroom. Behind me, Jacqueline called my name, and I wailed and reached for her, but nobody except us cared.

When we were back on the street, my father seized me by the shoulders. "You need to leave them alone, Phoebe," he said. "They need time to process this."

I let out a rueful laugh. Time wouldn't change what was happening to Jacqueline. Time would just get away from us, and then it would be too late.

My father kept talking at me, and I breathed in, ready to scream, but as I looked past the sidewalk, something inside my chest twisted.

We weren't alone.

Down the block, Lisa leaned against her family's sagging mailbox, her bare feet slick with grass. Closer still, there was a creak of an old wooden swing, as Helena rocked back and forth on her porch, grinning at no one in particular. Across the street, Violet stared out from her bedroom, her gaze flicking up at us whenever she thought we wouldn't notice. Even Dawn's front window was dark with her silhouette.

Why were they watching? Had they heard Jacqueline's screams? Maybe. But if so, why hadn't the whole neighborhood heard? Why were they the only ones to respond?

My father droned on, lecturing me as though he had a right, and rage blossomed inside me as I remembered what the men had said in the kitchen.

"Then maybe we should just give the doctors what they want."

My father hesitated. "I never said that."

"No, *you* didn't." I looked right at him, though I no longer recognized his face. "But you never argued with them, either. Right, Dad?"

I didn't wait for him to answer. I just ran. Down the sidewalk and away from the girls, who kept staring after me even once I was gone. I didn't stop until I reached my own backyard. Nothing looked familiar here, but I pretended not to notice as I climbed up to the treehouse and pulled the rope ladder up behind me so no one could follow.

)O(

All night, I thrashed and dreamt of them. The Rust Maidens, their bodies weathered and torn and no longer their own.

I woke up screaming, but unlike Jacqueline, I couldn't make a sound.

As the butterflies drifted by me, I blinked into this new day. It was Sunday. A day of sermons, a day of gathering. Usually a day that I hated, but maybe this one wouldn't be so bad. Even

111

the Rust Maidens had to be included in this. After all, their mothers and fathers probably thought they needed the Lord's blessings most of all. That meant Aunt Betty would bring Jacqueline, and I could see her then. I could talk to her.

I headed to the church alone, not bothering to wait for my parents or even change yesterday's clothes.

In the morning light, Denton Street was different. Overnight, new signs, cheerfully homemade, had popped up in windows.

Room for Rent. Please inquire within.

Upstairs bedroom available. Free breakfast.

Not every house had one, but there were enough of them to stir alarm in my guts. I stared at the signs, one after another, trying to divine their meaning until the truth flooded into me. The tourists needed somewhere to stay. And why let the out-of-towners go into the city when they could stay right here amongst the Rust Maidens themselves, the star attraction? I shuddered. The girls were becoming a cottage industry in spite of themselves.

Down the block, the congregation poured into the Presbyterian Church, and I waited on the lawn, desperate for some sign of Jacqueline.

But when Aunt Betty arrived, she was alone.

"Where is she?" I asked, blocking her path.

"Sick," she said, and pushed past me into the church.

The strident bells rang out in the steeple, and I stood, defeated on the steps. Poor Jacqueline. Too "sick" even for the Lord's blessing.

Inside, everything was normal, so long as you didn't look too hard.

In the back, several blue-haired ladies arranged stale cookies on paper plates. Usually the goodies were free, but today, with so many "newcomers"—the kind with cameras and greedy faces—the congregation was planning for its biggest bake sale of the year.

"To raise funds for a new roof," the women whispered, and I

hated them almost as much as the tourists.

As I expected, the rest of the Rust Maidens were here. Kathleen and her father flanked Lisa, whose wild eyes glistened like moonstone.

Doctor Ross and his wife and Violet, with her arms pricked and prodded and bandaged back up again.

Dawn, her face all shadows as she fidgeted in the pew, far from Clint's family and baby Eleanor.

The pastor's family in the front row. His always-smiling wife sitting next to Helena, with her pink cheeks and straight teeth and dressed collarbone oozing melancholy.

But this was a normal day, our parents had decided. So we listened to the sermon and crooned "How Great Thou Art" and smiled at our neighbors as if they were our friends.

The girls, however, knew better. They seemed to float above it all. I hunkered down in my seat and watched them. When she thought no one was looking, Helena glanced down the pew at Violet, who flashed her a small smile back. Then Violet looked at Dawn, who didn't smile, but didn't frown either. A lightness came to her face anytime the other girls were watching her, almost like she felt seen for the first time in her life. And Lisa, the strange one, the girl who knew better than anybody, sat back, observing the other three, grinning to herself.

I wondered what Jacqueline would see, what she could tell me if she were here, instead of resting alone at home, cross-legged in bed, shipwrecked from the world.

The pastor continued to drone on. "The Lord speaks to Samuel of acceptance when he says that—"

In the back, a tourist's camera flashed, and I grunted. *Acceptance.* That word was a talon raked on the inside of my chest. None of this was about acceptance. It was about bake sales and a lunch counter at capacity and extra rooms rented out in a time of need. The Rust Maidens shouldn't be accepted because it was the right thing to do. The Rust Maidens should be accepted because they were good for business.

The sermon ended early, but I didn't wait in line with the

others for cups of burnt coffee and overdone chocolate chip cookies. Instead, I marched home alone, and climbed up into my treehouse. I was eighteen years old, an adult, a woman if that was what you wanted to call me, and all I wanted to do on this Sunday morning was sulk like a child.

But I didn't sulk, not when I saw it there, waiting for me in the center of the treehouse. A sign from her, from Jacqueline. A triple moon etched into the floorboards.

This was our secret code. Freshman year, we'd found a picture of it in an old book about symbology tucked away in the back room of the school library.

"That mark is the devil's doing," Aunt Betty had said when she found Jacqueline and me doodling it on the margins of our notebooks, and that was all the encouragement we needed to adopt the sign as our own. Anything to vex her mother.

Jacqueline had been here. While I was gone, she'd been in the treehouse. These butterflies had probably nestled in her hair, and the wooden boards beneath my feet had lurched with her weight. Maybe she'd taken a sip from the tartan thermos. Maybe she'd called my insects by their names. This wasn't so different. In a way, everything was normal. Everything was like before.

I needed to see her. It was what I wanted, and what Jacqueline wanted too. My head high, I went to her. I marched up her front steps, and knocked on the door. But, of course, she didn't answer. I glared at the one who did.

"She wants to talk to me," I said.

Aunt Betty snapped her tongue, one hand still on the door, ready to slam it at a moment's notice. "Really?"

"Please, just let me see her for a minute." I hated myself for standing there and begging for what she had no right to deny. "You can be with us the whole time."

She snuffed out a laugh. "I don't think so," she said, and the door swung closed in my face.

That was when I saw them, glinting there in front of me. The silver locks installed on the outside. Ones that Aunt Betty could latch and unlatch when she left the house. This was what she had always wanted—to seal Jacqueline off from me and everyone else. To keep her safe in a way no one could ever keep my uncle safe.

But I couldn't leave my best friend here. I couldn't abandon her to whatever Aunt Betty thought was best. She wouldn't have a chance if I did.

My eyes blurred with tears, and I paced back and forth on the sidewalk. The government men's house loomed over me. Beneath the dripping gutters, a piece of old lattice sprawled sullenly in the former owner's garden. I stared at it, a plan swirling in my head. I could reach Jacqueline. It wasn't the best way, but maybe now, with everything that had happened, it was the only way.

I decided to wait until dusk to return. It seemed safer somehow with the evening as my unlikely accomplice, concealing me from my aunt. I would get to Jacqueline. We just needed a few more hours. I'd save her from this nightmare.

)O(

For Sunday dinner, my mother cooked honey-glazed ham and mashed potatoes with too much butter, and I had to sit there at the table and pretend we were a family.

"We still need to change the oil in the Impala," my father said to me. "Otherwise, that hunk of junk won't make it down the block."

I shrugged, not looking at him. "You're right. It probably won't make it down the block," I said. "It won't make it anywhere. None of us will."

I shouldn't have said that. I shouldn't have said anything. My parents certainly didn't speak again, not for the rest of the overcooked meal and not when I told them I was going out for the night.

"See you later," I said, and slammed the door behind me.

Out in the darkness, I crept through backyards until I

reached the government men's house. Not making a sound, I grabbed the piece of discarded lattice. Then, with a steady hand, I leaned it against Jacqueline's house like a ladder and started climbing.

Above me, the curtains in her bedroom fluttered. I neared the top, almost close enough to touch her window. Jacqueline was right there, that face that looked so different but still looked like her. She pressed her fingers into the glass, and I reached out, wanting to hold her hand, wanting to be there to do something, *anything*, for her. But as my palm pressed into the window, the lattice lurched beneath me. I froze, convinced that if I was entirely still, it would be enough to stop the inevitable.

It wasn't. The thin wood, already half-decayed, crumbled into dust beneath my feet, and I had just enough time to imagine how much it was going to hurt before I fell.

The crash of my body shook the earth. I landed right next to the porch, close enough to the front door that there was no way Aunt Betty didn't hear me. But I couldn't run. Curled in the overgrown grass, I could barely move. A gash six inches long bisected my calf.

Above me, the porch light flicked on, and Aunt Betty's voice sliced through the night.

"I told you I'd call the police, Phoebe," she said.

I folded into myself and wished I could disappear. She'd find me here. There was no way to hide.

But then something rustled nearby in the grass, and Adrian was suddenly standing next to me. He leaned against the porch balusters, making him the first thing she saw instead of her wayward niece, bleeding and coiled on the ground.

"Good evening, Betty." With one hand, Adrian waved at her, and with the other dangling at his back just out of her sight, he motioned me on. I dragged what was left of me around the house and into the shadows. Their voices echoed in the dark, and I held my breath and listened.

"I heard something, I'm sure of it," Aunt Betty said.

"Just me doing the rounds." I imagined Adrian flashing her that smile of his. He was skilled at convincing people he had good intentions. He almost had me believing him.

"Have you seen my niece out there?" she asked.

"Not tonight. Why? Do you have a message for her?"

I had to bite down hard to stifle a laugh. Aunt Betty with a message for me. The most she had to say were a few poorly-veiled insults and certain four-letter words.

Out front, they said their stiff goodbyes, and I tried to limp around the house and back to the street, but a shadow moved across my face. I looked up to find Adrian staring down at me.

"You'll need something for that," he said, and for once, I couldn't argue with him.

He helped me inside, into the place I still considered the abandoned house next door. But it wasn't abandoned, not anymore. It belonged to the government now. Just like the Rust Maidens. Just like the rest of us.

Upstairs, the single exposed bulb in the bathroom bathed our skin in jaundiced yellow. Adrian leaned over me as he cleaned the dirt and bits of grass out of the cut. He smelled of cedar and starched linens still dangling from the line. I stank of blood and iodine and fresh bandages. His fault, since he was the one wrapping me up. My fault, since I was the one who fell in the first place. No matter what I wanted, I could try a thousand times, a thousand different ways, and still fail.

I waited for him to bargain with me again.

I helped you tonight. Why don't you help me, Phoebe? Why don't you help them?

But he didn't make any requests. He just finished patching me up and tucked the iodine and the leftover roll of bandages back into the cabinet.

My toes wiggled on the tile as I flexed and unflexed my injured calf. Now I was just another Denton Street girl, looking like an open wound. I'd have to sneak inside the house tonight if I was going to avoid questions from my mother about what happened.

117

Adrian escorted me back downstairs, but when I got to the door, he touched my arm to stop me.

"Just so you know," he said, "the doctors set up appointments for all the girls next week. Maybe you can talk to Jacqueline then."

A knot formed in my throat. "Appointments?"

"At the clinic downtown," he said. "The doctors aren't making progress with their home visits, so they want to run a few more tests."

Tests. What that could mean was anybody's guess.

I nodded. "Thank you," I said, and meant it.

That night I slept in the treehouse again, and didn't awaken until my mother's voice called out for me.

"Phoebe, we need you to come down."

In the living room, my parents were already dressed for the day. Now I had to get dressed too. It was a morning of solidarity, when the families joined the fathers on the picket line.

"All the wives and children will be there today," my father said flatly.

I hesitated. "*All* of them?"

"Every one of them," my mother said and poured herself a drink. "That means Lisa and Dawn too."

I heaved down an uneven breath. "Do you think that's a good idea?"

My father wouldn't look at me. "Would you rather we ignore them?"

I knew what he really meant. *What would make you happy, Phoebe? Is there anything that we can do with those girls that you won't complain about?*

I shook my head. "I just don't think we should put them on display."

This whole street was becoming a zoo, a menagerie of girls, and it was all so terribly wrong. We were supposed to love them, not sell tickets to their destruction. But that didn't seem to matter, not when bake sales and makeshift bed-and-breakfasts were the order of the day.

At the steel mill, a crowd of two hundred had already formed by the time the families arrived to support our fathers. Photographers from *The Plain Dealer* and *The Post-Gazette* and *The Times* were there, official badges dangling around their necks like limp nooses, but they had to get in line with the other tourists. There was no special VIP treatment for those who boasted credentials and had planned to be here to cover the labor strike, even before the girls got sick and became the featured entertainment.

Alongside our fathers, we gathered next to a rusted chain-link fence that separated us from the mill. All of us pretended this was the same as always, and that we only had an audience because these spectators cared about things like unions and fair wages and sticking it to the man. The strike routine was simple enough: there were signs and chants and garbage tossed at the scabs, those men foolish enough to cross the picket lines as temporary workers for the mill.

"Traitors," our fathers yelled, and I wondered what they knew of the word.

All the while, Lisa and Dawn wandered. The tourists and photographers oscillated between pictures of our fathers and pictures of these wraiths, their bodies swathed in bandages as if prepared for ceremonial burial.

In the midst of the crowd, I closed my eyes and struggled to catch my breath. When I looked again, Lisa was standing right in front of me. Her face glimmered in the sunlight, the skin across her cheekbones stretched taut, revealing something the color of pewter beneath.

She smiled, and her thin, glinting lips flashed at me. All the skin had peeled away from her mouth, and now her lips were like mirrors, reflecting me back at myself.

"None of them know yet, do they?" she whispered, a faint sound of gravel in her voice.

I stared at her. "Know what?"

"That it's all too late." She leaned toward me, and I inhaled the scents of brackish water and earth and heat. "But you know, don't you, Phoebe?"

"No," I said, my throat dry. "I don't."

"Sure you do. Even if you don't want to admit it." She smiled again, but I wouldn't look at her lips this time, at the distorted funhouse version of myself.

"Lisa," I started to say, but then she was gone, vanished back into the throng without another word.

Nobody heard her speak to me. They were too busy with our new guests. The mill owners had appeared on the other side of the fence, wearing their polyester suits and their phony smiles.

"We want you all back at work as soon as possible," they said. "But you'll have to be reasonable."

Reasonable to them meant fewer bonuses, fewer benefits, and most of all, fewer workers. Our fathers hollered insults, and the mill owners shouted them down with niceties and lies, and no one noticed the tiny, wet girl snake her way through the crowd. Not until Lisa had stepped forward and was already at the rusted chain-link fence did anybody realize she was there at all.

"Is that one of them?" a mill owner whispered to another, and they all nodded, their eyes wide, the thick sinews in their thicker necks pulsing.

Lisa smiled, vaguely content they'd recognized her. But she wasn't done. She reached out slowly, her ridged fingers almost uncertain of themselves, like she was testing out a theory for the first time. Apparently it worked, because all at once, her hand went right through the fence. I stumbled back a step, not ten feet away from her. This couldn't be real. It wasn't that her fingers went into the gaps in the links, but her fingers went into the links themselves, her metallic bones fusing with steel.

She pulled out her hand and did it again. Over and over, her skin letting out wet popping sounds each time.

A shiver ran through the crowd. This was everything we didn't need. I felt my body rise up, and I wanted to run to Lisa, to stop her before it had gone too far. But it was already too late. They'd seen it. Everyone here, the tourists and the reporters and our own families, had witnessed what she could do. My parents were here as well, their mouths as slack as the rest.

And the girls weren't done yet. From the edges of the throng, Dawn emerged. Lisa, with her eyes glinting, held out her free hand. Like a friend. Like a sister. Together, the two girls stood at the chain-link, and Dawn's hand plunged into the metal the same as Lisa's. They were both in front of it and part of it.

No one moved or spoke or even took a breath. Not until Kathleen broke the stillness with a wail.

"Lisa, baby!" She shoved through the crowd and threw her own body around her sister's, as if she could conceal what Lisa had done. "Come away from there, okay?"

Quivering, Kathleen led Lisa away, but even while her older sister looked ready to break into pieces, Lisa wasn't the same. Her shoulders back, she glanced at me as she brushed past. The stillness on her face, how perfectly gratified she looked with what had happened, left me chilled, and I turned away under the weight of her impossible stare.

As the two Carter girls disappeared into the already ruined day, the mill owners huddled together, murmuring in wild collusion. Their faces white as blank paper, they whispered and nodded and nearly screamed before rushing as a group into the building, back to their air-conditioned offices where no teenagers could hurt them. They didn't turn back once.

At first, I was certain this was why the girls had done it. To spook the mill owners. But no, that couldn't be it. Lisa and Dawn had barely looked at them. They'd focused instead on each other. This had nothing to do with the steel mill or our fathers or the reporters from major newspapers. The girls did this because they wanted to. Just to see if they could.

Nearby, everyone clambered for a closer look at the fence, pretending the chain-link was the problem and not the girls. Her head down, Dawn skittered out of the way. People should have been crowding around her, demanding how she did it, but nobody bothered. She slid so easily through the crowd, and it was almost as if she'd made herself invisible, unseen by everyone except me.

I kept staring at her, kept wondering what it would be like to be her. She scanned all the faces around us, slowly, before her gaze turned to me. Instantly, I felt caught. In a way, I was, because she took my staring as permission to shuffle over to me. We stood quietly together as she gathered the courage it took to speak.

"What's she like?" she whispered at last.

I gaped at her, not certain who she meant. Then the answer twisted deep in my chest.

Eleanor. Dawn had given birth to her, but other than the delivery, they must not have let her see the baby, or hold her, or do any of the normal things that other mothers take for granted. The doctors probably felt they couldn't trust Dawn, not with those arms of cut steel and that body where her water never stopped breaking. That meant she didn't even know her own child. But I did.

My heart heavy in my chest, I shrugged. "She's a baby," I said, grasping for something better. "Aren't they all the same?"

This was the wrong answer, and I knew it. Dawn wouldn't complain, though. She probably didn't remember how. With her face down, she just nodded, ready to return home soon. Ready to go back to prison.

"She looks like you," I blurted. "Or… how you used to look."

This wasn't what I'd meant to say, and it wasn't even really true, but it was the right answer, because Dawn instantly brightened. She reached out for my hand, and it took everything in me not to recoil from those fingers, each one trimmed with jagged metal and glass.

"Thank you, Phoebe," she said, and I thought how much her hands felt like Jacqueline's. Painful and dangerous, but familiar too.

Dawn smiled, the first real smile I'd ever seen on her, before she disappeared back into the crowd, at ease in spite of everything.

Behind me, some of the men gathered closer to the chain-link fence, testing the metal with their own hands, discovering to the surprise of no one that their fingers weren't so nimble as the girls'.

"How did they do it?" they asked. "And what does it mean?"

"It was just a trick," the mothers whispered, and they all tittered in agreement, because it was easier to do that than try to understand the truth.

But Lisa was right: it was too late. Too late to convince anyone that the Rust Maidens were like us, just normal girls feeling a bit under the weather. Our fathers jolted away from the fence, suspicion boiling in their eyes, and the mothers' whispers turned to ugly barbs in their mouths.

"This isn't safe," someone said. "*They* aren't safe."

In an instant, our lives had changed. Lisa put her hand on that fence, and the girls became something else. Something dangerous in ways we couldn't understand.

Things couldn't last like this. Not for much longer, not if the strike didn't clear up soon like some nagging cold.

Though the summer swelter draped heavily on my shoulders, I crossed my arms in front of me and shuddered. The flame of the mill burned bright overhead, but its warmth might as well have been a thousand miles away.

NINE

On Wednesday, I dressed before dawn. It was the most important morning of the week. The day the Rust Maidens were due at the clinic.

After the debacle at the picket line, I'd offered to take Kathleen and Lisa to the doctor's appointment. Their father was too drunk to drive anywhere any time of day, and nobody else would ride alone in a car with them. Everyone used Lisa's trick with the chain link fence as their reason, but after years of not trusting the Carter girls, that was only an excuse.

I wanted an excuse of my own. A pretext for going to the clinic. Anything to have a chance to see Jacqueline. I was the opposite of everyone else on Denton Street, but in a way, just as bad.

Downstairs, my mother was already awake.

"It's hot today," she said. "You sure you want to wear that outfit?"

I glanced down at my heavy bell bottoms and scoffed. "Since when does me being overdressed bother you?"

She gripped her second morning cocktail tighter, not looking at me. "Just trying to be helpful, Phoebe."

Shame burned my cheeks. For once, she was only being a mother, concerned and kind and brimming with unwelcome advice. But I didn't want to explain why there would be no skirts or dresses for the next week, temperature be damned. This was my punishment for toppling from the lattice. Any way to conceal my still festering wound.

A knock at the door. Lisa's crystalline giggle leaked through from the other side. My mother and I both froze, caught off-guard by that sound, so metallic and otherworldly.

Then my mother grunted out a laugh.

"Have fun with *them* today," she said and poured herself another drink, as I went to the door alone.

Outside, in the driveway, Lisa slid into the backseat, humming a nursery rhyme out of tune. Kathleen got in next to her, leaving me to chauffeur.

With all the doors locked, I exhaled for courage and turned the key in the ignition. The Carpenters' "We've Only Just Begun" blared through the speakers. This jolted me. Had it been that long since I'd driven anywhere? Was that day at the shoreline, graduation day, the last time I'd started the engine? It must have been. I wouldn't have left it on this station.

Maybe this was a good sign, though. A sign from Jacqueline. After all, we would be together today.

What I didn't expect was to see her so soon, not even a half mile away from the house. Except I wasn't the one who spotted her.

"Should we stop for Jacqueline?" Lisa asked, her long gnarled finger pointing languidly at the bus stop.

There Jacqueline was at the end of Denton Street, waiting alone for the RTA.

The Impala shrieked to a stop, and I threw open the driver's door.

125

She wouldn't look at me. Nearby, a red-nosed man in tattered corduroys lumbered past, gripping a brown bag-wrapped bottle and cursing at the sun for daring to shine.

"What are you doing?" I asked Jacqueline.

"I'm fine, Phoebe," she said. "I don't need a ride."

That was a message from Aunt Betty. She was working at the corner store and couldn't take Jacqueline to the appointment herself. But she wouldn't let her come with me, either.

Kathleen cracked the backseat window. "Get in," she said. "We're going to be late."

I stepped out of the Impala and moved toward Jacqueline on the sidewalk. Not too fast, not too close. I didn't want to push this time.

"Please," I said. "Besides, it's not safe for you to ride the bus looking like that."

Looking like you, I meant. Since the last time I saw her, the skin across her face had thinned, just like Lisa's, and hints of pewter-colored bones peeked out behind the apples of her cheeks.

But Jacqueline didn't budge. "You and I aren't the same now, Phoebe," she said. "We haven't been the same for a long time."

I stared at her, pain churning inside me. "That's not true," I whispered.

"But it *is*," she said. "You can't keep trying to save me all the time."

I exhaled, ready to say something else, to argue with her, but the red-nosed man in the corduroys was right next to me, groaning in my ear. With a careless, greasy hand, he shoved me into the gutter and lurched forward to take hold of Jacqueline. She cried out, but he didn't let go, not even when her body sliced open his palms.

"You're one of them freaks," he slurred. "This is all your fault. Everything going wrong is your fault."

I pulled myself to my feet, furious that I hadn't anticipated it, that I hadn't been able to stop him in time. By now, Kathleen was out of the car too, and together, she and I screamed and did our best to pry the man off Jacqueline. He struck me across the face, his fingers smudged with nicotine and smelling of Boone's Farm apple wine. But I didn't stop, I wouldn't stop, not until she was safe.

An open palm to his jaw—my palm this time—and he stumbled backward, but didn't let go. Instead, his hand tighter than before around Jacqueline's wrist, he yanked her farther from us, down the sidewalk and into an alley. With dark tears streaking her cheeks, she cried out, that discordant but horribly beautiful wail.

The sound buzzed through our veins, doubling us over, but it wasn't enough. Though half-dazed, this man wasn't done with her yet. He pulled her body closer to him as he thrust his face at hers.

"I'll stop you, I'll stop all of you," he was saying, and I struggled toward them, dizzy and terrified I'd be too late to help her.

Then a voice behind us stopped the world.

"Please leave her alone." Lisa, now out of the car. Ethereal but calm. "Or you'll be very sorry."

The man stopped and gazed at Lisa, at the unknowable look on her face. He didn't understand much, but he suddenly realized he'd gotten more than he expected here. His grasp gone slack, Jacqueline yanked her hand free and wiped his blood from her puckered skin, but she didn't run. She just stared into him, something dark brewing behind her eyes.

Lisa pushed past me and joined Jacqueline in the alley. The man backed slowly away from them, until he hit the wall and his trembling body slid down the crumbling brick.

"I hope they take you all away," he mumbled.

"Do you now?" Jacqueline asked, and moved toward him. Lisa moved toward him too. They were both standing over him now, their bodies sharp and dangerous and ready.

With a smile, Jacqueline lifted one arm over her head, those broken glass fingernails glinting in the sun. Lisa made the same motion. The man's eyes grew wider, and he let out a strangled moan, but he didn't fight back. He already knew that against these two girls, he was going to lose. They would rip him to shreds with no more than a flick of their wrists.

Everything in me seized up. I couldn't let this happen. Jacqueline wasn't a monster. She was my best friend. I still knew her, even if she believed we weren't the same anymore.

"Jacqueline?" At her side now, I reached out and carefully took her hand, holding it in mine the same way I used to. The way that reminded her who she was.

Sighing, she lowered her other arm. "Let's go, Phoebe," she said.

The Impala took off down Denton Street, the bleeding man back on the sidewalk and lobbing insults at us until the car was out of sight.

We drove the rest of the way across town in silence.

◗◖

The clinic was like every other medical facility. The labyrinthine layouts, the inexplicably beeping machines, the stench of bleach masking the slow crawl of death. Hospitals were confusing places that pretended to be orderly, that pretended to make sense. Places that told us to trust them, even though they offered us little reason to do so. People went there to die, didn't they? Shouldn't that give us all the reason in the world to be leery? Even cemeteries were more honest. At least people who entered those gates for a stay were already dead.

At nine o'clock sharp—the official appointment time—all the Rust Maidens were here, one after another, kept apart in their separate rooms. We didn't even see Violet or Helena, but Lisa was housed next to Jacqueline. We knew because we could hear her babbling nonsense through the paper-thin walls.

"Can you hear them all?" Lisa asked. "Their heartbeats sound like symphonies."

Kathleen cooed. "It will be all right, baby," she said. "Everything will be fine. Just lie still for a little longer."

In our own tiny prison, I stood against one blank white wall.

This was a courtesy they extended to us: the doctors let us stay with the girls for a while as they drew test tubes of blood and took vital signs and biopsied samples of their skin without anesthetic. It hurt us more than it hurt the girls.

"How are you feeling?" I asked Jacqueline when we were alone, and I hated myself a little for sounding just like the others. The doctors, the nurses, all the people with so little investment in them. I should have had something better to say.

"I'm tired, Phoebe," she said. "We're all tired."

All. The five of them.

"How do you know?" I stared at her. "Did they tell you that?"

She shook her head. "I can just feel it. It's strange. It's like I'm still me, but I'm something else now too."

I clasped my hands in front of me to keep from shaking. "Are you scared?"

She chewed her bottom lip and pondered the question, a curious expression twitching across her brow. I held my breath. But when she finally looked ready to answer, another orderly thrust into the room, a needle in hand, and the moment between us was lost. I didn't know for sure if she was afraid of her own body and what it was doing to her, or if she was afraid of everyone else who couldn't understand, or if she wasn't afraid at all.

When it was time for the X-rays and the stirrups and all the things too invasive to mention in polite company, the doctors put the Rust Maidens on stretchers, one by one, and stole them away from us. I held Jacqueline's hand for as long as I was able, until the nurses wrenched us apart. Even then, Jacqueline watched me all the way down the hall, flashing me a small, sad goodbye just before they rounded the corner and she was too far for me to reach.

I lingered in the waiting room for three hours with the other family members. Kathleen, and Dawn's mother, and the pastor and his wife. Doctor Ross, too. No longer armed with his scrubs and stethoscope, he looked just as lost as the rest of us.

In the early afternoon, five doctors, all of them men, brought us what they pretended was news.

"There isn't a name for what the girls have," they said, and this explanation went on a long time, with talk of case files and official procedures and things that only mattered if you were a ticker-tape bureaucrat.

"Their bodies have already changed so much," the doctors said. "We can't remove all the foreign body substances without—"

They didn't have to finish that sentence. We could finish it for them. *Without killing the girls.*

The girls, our girls, the one who might be too far gone now for our help.

I stepped forward. "If we can't reverse it," I said, "then how do we stop it? Or slow it? Or do anything?"

The doctors all gave me the same stiff, patronizing smile. "That was why we brought them here today. We obviously don't have all the results yet—"

"But?" Everything in my body was chilled. "You already know something, don't you?"

"Yes. Or at least we have an initial prognosis."

Incurable was a word nobody in the room was brave enough to use. *Terminal* was another. But we all soon understood both of these things to be true.

"We'll send them home with some supplements," the doctors said. "That might help to slow the progression."

They passed out prescriptions like they were consolation prizes. *Well done on the chintzy game show of life! Though we're sorry you've lost your daughters, please enjoy this parting gift! But first a word from our sponsor: the city of Cleveland, where young girls wither to rust and die just to get out of town.*

With my eyes squeezed closed, I swallowed the fury in the back of my throat like it was a glob of snot before I looked at the doctors again, everything in me shaking and furious.

"You already knew this," I said. "You already knew from the home visits that this was hopeless, didn't you? Why bring them here? Why poke and prod them like that?"

The doctors weren't expecting this. They weren't expecting

me to say the truth. The older ones were smart enough to shut up, but one of the younger doctors just shrugged.

"For research," he said. "It's beneficial to track these things."

These *things*. These girls. These guinea pigs.

I was already across the room, my fist buried in the young doctor's smart mouth, before anybody could stop me. Of course, with the blood running down my hand and him wailing like a swaddled infant, they stopped me soon enough, wrestling my still-flailing body into the hallway and pinning me against the wall. They waited on security to do the rest.

But a minute later, it wasn't security that arrived. It was the government men, all three of them. The two I didn't know, and the one I wished I didn't.

"That will be all for now," Adrian said, and dismissed the doctors, who glared at me and grumbled and went back into the waiting room to answer more pointless questions from equally pointless parents. After all, soon they wouldn't have daughters anymore. And what was the purpose of a parent if they didn't have a child?

Adrian stared at me, a bemused smirk growing on his lips. "You really get yourself into it, don't you, Phoebe?"

I should have been grateful. In county jail, I would be no use to Jacqueline. But all I could feel was the rage sizzling in my veins. Rage at how everyone, me included, had failed the girls.

"Don't talk to me like that." I spat the words at him. "Don't pretend we're friends."

Adrian hesitated. "I'm here to help you."

"Please stop," I said. "You can't keep trying to save me all the time."

Instantly, those words took my breath away, the fact that out of all the possible things to say, I'd chosen that. The same thing Jacqueline said to me only hours ago. The same thing that cut me to ribbons inside.

Adrian took it better than I had. "I apologize, Miss Shaw." He smiled at me. "Next time, I'll be sure to let them arrest you."

He turned away, and I didn't stop him. I just leaned against the wall and tried not to bang my head repeatedly against it.

After the appointment, with the Impala rocketing down Cedar Avenue, Kathleen and I said nothing to the girls. It didn't matter. Jacqueline and Lisa watched each other in the rearview, their eyes swirling with secrets, and it was clear they already knew. They probably knew the truth before the doctors did. That they were hopeless cases. We were losing them even as they sat right in front of us, dying in plain sight.

We needed to head back to Denton Street, to get the girls home, but I didn't consider that neighborhood a good home to any of us right now. I couldn't take the girls back to the place everyone expected them to die. Not yet. So I took us somewhere else instead.

Bayton Beach was as quiet as the grave, and that was what I wanted. A chance for us to relax, just for a moment, and for me to figure out what we were going to do next.

A small laugh bubbling up her throat, Lisa wandered along the beach, dipping her bare feet into the dirty sand. Kathleen plodded behind, always watching.

Just beyond the shore, the water blossomed in vibrant shades of green. An algae bloom, from the cocktail of chemicals all the factories couldn't stop churning into the water. According to the hopeful do-gooders across the city, things were getting better. They kept telling us the lake was cleaner now than it had been when we were kids. Days like this made you wonder what kind of fools they took us for.

Sitting cross-legged in a sea of old crumpled *Plain Dealers* and broken beer bottles, Jacqueline cleared a spot and traced a triple moon in the sand with the tip of one sharp finger.

"It's not your fault," she said.

I studied her ever-changing face, glimmering in the sun. Since this morning, a thin seam had appeared along her left cheekbone, exposing a sliver of rusted bone beneath. "What isn't my fault?" I asked.

"Everything." She laughed. "You blame yourself for all of this, but it isn't you. And you can't stop it. Nobody can."

"I won't believe that," I said. Nearby, Lisa splashed in the verdant water, and Kathleen called something indistinct after her. "There's always hope."

Jacqueline smiled, and the whole world lit up around us. "That's true. But maybe hope doesn't look the way you expect it to."

I wanted to ask her what that meant, but I knew she wouldn't tell me. So I asked her something else instead, something familiar.

"I'll race you to the sun?"

Jacqueline shook her head, the edge of her thumb rubbing the place on her arm where the doctors had removed vial after vial of blood.

"Too tired to run," she said, and I nodded, a knot in my throat.

"Lisa?" Kathleen's voice down the beach, strained and scared. "Where are you?"

I shielded my eyes from the sun and searched the water, but there was no one there. No splashing in the waves. No form at all. Lisa was gone. Devoured by Lake Erie.

Kathleen screamed, and I scrambled to my feet to help her search. Together we dove into the water, sinking beneath the waves, our eyes open, desperately looking for someone who wasn't there. The murk and algae rose up into our mouths, and we spewed out the waste of Cleveland, but still, we searched, coming up for air only when we needed it.

"Lisa?" I screamed her name to the sky, but it seemed so useless. If she didn't want to be found, why would she answer?

"Phoebe, where is she? Where is she?" Panic sliced through Kathleen's words, and she dove down deeper this time, so deep that I was afraid she wouldn't come back either.

"Kathleen?" I bobbed on the surface, my body suddenly cold. "Are you here?"

The whole world went still, and I couldn't breathe. I looked to the shore, where Jacqueline was still sitting, the same way that I'd left her. From here, I couldn't see her expression. What was she thinking? What did she know?

At once, Kathleen surfaced, her face pale, almost blue. She'd stayed under too long. I grabbed her with both hands, taking her by the collar, the only part of her I could keep hold of, and I dragged her through the water and back to the sand. Jacqueline clambered to the edge of the shore to help me.

"Don't," Kathleen murmured as we cleared out a clean space for her. "We have to find Lisa. Have to find her."

"There," Jacqueline said and pointed out to the lake with her glassy finger.

Lisa waded there, blinking up at us from the depths. As if she never went anywhere at all. Or as if the water gave her back to us. This time, anyway.

Without a word, she returned to shore, and still half-delirious, Kathleen wrapped her arms tight around her little sister, not noticing where the edges of Lisa's body jutted into her.

Over Kathleen's shoulder, Lisa gazed at Jacqueline, and Jacqueline looked back at her, the two of them knowing something, but not saying it. Their secrets were barbed thorns they couldn't share with anyone, least of all us.

The sky clouded over, and thunder rumbled in the distance.

"We need to leave," I said. "Now."

The rain arrived before we got back to the Impala. Together, we took another drive across town in silence. In the backseat, a still-panting Kathleen curled into Lisa, and for the first time, she looked like the younger sister.

At the interstate crossing, Euclid Avenue was closed down, a detour for our day from hell. With a sigh, I followed the signs, not realizing until it was too late where it would take us.

Right past the picket line.

In a flurry of screams, there were the men, marching back and forth, chanting with their signs, everything as it had been only a few days ago when I was there, and Dawn and Lisa put their fingers through the chain-link. Except now, with no girls on site, they could pretend that things were normal, that this was a normal strike, not one where they had to return each evening to daughters they no longer recognized. Kathleen and Lisa's father was there, and Dawn's father too, the picket duty their excuse for not being with the girls at the clinic today.

And, front and center, there was my father. My strong father with his stern face, chanting for his job. Chanting for our future.

As the Impala passed, he looked right at me. Then his eyes shifted, and he saw Jacqueline in the passenger's seat, her gaze set blindly on some faraway point.

He knew. He knew I'd disobeyed him and Aunt Betty, that I would keep on disobeying them for as long as I could help Jacqueline. That she was all that mattered to me.

I expected him to scream or scowl or run after the car. But he didn't. He only turned away, pretending never to have noticed in the first place. I exhaled and kept going, back around to the other side of Euclid and down to Denton Street on the West Side.

Staying quiet. That was the only way my father could say he was sorry.

Back home, Lisa and Kathleen skittered away to their house, not even bothering to say goodbye. After everything this afternoon, I couldn't blame them.

Jacqueline had to leave me, too. Aunt Betty's shift at the corner store was ending soon.

"I love you, Phoebe," she said.

Then she disappeared down the sidewalk. I watched her go, and wished I could do anything to make her stay.

Upstairs, my calf aching, I shivered out of my jeans and sat on the edge of the tub, cleaning out the cut from the lattice. It was oozing yellow and probably needed stitches, but no way was I going to a hospital, not after today's appointment. I never wanted to go to a doctor again.

Footsteps in the hallway, and the bathroom door swung open. No knock, no other warning. My mother was on the other side.

"Phoebe, I was wondering if you could go down to the corner store and pick up—"

There was no end to that sentence. She just stared at me, her mouth slung open and face gray.

I stared back, a brown bottle of peroxide still poised in my hand. "I'm just cleaning a cut," I said, before I realized it. She didn't know it was from the lattice. She thought it was something else. Something worse.

"I'm fine." I reached up and pulled her closer. "See? No rust or glass or anything in there. Just normal blood and pus."

It should have been the grossest explanation. She should have turned up her nose at me and sashayed out of the room for another drink.

Instead, she let out a tiny howl and collapsed in my arms. The scents of cheap gin and her favorite Avon perfume hung heavy in the air, clinging to my body, as she held me close and sobbed.

"I thought…"

"I know," I said.

"This summer," she whispered, her voice thin and afraid, "with the strike and the girls and everything, I already feel like I've lost your father. I can't lose you too."

I entwined her fingers with mine. "Don't worry," I said. "I'm right here."

She held me tighter, and I buried my face in her long hair. I wanted this moment to matter. I wanted to tell her everything, how frightened I was, how lost. But I said nothing, and I felt nothing too. All I could do was wish my mother had been right. That I was changing. Then I could be like Jacqueline. Then I could understand my best friend the way that I used to.

That night, it was TV dinners and TV news, the bad kind. As if there were ever any good updates about the world. Washington State was still cleaning up the mess that Mount St. Helens had made last month, and another old-time actor had died. They all seemed to be doing that lately, like it was the latest Hollywood trend and everybody who was anybody had to get in on it. One foot in the grave or bust.

Then "Union Update" flashed across the screen in black, block letters, and all the breath in the room seized up at once. My parents and I watched the flicker of the screen, waiting for what would come next.

The newscaster with the shellacked hair and the Miami tan cleared his throat, anything to delay him from having to say it, those words we always knew we'd hear.

"At the steel mill, union negotiations have broken down, and management announced today that it will close the doors to the mill indefinitely sometime next week."

The newsman turned to the second camera, a shift that spanned an eternity.

"This story is developing, and we'll provide more information as we receive it."

He moved on to the Indians score, another loss to the Detroit Tigers, and that was it. The update we were waiting for, the one we'd feared. Sometimes the only satisfying answer, the only one that would make you stop wondering, was the only one you never wanted to come.

But I couldn't believe it. My ears ached with the echo of those words, and I was certain I'd misheard the far-too-cheerful newscaster.

I looked frantically between my parents. "What does that mean?"

My mother swallowed the rest of her drink in one gulp, the best answer she could give, and my father's mouth was a straight line, so stiff and emotionless that I couldn't understand it. In this moment, in this house that was so familiar, I couldn't understand anything. It was like I'd stumbled onto a set that was made to look like my life, but it was only a cheap imitation. Push on the corners, and it would all collapse around you.

"They're closing down the mill," my father said. "That's what it means, Phoebe."

I collapsed back in my chair as the green beans and veal parmesan turned cold in my lap. Our future, new and ugly and wrong, settled over me, so much heavier than I'd ever expected it.

Then I imagined her. In the house down the street, behind

lock and key, Jacqueline was probably in front of the television too, her TV dinner growing as cold as mine, as she heard the same news and realized the truth.

That everything bad was about to get so much worse.

TEN

The neighborhood wives had made up their minds. Over Virginia Slims and pitchers of before-noon Bloody Marys, they held a meeting during the last weekend of June and took a vote to make it official.

The Fourth of July block party would go on as planned. They announced it in front of the congregation on Sunday.

"No reason not to celebrate," they said, and in the back pew, I chirped out a laugh.

No reason. Not the closing of the mill, not our girls transforming into monsters, not the end of everything as we knew it.

No reason at all.

We were going to pretend that our lives were normal, even if it killed us, even if it suffocated what little lingering hope we had left. Bring on the barbeque.

A permit was obtained from the city to close off the street, and every house broke out the Weber grills and twenty-pound bags of charcoal. Dozens of grim-faced parents and jubilant tourists lined the streets. Our fathers, their hands no longer holding picket signs, gripped onto metal tongs for dear life and pretended one good cookout today could be enough to make up for all our loss.

By nine a.m. on July 4th, Denton Street reeked of charred flesh, and it turned my stomach to acid. With my knees folded into my chest, I sat in the middle of the sidewalk with my tartan thermos, topped off with whatever I could funnel from the liquor cabinet. These days, my mother was emptying every bottle in the house faster than I could keep up, so today's cocktail was a noxious mix of Jim Beam, vermouth, Maker's Mark whiskey, and the last three drops of Triple Sec. I swallowed the concoction quick so I didn't have to taste it.

Across the street, the government men's house was dark. All three of them had departed after breakfast, a mountain of file folders in their arms.

"Heading to the clinic," Adrian told me when I saw him in the driveway, loading up the backseat with his questionable papers. I'd been hanging around Jacqueline's house, hoping and failing to catch a glimpse of her. I looked at him in the rising sun, and a string of questions budded on my lips: *what are you doing? What are you planning? Can I come too and eavesdrop on your conversations?*

But with his eyes dark, Adrian didn't look eager to answer, and I wasn't eager to ask—not this early, not on this terrible, celebratory day—so we just waved goodbye to each other and went our separate ways. I could always break into the house later and steal his notes.

Besides, there was plenty to keep me busy. All down the block, there were helium balloons and homemade relish and crowded picnic tables, each one bedecked with citronella candles to ward off the mosquitoes, as though they were our only problem today. And there was enough liquor for every man, woman, and child in the neighborhood to drown in. Whatever the other mothers hadn't already quietly gulped down wholesale was up for grabs.

By noon, you couldn't find an eye on Denton Street that wasn't glassy.

Even the tourists imbibed on our generosity, pretending they had the same woes as we did. They milled about the neighborhood, their ever-flashing cameras dilating like eyeballs in our faces.

Unlike a week ago, nobody wanted them here, not anymore. We'd prefer to mourn what was left of our lives in peace. But with our spare bedrooms rented out and bake sales popping up every other day, we needed the money. Right now, not one family on the street could afford to turn away a single penny. So in spite of ourselves, the tourists stayed.

The Rust Maidens, though, weren't welcome to the festivities.

"They wouldn't enjoy it anyhow," the preacher's wife said, her smile twitching at the corners. "Helena prefers solitude these days."

More like everyone on Denton Street preferred solitude for them.

Now with everything cascading away from us, there wasn't any make-believe acceptance left for the girls. Kathleen shepherded Lisa through the crowd, the ratty afghan draped over the tiny girl. Nobody offered them a drink or a slice of apple pie or a kind word.

"Why didn't she leave her at home?" someone whispered. The other families had been far more considerate. Their girls were where they belonged—not among us.

Violet opened her bedroom window, and her camera lorded over us as she captured the faces of her captors.

Helena sat on the porch with nothing but her Bible for company.

Dawn paced in the darkness of her parents' parlor, back and forth, her feet probably wearing away the varnish from the floorboards.

Jacqueline was marooned out of sight in her room, the locks on the doors sealing her in, while Aunt Betty socialized and smiled and acted like nothing was wrong.

In the street, we all acted like nothing was wrong too. We sipped our drinks, spiked with whatever was convenient, and we chewed our burgers, tasteless and dry. We wanted to talk about them. We wanted to say the truth, to scream it, to confess our fears. But we couldn't. We'd practiced keeping quiet for so long that now, when we needed to speak the most, we'd forgotten how. And anyways, what was the proper way to bid farewell to everything you'd known? Even if we hadn't sewn our lips shut years ago, there still might not be words for what we needed to say.

Not everyone was so harried. Clint roamed free-range down Denton Street, drinking up whatever cup was passed to him. Part of me hoped somebody would lace one of the punchbowls with arsenic and put him out of the misery he caused the rest of us. In mid-June, he'd started in on a new girl in Parma Heights. He'd met her downtown at Kaufmann's, and everybody knew she was the destination when he took the city bus each night after dark. Even in her seclusion, Dawn had figured it out too, though I doubted she cared at this point. It was probably a relief that Clint's clumsy hands would never again try and fail in the dark to flick open the clasp on her bra, or that she would never have to hear his voice, like a dull razorblade, making hollow apologies for his backseat failures.

Sometimes, change was a mercy.

Just before dusk, somebody lit a pack of sparklers and handed them out to the smaller children, and for a bit, the whole neighborhood looked like it was on fire. The rest of us ate until we were stuffed, and then we waited an hour and ate some more. There was nothing else to do besides dine and drink and pretend we weren't dying. While grubby faces piled condiments high on stiff hamburger buns, Eleanor curled in a bassinet and sobbed. Her cries set everything in my body humming, and I wanted to tear at my own skin to make the feeling stop.

Poor little Eleanor, unwanted and motherless. And more or less fatherless too.

"Why do babies do that?" Clint sneered at her. "What does

she have to be upset about?"

I took another sip from my thermos. "To start with, I'd say a great deal."

Clint's mother did her best to rock the cradle carefully, like a good grandmother, or at least the best grandmother she could be under the circumstances. But it didn't matter. Eleanor wouldn't stop crying.

The air shimmered with heat, and the cocktail-drenched voices rose and fell around us. Everything was normal one moment, barbeques sizzling, parents laughing nervously, the baby sobbing. Then suddenly, the world split in two, and she was here, a ghost in our midst.

"I can help her," Dawn whispered.

No one had seen the shadow disappear from her parlor window or heard when the front door creaked open. She simply strolled down Denton Street, her body dripping and her gaze sharp, set on one thing in this entire world.

Eleanor blinked up at her mother and cooed.

Clint hesitated before a smug grin curled on his lips. "Sure, darling," he said. "Give it your best try."

He held the baby while Dawn moved nearer. She wasn't allowed to embrace Eleanor, but this didn't seem to disappoint her. After all, this was the closest she'd been to her daughter since the delivery.

All around us, no one else spoke a word. The whole neighborhood watched, hearts frozen, as Dawn peeled up the front of her tank top and breastfed Eleanor. The baby fussed for a moment before latching to her mother.

I stepped forward and held my breath. I wanted this for Dawn, but not here. Not with an audience of so many people that didn't trust the girls.

But Dawn didn't seem to notice anyone except her daughter. She moved closer still, and the exposed bits of her cracked flesh glinted in the flash of the children's sprinklers, her skin gray and peeling and damp, all of it concealing the corroded metal beneath. When she finally pulled away, a thin stream of milk the color of rust and brackish water dripped down her chest, and Eleanor's babbling lips were stained red.

Clint's mother stared at Dawn. "What *are* you?" she asked, her voice blistering with disgust. "And what are you doing to her?"

"I'm trying to be like you," Dawn said, almost whimpering. "I'm trying to be a mother."

The neighborhood women were all together in a line now, their mouths pursed like rosebuds.

"You'll never be like us," they said, and they didn't have to say more. Like them. Like good mothers. Dawn would never know the simple pleasure of just rocking her child in her arms, holding her baby as she fell asleep.

In a flurry of acrylic hands, they yanked Eleanor away, swooping in to rescue the child from her own mother. Wailing, Dawn tried to fight them, tried to keep some part of her body tethered to her child. The palm of one hand, or a tip of a rusted-out finger, anything to be near her. But the other mothers were too fast. They'd already closed ranks around Eleanor.

"We'll make sure she's safe," they said, and that was it. The cruelest insult, the words that pressed the thorn deep into Dawn's heart. Her future was lost to her before she'd even had a chance to fully imagine it. To imagine being a mother to a child she never asked for.

Dawn's face twisted, and something in her shifted. Though she didn't look entirely human—hadn't looked human for weeks now—that didn't matter. The expression that washed over her was unmistakably her own. For a moment, she was just the same scared girl she'd always been, a girl with more pain than one person should ever have to carry. Nearby, Eleanor started to weep in the circle of mothers, and Dawn was weeping too. Dark tears stained her cheeks, and her whole body quivered, the thrum of her anguish vibrating through what was left of her bones and into the hot concrete beneath us.

I inhaled a sharp breath, realizing it was too late to stop what was coming next. What had always been coming perhaps, even if we hadn't realized it until now.

With her head tipped back, Dawn let out a wail, and the sky cracked open.

This was different than Jacqueline's scream, deeper somehow, and stranger too. It was the hot screech of metal and the carriage of heavy earth and a thousand restless waves at midnight.

The sound pierced my skin and went into my marrow, shaking me the same way it shook her. But hers wasn't just a howl of agony—it was a cry for help. A beacon to the others. Something meant to bring them together.

And in their solitude, they heard her. Each of the girls, ready and waiting for this. At once, there was no one in Violet's bedroom window, or on Helena's porch swing, or in Jacqueline's house. They were here instead, materializing among us, both part of the throng and somehow estranged from it.

Lisa, the only one who hadn't taken to her expulsion, was the last to go to them. She looked from the girls to her sister and back again before she steadied herself and shed her afghan like an unnecessary skin. With Kathleen pleading quietly behind her, Lisa threaded through the crowd and joined the others.

There they were, together for the first time in front of us. They didn't speak. They didn't have to. They were everything we'd never realized. All five of them, gorgeous and fearsome and not at all the girls we thought we knew. We remembered them as quiet, as sweet, as familiar.

We didn't remember them as powerful.

Their flesh steel-plated shields against us, their bodies leaking gray water that could fill up our lungs in a heartbeat. Those eyes that watched us and saw everything. There were more of us, to be sure, but against them, we somehow doubted our odds.

Aunt Betty shoved through the crowd. "What are you doing?" She glowered at Jacqueline. "Go back home. Now."

But that wasn't going to work. Her eyes dark, Jacqueline shook her head, and the other girls mimicked the motion. Five faces swinging back and forth, pendulums that measured our world, that divided us between the moments before this and all the terrible moments that would come after.

The parents and the tourists stared at them, plastic cups suspended in midair and hot dogs sizzling into char on the grills. Something had changed. We understood this, even if we couldn't string the syllables together to say it. The girls were no longer safe. They were our enemies now, here and ready to make a stand. Not that any of us, even the Rust Maidens, knew what that meant.

The neighborhood moved closer to the girls, a random smattering of parents flailing this way and that. They were desperate to take hold of them, to do their best to stop the blossoming insurrection, even if they weren't sure they could win. Winning almost didn't matter. We certainly couldn't stand back and let them rebel like this, not with an audience of outsiders. There was decorum to maintain, a sense of authority over our own. Because what kind of men would our fathers be if they couldn't control five little girls? And what kind of women would our mothers be if they didn't stand behind their husbands?

They were closer to the girls now, expecting at any moment that the five of them would scatter. Every moment, they were disappointed. I knew I had to do something. I couldn't stand here and watch, a bystander in my own life. I couldn't let them grab the girls and never let them go.

With a single, fluid movement, I surged forward and blocked the girls from the gathering crowd. I wasn't enough by myself, but at least there was someone standing in our parents' way. Sneering, the mothers and fathers fell back a few steps, uncertain what I had planned. I was uncertain too, but I had to do something before the crowd closed in around me.

All my muscles constricted, and I seized Jacqueline's arm.

"Go," I whispered. "Get out of here. Together."

This turned an invisible knife deep in my chest. Jacqueline, headed where I couldn't follow. But it wasn't permanent. It was just for now. Until we could figure out how to stop this, how to make all this better somehow.

With our parents pushing nearer, their breath heavy and stinking of booze, I squeezed Jacqueline's arm once more, a bid for her to go before it was too late. What was left of her skin felt cold and unfamiliar, but strong. She stared into me, and without a word, she understood. The girls joined hands and walked down the street as if there was no other way.

I wanted the five of them to run and not look back. Away

from Denton Street, away from Cleveland, away from the so-called Great Lakes. I wanted them to flee to somewhere they didn't know, and that didn't know them.

But that wasn't how this worked, and I should have realized that. They were girls who belonged here, maybe more than we did. The five of them marched to the end of the cul-de-sac and, without hesitation, they opened the front door to the abandoned mansion. Like this had always been their plan. Like the place was waiting for them, unlocked and eager, brimming with the hope for a new family to reside within.

Not one parent went after them.

We'd seen their strength now, their collective power. Nobody could separate them, not tonight, not if they wanted to be together.

With idle chitchat seeming altogether impossible now, the barbeques soon broke up. Charcoal was doused with water, and everyone murmured their goodbyes, pretending nothing out of the ordinary had happened, not saying what they were thinking. *Thank you for the hamburgers, Midge. Hope your mutating daughter comes home in the morning.*

Not that anyone really expected the girls to come home.

Nearby, the tourists lingered in the street, looking wearier now, as though suddenly questioning themselves on why they were even here in the first place.

My head heavy, I turned away from everyone and followed the outlines of wet footprints, gazing at Jacqueline's most of all. Her steps were different than the rest, always soft as a ghost's, like she was never really there.

But these prints weren't the only markers of the girls. All along Denton Street, I saw what else they'd left behind, the pieces of who they were and might not be again.

Bible pages fluttered in the wind. Helena's faith, abandoned on a porch swing.

Empty film canisters lined up on Violet's window sill.

Shame, and not much else, hidden behind the blinds of Lisa's house.

For her part, Dawn had nothing to leave behind. Nothing

except the wide-eyed infant who cried out again in the night, wanting only one thing in the world and having that one thing denied to her over and over.

Because I couldn't help myself, I stopped in front of Jacqueline's house. Aunt Betty was collapsed on the front porch, sobbing. Everything she'd tried had failed. Even the prison she'd built for her only daughter hadn't been strong enough. The exterior locks, brand-new only a week ago, were now rusted out and broken, as if Jacqueline's touch through the door was enough to destroy their power.

Enough to set her free.

"What have you done?" Aunt Betty wailed, and I didn't know if she was asking me or Jacqueline or herself. I just stood on the sidewalk, my hands folded and quivering in front of me, and said nothing, but wondered the same question.

Overhead, a light dimmed. With the last of the temporary workers filed solemnly through the back door, the flame above the steel mill winked out. I glanced up and saw it happen. It was just a moment. There, and then vanished. Snuffed out. Our beacon gone, our lives gone.

But there was another light now. Inside the mansion, a single candle illuminated the front room. I inhaled, and even from here, I could smell the citronella. A pillar swiped from a picnic table on the girls' long walk down the street, something to guide their way. I crept closer until I was standing right in front of the mansion's cobblestone driveway—me, the guest who wasn't invited— and for an instant, I could see her there, watching me out the window. Jacqueline, a face like a lost wraith. But like my friend, too. Like the only one I'd ever trusted.

Then the moth-eaten curtains fluttered closed, and she was gone.

ELEVEN

Back in my parents' nearly empty house, I replay the evening, the unreality of it all.

The three of us trespassing in Helena's house, listening for lost voices.

The glimmer of that wound on Quinn's arm, still fresh and weeping.

The quiet expression of her face, perhaps already an acceptance of what's to come.

It's on repeat. This whole city is stuck on repeat. A cycle that, no matter how hard we try, we can never seem to break.

I didn't tell Quinn what I saw. I don't know if it would have helped if I had.

Maybe I'm wrong. Maybe that glint beneath her skin isn't what I think it is. Even after all these years, I still can't invent better lies to tell myself.

I curl in the corner of the living room, tucked inside my orange-lined sleeping bag, purchased on sale at Sears forty years ago. It was the best my mother could find for me, the only thing she hasn't sent to storage or to her new one-bedroom apartment in Lakewood. She traded down to have enough money for my father's care.

Upstairs, the floorboards creak. My mother's awake, haunting the house that used to be hers. The wreckers are due at our doorstep in six days. Now we're practically squatters in our own lives.

I turn over on my stomach and stare into the dark. It won't be long until we're gone from here. This isn't my battle to fight. It's never been mine.

But that doesn't mean it doesn't still feel like mine.

I squeeze my eyes closed and tell myself this time will be different.

This time, I'll stop it.

)O(

The next morning, my mother leaves early to visit my father. She asks me to come with her, but I shake my head.

"I'll meet you there later," I say.

Once her car heads down the street, I hesitate in the living room. I know what I should do: I should go upstairs and finally clean out what's left of my life. The bedroom needs to be emptied before the construction crew tears it all down.

But that's not what I'm going to do today.

In the garage, I slip into the driver's seat of the Impala. The key is still tucked in the visor, and, holding my breath, I slide it into the ignition. The engine roars to life. Like it remembers. Like it always knew I'd come back.

As I pull out of the driveway, another house down the block collapses. Dawn's. The wrecker swings so effortlessly, and everything falls. In an instant, the picture window where she used to walk shatters in a spray of diamonds.

And there on the sidewalk, at the end of the cul-de-sac is Eleanor, watching her mother's childhood home fall. She doesn't see me leaving Denton Street. She doesn't see anything except what she's lost.

A wave of unease chills me. I want to drown out the sound of the construction, but I don't dare turn on the radio. I'm scared of what song will be waiting there to greet me if I do. I just keep going, and I don't look back.

The drive across town is worse than I expect. Even in daylight, this town looks like a funeral. I guess a lot of towns look like that now. They're saying this recession is the worst since the Great Depression. Though it's hard to tell the difference in a city that hasn't been in its prime for half a century.

According to the news, people are doing the smart thing and getting out. People on Denton Street, and people elsewhere too. They're fleeing to anywhere there are jobs, or they're simply being evicted from their lives in spite of themselves.

Then there's Quinn. She's getting out any way she can, too. Give it a week or a month at most, and she'll be gone. It's a familiar tale, and not just on this street, not just the Rust Maidens. Girls vanish all over. Odd girls, forgotten girls, runaways, the ones nobody cares about. She'll be another tally mark. There are too many places in the world that never stop tallying loss.

My fingers tighten around the steering wheel. This all seems so pointless, thinking I can help. What can I do? Is it even possible to break a cycle that's stronger than all of us?

Maybe not, but I'll try. It's all I can do now.

On the East Side, University Circle is the only area in the city that hasn't changed as much as I expected. The Case Western campus is still what I remember from my college visit in the fall of '79, everything so neat and proper, the brick buildings with their spiky turrets looming as reminders of the city's history, a past that isn't as tinged with tragedy as mine. It isn't all calamity in Cleveland. Sometimes I have to remind myself of that. Given a long enough trajectory, things have a way of working out. But so rarely is one lifetime long enough.

At the far end of East Boulevard, I find a narrow parking spot and feed the meter until it's full. That buys me two hours.

Nowhere near as much time as I need, but it'll have to do.

Out on the sidewalk, I tug my pea coat closed as my breath smokes around me. December is in full swing, kitschy lights and garland fleecing every streetlamp. I pay no attention to the make-believe cheer. The place I'm going is the last building in a snarl of storied institutions: The Center for Northeastern Ohio History. It's the smallest of the museums here, less than a quarter the size of the Museum of Art or the Museum of Natural History. But none of those bigger places have what I'm looking for.

I burst through the rotating door, and the cold of winter follows me in, my feet tracking ice and melancholy into the lobby. I've never been here before, but my mother's told me all about this place.

"It's a nice little exhibit. Nothing crass at all," she says every time she brings it up on the phone. "Maybe I should donate some of your old keepsakes to them. Your diaries and pictures of the girls."

I always sigh. "Do whatever you want," I say, knowing my response means nothing at that point. I've already been excused from the conversation.

"No, I think I'll wait until you come home. Then we can go through everything together." A long pause. The same pause she always takes when we talk about the museum. "I've told you before who the curator is, right? You know, I'm sure he'd love to talk with you."

"I bet he would," I always say, and hang up the phone.

Now here I am, in this place I promised myself I'd never go. I promise myself a lot of things. I can never keep my word about any of it.

At the front desk, a smiling docent, probably an undergrad preemptively working off her student loans, nods a greeting to me. I don't have any spare cash for admission, so I improvise.

"I'm an alumnus, class of '84," I say, and it's almost true. If my life had stayed its course, that's exactly what I'd be. It feels like telling this lie is the closest to the truth I can get without being there.

With an eyebrow raised, she stamps my hand and lets me in for free. Just like that. Me, the imaginary graduate securing her passage into alien territory. Everything about this city feels alien to me now.

I wander for a while, not sure where I'll find what I need. Even with a map, it's the usual rigmarole, the permanent installations everything I expect.

In the front room, steel and unions and the dying flame, this history still so potent you can practically smell the rotten-egg stench of sulfur, that familiar aroma all the mills once shared.

On the second floor, rock and roll and Alan Freed and the payola scandal. "Maybellene" and "Rock Around the Clock" and other Fifties tunes loop on repeat over the speakers.

The girls are a footnote compared to all of this. Few people caught wind of them outside of Ohio, and even some locals still believe the Rust Maidens are nothing more than a hoax. Five silly little girls who craved more attention than they deserved.

At least here in the museum, they're not treated like a prank. But what they are given isn't much better. It's one windowless room, small and tucked away in the back.

I pace up and down the cramped aisles, passing faded pictures and laminated headlines. The scent of these old things clings to me like stale cigarette smoke. I don't even know what I'm looking for. The truth, I suppose.

The curator's done his best with what he had, but there isn't much to go on. A few declassified government documents and five truncated biographies. The girls never had a chance to find out who they could be, so the museum had to settle with a series of banal facts and dates: when they were born (sometime in '61 or '62), where they're from (Cleveland, of course), and what they did in those eighteen short years (not much of anything, has nobody in this town been paying attention?).

In the corner, I find myself waiting behind glass. Inside a display case lined with dust, there's a pair of Polaroids snapped at the barbeque on graduation day. Both of them feature Jacqueline and me at a picnic table, not looking up at the camera, but looking at each other. Scheming our escape.

There I am, the girl I was. And there's Jacqueline, the change almost certainly stirring beneath her skin by then. Did she already know it? Was that why she gave me that look that day? A look like goodbye?

I squint again at the images. This isn't the same picture Violet gave us that day. She must have kept these two photos for herself, part of a portfolio she never completed. Her camera is here too, a smudged fingerprint still on the black shutter button. I imagine her hand, unsullied from the transformation, waving the undeveloped image in our face. Jacqueline and I weren't eager to take it from her that day. It didn't seem to matter then. Maybe it still doesn't.

My feet heavy beneath me, I keep going, keep hoping to find something. Down the hallway, there's another room, one marked with a simple sign.

Private. Employees Only.

The door is open, so I go in, uninvited as always.

These are the archives, the only place that might be able to give me the answer I'm looking for. The walls are arrayed in thick leather binders, dozens of them, maybe hundreds, stacked on metal shelves, their edges bursting with plastic-encased doctors' files and case reports from despondent family members in the weeks after, each page transcribed by hand. The spines on all these volumes look ready to split from being opened and closed too many times. From somebody viewing and reviewing the facts as they knew them, almost certainly disappointed with each new perusal.

I pick one binder at random and start reading. After a minute, the docent finds me. The blinking red light of the security camera on the wall must have given me away.

"Are you sure you belong in this place?" she asks, and we both already know the answer.

I belong here more than you, I want to say. This little undergrad doesn't know the first thing about the Rust Maidens, other than the horror stories her parents told her growing up.

"You heard about those girls from Denton Street, haven't you? Be a good little girl, or you'll turn out like them. And you don't want to end up a Rust Maiden, do you?"

My friends—the urban legend to beat all others.

"I already told you," I say, smiling, "I'm an alumnus."

As though that grants me an all-access pass.

The docent is still watching me. "What did you say your name was again?"

I hesitate, my lips twisting wordlessly, desperate to form whatever lie will keep me in this room the longest. But I must not have the energy for another fabrication, because I just shrug and say, "Phoebe Shaw."

It stifles my breath once again to hear it, but there it is. Who I am. My name, so long a stranger to me, now reclaimed even when I don't want it.

The docent nods. "I'll be right back," she says, and disappears out the door.

I only have a couple of minutes until she's checked out my story and discovers—surprise!—it's totally bogus. That will be enough time. It has to be enough time. I thumb through the pages, more desperate now, but it does no good. This is the same sort of drivel from the government files years ago. All empty statistics and empty anecdotes. Nothing meaningful. Nothing true.

Something shuffles down the hall, but I don't look up. I keep reading, keeping searching for that one piece of the puzzle I've always been missing. Whatever will help it all make sense. Whatever might stop it from happening to Quinn or anyone else.

I don't find it. Not here, not today. Probably because it doesn't exist at all. There is no answer for what I'm looking for, no smoking gun that will explain what I couldn't understand before.

The shuffling gets closer, and with a sigh, I look up.

As expected, the docent has returned. "Miss Shaw," she says, and I roll my eyes.

"What is it?" I ask, and go back to scanning the last volume I grabbed from the overstuffed bookshelf, eager to glean whatever I can before this moment is cut short.

I don't get much, before the docent's hand is wound around my arm. It's a tenuous hold, one I could break in an instant, not that that would help me much.

"The curator would like to speak with you now."

"I bet he would," I say, and place the binder back on the shelf, not hurrying about it, not showing that I care. Then I follow her to an office down the hall where she delivers me to my punishment: the curator sitting at a cluttered desk.

"Hello, Phoebe," he says.

"Hello, Adrian."

The docent closes the door behind her, and we're alone.

He smiles. "You're not surprised to see me here?"

I plop down in the chair across from his. "I thought I heard something about you getting a job at this place."

I heard something about you. More like, I heard everything about him. My mother gave me an obligatory update every few months for the past thirty years. When I would call home, she always managed to work him into the conversation.

"Adrian left his position with the government."

"Adrian's still around, working at the museum."

"Adrian is trying to make it right."

I always laugh at that last one. None of us can make things right now. That's what I keep learning, over and over, a lesson I never seem to master.

I sit back in my chair, one arm slung over the side, and regard him through half-closed eyes. *This doesn't matter to me*, I'm trying to say. It's the same thing I'm trying to believe.

Seeing him should be the easy part of being home. I hardly knew him then. I know him even less now. This should be no different than passing a stranger in a parking lot.

He's almost sixty, practically an old man, his eyes crinkled at the edges and his hair faded to gray. Yet nothing about him feels old to me. He feels exactly the same. I shouldn't still want him. After all these years and all these mistakes and all these regrets, this shouldn't be happening. A grown woman acting the same as some swoony girl who can't get over a crush.

I feel like I should be better than this, but apparently, I'm not.

My hands fold and unfold in my lap. "Are you going to have me arrested for trespassing?"

He almost chuckles at this, but thinks better of it. "That wasn't my plan."

We do a volley of niceties—*so good to see you, it's been so long, how is the weather?*—and I think I might be able to slide out of here unscathed.

Then Adrian sets his gaze on me and asks with an offhand curiosity, "What is it you were looking for today?"

"Anything that could help," I say.

Instantly, I wish I could revoke the words. As always, I've revealed myself without meaning to. I do my best to silence my face as I fumble with every object within my reach on his desk. A stapler, some generic ballpoint pen, a picture frame that I turn to face me, certain that it'll be the beaming faces of his family. Instead, it's just the city skyline.

Adrian inspects me. "Something's happened, hasn't it? That's why you're here."

I say nothing, but that's more than enough.

He leans across the desk, and for an instant, I think he might reach out for my hand. He doesn't. "I could help," he says. "With whatever you need."

I don't like the idea of this, anything that could give him entry into my life again. I've tried so hard to escape this place, and now I'm whirlpooling back into it, as lost as I was at eighteen. But maybe he's right. Maybe he can help me. There might be things held back from the archives, secrets gleaned once it was too late, once the girls weren't around anymore to question.

But I won't ask.

"I should go," I say, and shift out of the chair.

Adrian exhales an unsteady breath. My leaving isn't quite

what he was hoping for.

"I'll show you out," he says.

He walks me to my car. Side by side, I'm close enough to touch him again. I breathe in and discover he still smells of cedar. Of course he does. Of course that wouldn't change.

Outside in front of the museum, we pass a half-finished foundation on the green space.

"What will go there?" I ask, my eyes trained on the spot, half-mesmerized, though not knowing why. It's only some displaced earth. Nothing remarkable. Nothing at all.

"We hope to build a monument there," Adrian says, each word plucked carefully. "Something for the girls."

It takes me a moment to process this, to understand that he means *my* girls.

"Like you have any right," I half-growl at him. "After everything all of you did to them. You didn't even know them."

"That's true," he says, inspecting the empty spot on the lawn. "But the one person who did know them won't remember. So somebody has to."

He smiles, and all the rage in my heart turns cold. Adrian knows he's one-upped me this time. I should have stuck around. I should have remembered. But I can't. It's too much even being here in this city again, so close I can practically hear the girls giggling. So close I can almost see Jacqueline peeking out her bedroom window.

I need to tell him this. I need to confess all of this to him and so much more. But instead, I just shake my head.

"Have a nice day," I say, and head to my car without another word.

Back in the driver's seat, I steer the Impala down Euclid and do my best not to scream.

One thing I know: I have to tell someone. If not Adrian, then somebody. If no one knows the truth, then how can I expect to change anything?

I'll find my mother. I'll tell her what's happening now, and what happened before, and what will happen all over again if we don't do something. If we don't do better than the last time.

Sweet Evergreen is only a mile away from campus, and I'm walking across the parking lot before I have a chance to reconsider. The lights are dim inside, all the harshness scrubbed right out of the world. A little too late for that, but nobody seems to care.

In the all-purpose room, visitors the same age as my mother crowd around spouses who no longer recognize them. Sometimes it seems we're all destined to spend our golden years saying goodbye.

I keep walking. This place is everything I expected and all that I feared. The stench of urine-soaked bedsheets doused with gallons of Clorox, as if it's an exotic perfume. My father, wasting away in a place where he—and everyone here—deserves better.

An orderly directs me to a room at the end of the hall. Inside, it isn't a terrible size. A suite, they probably call it, though it's not large enough to earn that title. At least my father has it all to himself. I wonder if that's a mercy or a punishment.

When I walk in, the room is empty, except for my father reclined in bed. There are no pictures on the wall, no décor at all except a couple of machines that beep at random intervals. I breathe deep. I must have missed my mother.

I'm ready to bolt, but my father opens his eyes and smiles at me. On reflex, I smile back. It's so easy to do, so easy to match that familiar expression. I can't leave him, not yet, so I sit for a while.

"Have you met my daughter?" he asks me, his eyes bright.

I stare at him. "No," I say, "I haven't."

"A good girl, that one. Lots of big dreams." He exhales a laugh that startles the room. "And sure, all kids have big dreams. But my Phoebe, she's different."

Different. He's right about that, at least.

His words slur together, but I understand him. I've always understood him. Again, I wonder if it's a mercy or a punishment.

159

He babbles on and then tells me about the treehouse he just converted for his daughter.

"What does she need that for?" I ask, projecting myself outside of this room and this moment.

"For bugs." He lets out a vibrant cackle. "I told you my girl is different."

I watch him carefully now, not sure I want to ask my next question. "Don't you worry about what the neighbors will think?"

Those neighbors, the ones scheming in our kitchen.

My father smiles. "Who cares about them?"

You did, I want to say. The urge to run again courses through me, and this time, it's too much. I excuse myself, but before I've reached the door, I turn back. I can't leave like this. I can't leave without saying goodbye.

I start to say something, but my father cuts me off, his gaze wide and bright and suddenly his own.

"You'll make it to the stars, Phoebe," he says. "You'll make it anywhere."

This hits me all at once, and I can't breathe.

"Thank you," I whisper, as his eyes glaze over, and he forgets I was ever here.

I don't get any farther than the hallway before my knees give out and I collapse to the ugly mottled tile. Orderlies pass by and nod solemnly at me. They don't have to guess why I'm in a heap on the floor. It's probably a normal part of their daily routine.

I finally collect myself and head to my car and what's left of my life.

Back on Denton Street, the Impala cuts out in my mother's driveway, but I don't go inside. She's not home yet anyhow, probably out getting more moving boxes to pack up the rest of the house. I don't want to be alone in there, so I trudge down the street to survey the construction crew's damage.

A figure is already there on the sidewalk, in front of the spot where Dawn once lived. I exhale, relieved to see a familiar shape.

"Quinn," I say, my voice cracking in half.

But then the shadow moves, and I realize it's exactly who

I should have expected. The same person who was here this morning.

Eleanor.

"It's okay," she says. "I'm never the one people are hoping for."

We stare at the rubble. The broken glass and shards of old window frames have fallen into strange shapes. Things that look like crescent moons. Eleanor probably thinks this is a sign from her mother. I think it's a sign from Jacqueline. It's probably nothing at all, just a haphazard pattern we're reading like wet tea leaves in the bottom of a cup.

"What happened to them?" she asks, not looking at me.

"I don't know." I edge past the sidewalk and onto what used to be the front yard.

Eleanor follows. "Maybe if I was Quinn, you'd tell me." She's right behind me, her breath hot on the back of my neck. "I know why you've taken to her so much. I've seen the pictures. She looks like your cousin. You think if you save Quinn, then it'll be like saving Jacqueline. But you can't help any of them, and you know it."

Every muscle in my body seizes up, and I glare at her. Then one by one, my fingers curl into fists. This should deter her, but instead, her eyes flare, and she looks emboldened by it.

"Go ahead." She moves toward me, her chin raised an inch to give me a better target. "Then maybe after, we can talk."

Both my hands go limp at my sides. This is ridiculous. I should tell her about her mother. I should tell her everything.

But when I open my mouth to speak, the words won't come. The words never come.

"It's hard to explain," I say at last. "You weren't there."

That's a lie, though. Eleanor was everywhere that summer. She saw more than she knows.

"She never even got to hold me," Eleanor says, half under her breath. "What kind of mother never holds her own child?"

"It wasn't her fault," I say. "None of it was her fault."

Another shadow, someone else who isn't to blame. Quinn,

appearing in the yard next to us as she dodges around splintered wood and tufts of pink insulation.

Eleanor grunts. "We were just talking about you."

"Hello to you too," Quinn whispers, but says nothing else. She just moves closer to me, shivering in her short sleeves. No coat in subzero weather.

I'm removing my jacket for her when I see it. The spot on her arm, the size of a silver dollar now, gray and weeping.

My throat closing up with dread, I pass her my pea coat and look back at the ground. In the rubble, the shapes have shifted slightly. The points of the moon are a little sharper, the curves a bit more elegant. Not because of me or Eleanor, but because of Quinn. These signs aren't ours. They're meant for her.

"Your arm," Eleanor says and moves toward Quinn. "It's gleaming."

At once, Eleanor recognizes what it is. The daughter of a Rust Maiden doesn't need this explained to her.

"What's wrong?" Quinn asks, but Eleanor just shakes her head.

She and I both want to break this cycle, but we don't know where to start. Doctors can't help. The government can't help. Archives and museums and the collective history of this city can't help. If everyone else has tried and failed, who are we to fix it?

My eyes bleary, I glance down the block at Jacqueline's house. It stands almost alone now. No homes on either side of it, and a dozen notices tacked to the front door. It's scheduled for demolition the same day as our house, but it might not be abandoned yet, either.

The curtains flutter, and I hold my breath, but no one appears in the window.

"What do we do now?" Eleanor whispers.

"I wish I knew," I say, and because I'm too tired to fight it, the tears come.

They don't stop.

TWELVE

The night the Rust Maidens went into the mansion, a storm descended on the Midwest. It swept across from Omaha, sliding through Cleveland sometime the next morning. Winds hit highs of sixty miles per hour, and the skies went darker than sorrow. People died all over, dozens of them, and campers and boats upended and overturned, their snarled remains left for the junkyard.

It was an all-out assault on summer, or perhaps it was summer assaulting us. For what we'd done. For what we would do.

They called it the "More Trees Down" derecho. That year had been a strange one, even without the girls' transformations. Heat waves and storms by the score, so many that the July Fourth gale was merely one in a line of odd weather anomalies in the region. This particular tempest got its name because some farmers feared that by the time 1980 was done with us, we'd have no trees left. Our oaks and pines and maples just kept coming down, one after another, leaving us with so much firewood that we'd never be able to use it all.

As I listened to the radio crackle in the Impala, the DJ spouting off updates about the maelstrom, my chest tightened. Although I knew it didn't make sense, this one felt like it was meant for us. All those people in Nebraska and Illinois and Indiana had gotten caught in a storm that had nothing to do with them. This was our punishment for all the ways we were failing.

In the afternoon, when the worst of the gusts had passed, I slipped out into the backyard and collected the fallen limbs into a heap on the patio. I piled them next to the Weber grill we'd probably never use again, not after yesterday and all the terrible images already crystallizing in our neighborhood's memory. Our lives were becoming one long nightmare from which none of us could awaken.

When I finally couldn't take not knowing another moment, I climbed up the rope ladder to survey the damage in the treehouse. Protected by the plastic sarcophagus draped over all the windows, my bugs had mostly escaped the winds, but not entirely. A few tattered monarchs were waiting there to greet me, their corpses limp on the floorboards, wings frayed like torn wedding lace. The sight of them, their bodies battered by the wind, clutched my throat so tightly I feared for a moment I'd forgotten how to breathe altogether.

Someone hollered on the street below, a nothing command that broke this trance, and life trickled slowly back into me, even though I didn't ask it to. Even though I didn't want to be here. But there was nowhere else to go. My teeth clenched, I edged around the bodies to the potted milkweed, withered now from the summer heat, and pulled out a flask from the corner. No-name whiskey in this one, cut with water to top it off. For the rest of the day, I sat with the dead butterflies, drinking and sobbing and repeating over and over how sorry I was.

At sunset, I buried them in a green Tupperware canister beneath the tree. The elm had been a good home to them until it wasn't. This was what the butterflies had learned the hard way, what I'd learned too. As our lives assumed a new and unwanted rhythm, this became a summer of unlikely lessons.

Our fathers learned how to stand in unemployment lines.

Our mothers learned how to smile through bourbon-soaked tears.

And all of us learned how to live with the reality that the Rust Maidens were not a fad or a fleeting temper tantrum. It was, we soon realized, entirely possible that they had invented a new way to say goodbye.

"I don't know why they did this to us," my father mumbled on his way downtown to look for work. "And right now, of all times."

That was the accepted narrative of July: that for everything that had gone wrong that year, the girls were to blame. By their mere existence, the Rust Maidens had condemned us. Not on purpose, of course—I certainly never thought it was on purpose, anyhow—but that day at the chain-link fence was enough to get the mill owners running scared, with their tacky suits wrinkled and their jacket tails tucked. They couldn't bear the notion of those girls, so they cut the families loose. Better for the bottom line, they said, but that wasn't the real reason. The real reason was to dispel the nightmares about what might happen to their own daughters, those debutantes clutched close like heirloom pearls, hidden safely in the suburbs of Bay Village and Pepper Pike where the Rust Maidens couldn't reach them. At least, that was what the mill owners told themselves. It was an intricate web of superstitions and lies we spun for ourselves that summer. All the ways to save the girls—or save ourselves from them.

But they were still here. The girls moved about the mansion, restless all day and night. We watched them through the dusty windows, but they didn't return our gazes. Already, they had turned inward. Now that they were together, the outside world mattered less to them. We mattered less.

On Monday morning, after another round of spiked tea and stale biscuits, the mothers conspired together to call the city and see about having the girls evicted.

"They are squatters, after all," the women said, and while no one could argue, the staff in the downtown office were underfunded and overworked and not too worried about a clique of girls, no matter how monstrous, holding an impromptu slumber party in a place nobody cared about.

"We'll look into it," they promised, but never did.

But others on Denton Street were more than eager to keep track of the girls. The government men had stayed mostly out of sight since July 4th, locked up inside their rented house, but it was easy to imagine what they were doing in there. Analyzing doctors' reports, making calls back to Washington, and scheming. How their clandestine plans would turn out was anybody's guess.

I did my best to keep track of the girls too, or at least keep track of who was bothering them. At night, neighborhood children challenged each other to run up on the back porch of the mansion. You could see the little hellions there at the end of the cul-de-sac, their bikes tipped over on the asphalt, smudged faces glinting in the moonlight as they crept through the shadows and tapped on the door, lobbing an insult or two through the walls before they'd run.

It was a dare only the bravest would accept.

The more cowardly kids took to tossing pebbles at the windows, always from a safe distance. I'd catch the wayward imps when I could, slapping their little wrists, hoping I'd leave a big enough welt to warn them not to do it again, already knowing it wouldn't be enough. If they wanted to torment the girls, any punishment from me—someone no better than a stranger—wasn't going to change that.

On Wednesday afternoon, after chasing off three more kids and a few loitering tourists, I paced along the sidewalk. I would give the girls time. That was what I kept telling myself, even though everything in me said to run up and pound on that door, to tear at the lock, to break out the window. Whatever it took to get them out of there. To get *her* out. After all, if the bratty neighborhood kids could try to breach the threshold, why not me? I had more right to speak to those girls than anyone else on Denton Street.

Next door, a baby cried out, and the wail nearly cracked the sky. It was Eleanor. Through the open nursery window, Clint's mother scurried back and forth, looking lost, as a circus mobile rotated in an endless loop over the cradle. I never realized how close Clint's house was to the mansion. No more than ten yards separated the properties. If Eleanor could only look out her window, she'd easily see where her mother lived now.

Eleanor kept crying, and her tears made me want to cry too, so I turned away and started back home. I couldn't do this to the girls, anyhow. Not yet. I couldn't take this choice away from them. Jacqueline would leave whenever she was ready. But each night that passed, it seemed less and less possible that I might ever see my best friend again.

$$)O($$

The days slipped away from us, and July was half over before the first mother on Denton Street confessed what the rest of us had been quietly concealing for weeks.

Things in the neighborhood were disappearing.

Not girls this time; they were already long lost to us. These were little trinkets taken from backyards or porches or nightstands. An old necklace with a broken clasp. Lawn ornaments shattered in the storm and destined for the garbage heap.

"They took an old wheelbarrow from my garden," Violet's mother said. "What would they need that for?"

The women were gathered in our kitchen, taking up the same spaces the men had used for their meeting last month. Our house had become a neutral zone. No girls had changed here. That meant these walls must be safe.

I stood in the living room next to the empty turntable, listening to the soundtrack of the day.

"My suitcase," Kathleen was saying. "Totally ransacked. I'm

still not sure what they stole."

Probably not *they*, in this case. Probably Lisa. I couldn't imagine even the Rust Maidens put together were brave enough to sneak into the Carter house at night.

There was a long, anguished pause before my mother, her cordial glass trembling between her fingers, asked, "How do they do it?"

This was what unnerved them most of all. It wasn't so much that the girls were stealing trinkets. The mansion had been empty when they found it, so of course they needed accoutrements to make their stay there more bearable. Nobody blamed them for that. It was how they procured the objects that bothered us. Not one person had seen the girls since they'd fled the barbeques. Sure, we'd spotted an outline here or there, a scant figure scurrying past a window at midnight. But the girls out and about in the world wasn't something we could imagine anymore. We didn't even know if they still looked the same.

The preacher's wife spun the Lazy Susan on the table, around and around until we were all half-hypnotized. "We can't just leave them there."

"No, we can't," Violet's mother said. "Something has to be done."

I was in the doorway, listening to what they were saying. They weren't going to tolerate the girls much longer. I didn't know what the mothers would try next, but I needed to do something first.

"I'll talk to them," I said, and everyone in the kitchen turned to stare at me.

Aunt Betty exhaled a sharp laugh. "Sure, Phoebe."

"They listened to me before, didn't they?" I steadied myself against the wall. "The night they went into the mansion, I mean. Maybe they'll listen to me again."

Aunt Betty crossed her arms. "If you think you can do so much good," she said, "why don't you? Go knock on their door right now."

This was the last thing I wanted to hear. After everything.

After how long I'd waited, because I thought it was the best way. I thought we should give the girls time. But with all the mothers watching me, these women who already didn't trust their own daughters, I had to do something.

"Fine," I said, and moved for the back door.

It was one of those hot July days that made you crave Popsicles and ice floes and cryogenic freeze. I went onto the street, and the mothers followed me out. My entire way to the end of the cul-de-sac, their eyes tracked my every movement. Down the sidewalk, onto the front yard, and finally to the stoop of the mansion.

It was good that I was going in the daylight. It seemed silly to hide what I was trying. If anything, perhaps the rest of Denton Street would stop thinking of the girls as arcane and dangerous if only they took one visitor. If only they accepted me.

I knocked once and waited.

Nearby, sprinklers sputtered out water, and a jet heading away from Cleveland roared overhead, leaving a trail of white marshmallow fluff in its wake.

I knocked again and smiled back at the gawking mothers.

From somewhere behind me, a child shrieked and tossed a handful of pebbles. The tiny stones cascaded down my back, and I gritted my teeth to stop myself from running after the brat and wringing its neck.

Knocked a third time and tried not to look concerned, worried, frantic that the girls weren't going to answer.

Were they sleeping? Was resting all they did now? Did they rest at all? Really, what did I know of their lives now? Nothing. I knew nothing, and I was nothing.

"Jacqueline?" I pressed both hands into the door. "Please, are you there?"

For an instant, there was a fluttering on the other side, like a too-fast heartbeat. I held my breath and hoped. But then the noise was gone, and beyond reason, I understood that I was alone.

I stepped off the stoop and tried to peer through the windows. That was the first time I noticed it. All the glass of the mansion was blocked off with something gray. Thicker than spray paint, but just as opaque. Whatever this was, it had happened since last night. In just a few short hours, the girls had sealed us out in yet another way.

This was their way of telling us we weren't welcome.

I wasn't welcome.

"They probably put up curtains or blankets," the mothers murmured as I retreated down the street, shamed in my defeat.

"Well done, Phoebe." Aunt Betty smirked at me from the sidewalk. "Always the hero, aren't you?"

I glared back at her. "At least I did something," I said, and kept walking, all the way to my backyard where I climbed up to the treehouse to be alone with my bugs, and to have a better view of the mansion. The leaves were starting to thin from the heat, and I could see better from here. My personal box seat as I witnessed the end of our lives playing out.

Near the window, my foot crunched on something small. At first, my head whirled with the prospect of another injured butterfly, but that wasn't it. It was only a pod from earlier in the spring, where something went in and something else came out.

Chrysalises, I thought, and the girls rose up in my mind. Behind those dark windows, maybe their transformations wouldn't be a matter of degree. Maybe by the next time we saw them, there would be no more girls left. Only monsters.

I shook my head. No, not monsters. That wasn't my word. That was the word our fathers and mothers used. But even with the changes swirling beneath their flesh, nothing about the girls was monstrous to me. They were different, to be sure, but also beautiful in their own strange way.

I envied them.

Dinner that night was tasteless and unending. My father had left the television on before he came to the table, and a rerun of *Barney Miller* played in the next room, the laugh track punctuating the silence as my parents and I stared at our plates and tried to remember how to be a family.

"Did you hear about the graffiti at the mill?" My father

jabbed his iceberg lettuce with the tines of his fork. "*Pray for the Rust Maidens* spray-painted in front of the fence?"

"They think one of us did it." My mother took a sip of her bourbon. "Which is ridiculous."

"Of course they think that," I said. After all, who else would it be? Ever since I'd heard about it, I'd been trying to pick out the culprit on the street, but judging by the downcast expressions on our parents' faces, they all looked guilty.

My mother sighed and finally looked up at me. "I know you're doing your best, Phoebe," she said, and chewed her Salisbury steak carefully, so that she didn't have to say anything else. But she was thinking something else. Something she didn't want to say.

So my father said it instead.

"The neighbors have been talking about you. They think you've made things worse."

I choked up a laugh. "Me? *I* made things worse?"

My mother nodded, her fingers wrapped bone-white around her silverware. "You shouldn't have told the girls to leave. It hasn't helped any, having them hiding in that mansion."

And if they'd stayed? I wanted to ask. *Would that have helped them?*

But this time, I didn't say anything. I didn't scream or make a scene at the table or beg my parents to be on my side, just this once. Instead, I quietly excused myself from dinner. Then I waited on the front porch until the dark car down the road left its driveway, and Jeffers and Godfrey went out. Headed downtown, probably, to the Rib Room at the Charter House. How nice it must be to dine out every evening on the taxpayers' dime.

When I was sure they were gone, I walked down the block, the spare key in my pocket, and unlocked the side door of the government men's house.

Adrian was upstairs, poring over the latest doctors' reports in bed.

"Still not fond of knocking, huh?" he asked, barely glancing up from the file folders strewn across the mattress.

I moved toward him, past the window that looked out on the street. In the daylight, you could see the mansion from here, still gleaming as if new and occupied and wanted. But in the evening, there was nothing but shadows.

"Any updates?" I asked.

"Nothing useful." Adrian looked up at me, practically right through me, before he motioned to the tangle of papers. "Feel free to read them yourself, though."

It was strange every time he let me do this. Rifle through what wasn't mine to see. But I didn't argue. I edged nearer to his bed and picked up the papers that were fanned out on the sheets. Here the girls were, on these pages, as close as I could get to them. They were all numbers. Normal blood pressure, normal temperature, normal heartrate. Nothing else normal, but they still had something human about them.

"Is this it?" I asked, already knowing the answer.

Adrian wouldn't look at me. "I'm sorry."

I swallowed back a well of tears that I didn't realize was coming. A sob at my own uselessness, at how I'd never reach Jacqueline in time. Even if I could reach her, I wouldn't be able to change anything.

"We need to do something," I whispered.

Adrian nodded. "I know."

But neither of us had any idea of how to help the girls. The most we could do was help ourselves.

Adrian reached out for my hand. It was a small motion, the closing of the gap between us. I didn't move or pull away. I just closed my eyes and savored the way his fingers entwined with mine. Wanting his touch. Wanting him.

But then my eyes snapped open, and I did my best to recalibrate myself.

This was all wrong.

He was in Cleveland for the worst reasons.

I was in his bedroom for the worst reasons too.

I dropped the papers on the bed and moved away from him, toward the door I didn't want to walk through. I didn't want to leave, but I wasn't sure I wanted to stay either.

Behind me, Adrian sighed, and I heard the rustle of folders, stacked and tucked away.

"You don't have to go, Phoebe," he said, the remark tossed off almost as an afterthought.

But it wasn't an afterthought, and we both knew it.

I wavered in the doorway, looking back at him, knowing what I should do. I should go home and take a cold shower and start again tomorrow. I should make the right choice.

But I already knew I wouldn't do that.

With my gaze set on the window and the darkness beyond it, I stepped back into the bedroom and closed the door.

THIRTEEN

Before dawn, I moved noiselessly through Adrian's bedroom, not wanting to wake him as I searched the floor for my scattered clothes.

In the dark, his scent like cedar clung to my skin, and I closed my eyes and breathed him in. Part of me wished being here had meant nothing to me. But that wasn't true. I wanted him even now, even as I was doing my best to make a silent escape.

Running. That was my answer to everything.

Shame boiled in my belly. Last night had been a mistake, but one I was practically destined to make. Jacqueline had called it weeks ago, back when she was still around to cast her vote on topics like boys and booze and silly everyday things that never seemed to matter before.

With my dress zipped up and feet shoved into unlaced boots, I was halfway to the door. Almost done. Almost free. But when I turned back, just to glance at him one more time, there he was, watching me. Adrian, his body tangled in the sheets. Looking like all the trouble he'd promised me from the start.

I froze, caught under the weight of his stare.

"You could stay a little longer," he said, his voice soft and honeyed and thrumming down into my blood. My muscles went weak for an instant, and I wanted to climb back into that bed. Let the morning pass and the afternoon and another evening. Just wrap myself up with him and keep on forgetting.

But that wasn't how this worked.

I shook my head. "I need to go."

Though where I was needed was anybody's guess.

Adrian sat up in bed, something in him shifting. "You should probably know," he said. "We're heading back to Washington soon."

I suddenly couldn't breathe. It all unspooled in my mind: Adrian gone, this house empty again, a party spot with nobody left to party with. But what did I expect? Of course they'd leave eventually. This was a case for them, not a life sentence like it was for us.

I wouldn't look at him. "When?"

"Next week," he said, and then added slowly, "Why don't you come too?"

I almost laughed at this. Me in DC. Doing what exactly? Lounging around Adrian's apartment? Shacking up with a man I didn't know and didn't entirely trust?

"I don't think so," I said. "I should stay."

"Why?" he asked, and the question caught me by surprise.

There were so many reasons I should be in Cleveland. For Jacqueline. For the girls. For college too, I guessed, but that seemed like someone else's dream now, something so distant I might as well be reaching for the sun.

Adrian hesitated, his eyes dark. "There's nothing here for you, Phoebe."

That twisted deep in my guts, the bluntness of the statement, and the truth of it too. There was nothing here for anyone anymore. But I couldn't admit that.

"You're wrong," I said, and left the bedroom door open behind me.

Downstairs, I moved for the back door, not realizing at first that I wasn't alone.

Jeffers and Godfrey sat at the kitchen table, their stiff toast crisped around the edges, uneaten on paper plates. I stood in front of them, pretending I was invisible. It worked, more or less. They spoke as if I wasn't there, as if I was air.

"I hear we have a guest," the one I supposed was Jeffers said. "Should we offer her coffee?"

"Why would we do that?" Godfrey gnawed his bottom lip. "Besides, she's already gotten what she came for."

Jeffers grunted and leaned back on one leg of his chair. "Adrian, always the heartbreaker."

His eyes rolled back in his head, and he pretended to swoon. Imitating me like I was some silly little lovesick schoolgirl. Like I was common, the most recent in a long line of conquests. Maybe they were right, maybe that was exactly what I was, but right now with them guffawing at me, I didn't care. My hands curled into fists, and I imagined pulverizing the bones in their faces until all they could see was blood. But then I thought better of it. Try as he might, Adrian probably couldn't convince them not to arrest me for that.

I moved for the back door, but at the last minute, I couldn't help myself. I kicked that balancing leg of the chair, and Jeffers went down. Or maybe it was Godfrey. Either way, he hollered an obscenity at my back. I smiled and disappeared into the day.

At the end of the street, the mansion gleamed in the morning light. I wanted to go there. I wanted to try again to talk to Jacqueline. But she wouldn't answer if I did.

Besides, there was someone else standing near the street watching me.

Kathleen, on the sidewalk in front of her own house, sucking down the last of a cigarette. I held up my hand in a half-hearted wave, but she didn't return the gesture. From the look on her face, she had an entirely different gesture in mind. She must have seen me leave the government men's house. An early morning exit. She knew what that meant.

My feet heavy, I approached her, and immediately regretted it.

"At least someone had a fun evening," she grunted, the accusation sizzling in her voice. "Fortunately, a few of us were working. Trying to fix things."

I scoffed. "Like how you fixed things with your first article?"

She glared at me and then exhaled a puff of smoke in my face. "And exactly what have you done, Phoebe?"

Everything I can, I wanted to say, but she didn't wait for me to respond. She dropped her cigarette and crushed it under her the sole of her black Oxford dress shoe, the same way she'd like to crush me, no doubt. Then she was gone, headed back into that godforsaken house. To her typewriter, probably, off to finish her latest story. Hopefully, this one wouldn't be so disastrous.

I stood on the empty street, baking in the already hot sun. I wondered what I would have said to her, if given the chance. I wouldn't have asked for absolution, that was for sure. Nothing in me felt as sorry about last night as I felt sorry about everything else. This was a decrescendo on the long mistake that I called this summer.

Jeffers and Godfrey, mocking me at the kitchen table, flitted again through my mind. They could be doing anything other than taunting a teenager. They could be helping. As though that was ever part of their agenda.

They did, however, have one good idea. Coffee.

The bell in the corner store dinged over my head, and Aunt Betty glanced up from the counter, already glaring like she knew I was coming even before I did.

I took the stool on the end, not saying a word. She filled a white Styrofoam cup to the brim, and we stared at each other for a while. This should have felt familiar, almost safe, all things considered, but now a different kind of loathing brewed behind her gaze. She blamed me, the same way that everybody blamed me. Like I wanted the girls to go to the mansion. Like I was the one keeping them there.

I wanted to ask her if she'd seen Jacqueline, or if maybe anything in the house had come up missing. I also wanted her to talk to me. About any early signs of the transformation, or why Jacqueline might have changed in the first place. Nobody could tell us that part. The doctors and the government men and the parents—none of them could understand why normal, healthy girls were now anything but.

But then a shadow passed over my face, and by the time I looked up, Clint was already sidling up next to me at the counter. I had to bite down to keep myself from gagging at the sight of him. My first love, as nauseating as a hangover.

"Hi, Phoebe." He gave me an ugly grin. "How are you this morning?"

"Fine," I said and stared straight ahead at the wall, hoping if I didn't look at Clint, he would cease to exist.

It didn't work.

"I would think you'd be doing better than fine." He paused, savoring the moment. "I saw you leaving his house this morning."

He didn't say Adrian's name. He didn't have to. The coffee pot still suspended in her hand, Aunt Betty raised an eyebrow at me, and I sighed. Was everyone out with their binoculars at sunrise? And if so, why weren't they watching the mansion? That seemed like a better target than me. But this was our problem, wasn't it? Always watching and worrying about the wrong things. If we could refine our focus, then maybe we wouldn't have lost the girls in the first place.

Clint was still staring at me, gauging my reaction. "So," he said, "have a good time?"

"Sure did." I looked at him and smirked. "It was immensely better than a backseat."

At that, he grimaced, but didn't retreat. That should have been enough to scare him away, but apparently everything was going to be hard today, even chasing off exes who possessed all the charm of a housefly.

I took a long sip of coffee. "What do you want, Clint?"

By now, Aunt Betty had wandered down to the other end of the counter, where Doctor Ross's wife was ordering two pounds of ground beef for the family she no longer had. Clint waited until he was sure they couldn't hear before he leaned into me, so close I could taste last night's whiskey curdling on his breath.

"We're going into the mansion tonight." Something in his eyes sparked, and he waited for me to respond. As if his plan was the best I'd ever heard.

I sighed. "We? Who else is going?"

"A couple of the boys." With a cocky grin, he leaned back. A little too far, since he nearly toppled off the stool. Face blotched red, he regained his balance and moved in to me again. I held my breath. "Mr. Carter is helping us too."

A shudder ran through my body. Lisa and Kathleen's father. The notion of him helping anyone made me queasy. He didn't help people. That meant he had other plans. Ugly plans. A punishment doled out to a wayward daughter, perhaps.

I shook my head. "It won't do any good," I said. "I've already tried to get in, Clint."

"You knocked at the front door." He crossed his arms and leaned on the counter. "We're not going to be that polite."

My heart squeezed tight in my chest. No, I couldn't imagine Clint or Mr. Carter or the other boys being polite. But I could imagine them forcing their way in and cornering the girls and telling them they didn't have any choice in the matter.

No way were they going without me.

"When?" I asked.

Clint smiled. From the moment he walked in, he knew I'd agree. "Meet us in the mansion's backyard at midnight."

Then he was gone, a shadow moving through the store and out the door. The bell dinged, and my coffee cup went cold in my hands.

I waited through the afternoon, cross-legged on my bed, gazing down at a street that no longer felt familiar. Adrian called the house twice, and though he could almost certainly see me sitting at my window, I didn't answer the phone.

))O((

At midnight, they were already in the backyard of the mansion. Clint and Mr. Carter and a few others that I didn't know. Boys who weren't from this neighborhood.

And someone else. She fussed in Clint's arms.

Eleanor. He'd brought Eleanor.

"What are you doing?" I gaped at him. "Why is she here?"

Clint stared back, blank-faced, and shrugged. "I want Dawn to come out," he said. "What better way than to show her what she's missing?"

Now it all made sense. Clint would do anything to get out of caring for Eleanor. He probably wanted to drop the baby inside the door and call it a day.

Mr. Carter lit a Marlboro Light and grunted at me. "You never said anything about that one being here."

"Phoebe knows them better than we do," Clint said. "Maybe she can talk some sense into them."

Sense. Like any of this made sense.

The men took out their bag of tools—a hammer, a crowbar, even a couple of screwdrivers for good measure—and pried open the back door. But even once the house was open and waiting for us, we all hesitated, suddenly unsure of ourselves.

Then Clint took an uneven step forward. "Dawn?" he called into the darkness before disappearing into it. The other boys followed him, leaving only me and Mr. Carter out in the night.

"Are you ready, girl?" he asked with a sneer.

"You bet," I said. "I just wonder if the rest of you are."

Inside, the mansion looked like an industrial apocalypse. We entered through the kitchen and crept into the main living room. Everything smelled of earth and brackish water and the vague sickly sweetness of something decomposing.

As we moved, our flashlight beams dancing across the walls, the whole house swayed around us, as though it could barely support its own weight.

We stayed toward the perimeter of the room, and I ran my fingers along the old paneling, rough and oddly cold.

I stopped at the front door. It was blocked off from the inside. Everything here was blocked off. All of the windows were dark. None of them were soaped or blanketed like the neighborhood mothers had claimed. They were sealed, gray decay and rust filling every space, sealing out the sun. Some of the rot was from the stolen items—the missing wheelbarrow had been vivisected and merged into the mosaic—but most of this rust must have come from the girls. Their own personal creation, an art project gone awry. The walls bowed under the heft of the decay, drywall sloughing off to the floor like snowfall in February, the room creaking and straining with our every step.

"What did they do to this place?" Clint murmured.

"It's a cocoon," I whispered. The girls had turned the mansion into a cocoon.

But other than the rust and rot blocking off the windows, there was no other sign of them. No noise at all except for our steps, clumsy as we were in the dark.

"Where are they?" one of the boys grumbled as they went off to search the rest of the first-floor rooms. Of course, he was disappointed. They were here for a confrontation, a fun little chance to pick on someone. Finding the Rust Maidens would be so much better than their usual pranks, like pulling a girl's pigtails. The boys might even get a reward if they managed to bring them out.

"They must be up there." Mr. Carter shined his light on the winding staircase, dark and unwelcoming. He tried not to quiver.

I grinned. "After you, then."

The steps dipped under our weight, and I held my breath, unsure if they could sustain us. But the house held fast. For now.

"Lisa?" Mr. Carter called, his gruff voice shaking the already fragile walls. "No more games. You get out here right now, girl."

No one answered. He tried hollering her name again, like that was all she needed to come out, a little bit of coaxing. I shivered, not wanting to hear his awful voice anymore. Without a word,

I broke away and slipped down a narrow hallway. The corridor was longer than I expected, and turned suddenly, an endless coil of sagging walls and flecked-off paint. The ceiling sank over me, and I felt like I was being swallowed whole.

The boys cajoled each other somewhere behind me, but I was soon out of their reach, all alone in this place where I didn't belong. Where none of us belonged, except the Rust Maidens.

I kept moving, kept telling myself that Jacqueline would be here, somewhere. That it wasn't too late.

Something in the gloom sighed, and it sounded close, so close. But there was nothing next to me. Nothing in front or behind. The flashlight beam held steady in my hand. I wouldn't look above me. I wanted to find Jacqueline, but if she was there hanging from the plaster overhead, I wasn't brave enough to see it yet. Because girls couldn't cling to the ceiling. And they had to still be girls, didn't they?

At the end of the hall, a door was ajar. I froze, and wondered what I was doing here. I should go back. I should leave this place altogether. This mansion, this street, this whole damn town.

But I couldn't do that to her. I couldn't abandon her.

The tip of my boot eased the door the rest of the way open, and I went in. Almost immediately, I regretted it. Inside, the room reeked of vinegar and ammonia and metal. My eyes watering, I covered my mouth with my free hand and tried to turn back. But it was too late. Instantly, I was caught in a tangle of something thicker than spiderwebs. I flailed in the shadows as the flashlight passed over dozens of strings and clothespins. Laundry lines, but not quite the same. These were strung with hundreds of pictures.

A darkroom. That was what this was. Violet's darkroom. A final rebellion against her parents for what they'd denied her.

My eyes adjusted, and the setup emerged around me. Dishpans of shallow liquid dotted the floor, and in the corner, gathered together, were bottles of Spotone and stop bath and developer. That was what they'd stolen from Kathleen. Her photography chemicals.

The pictures dangled in front of me, still trembling from where I'd disturbed them. With the flashlight shaking in my hand, I picked the photographs off the line, one by one.

A waistline corseted with metal that could never be removed.

A hand on a table, all five fingernails gnarled and overgrown with shattered glass.

Something dark and shiny. An eye perhaps, watching me from somewhere I couldn't see.

My fingers quivered and gripped the thick white paper. The prints were all muddy. I could guess why. There was no sink in the room. To rinse the images, Violet had to use her own body, the murky water almost certainly drained out of her, strange and thick as amniotic fluid. But the tactic had worked. The images had developed.

My flashlight beam searched the room. Something else was missing too. There were no red lights dangling overhead, no electricity wired to the place anymore. How could Violet work in here, dipping the pictures and pulling them out at precisely the right moment, before the images went past developing and kept bleaching out in the chemicals?

Dread coiled through me. It was simple, really. That light was meant to aid human eyes. But you didn't need a red light to develop pictures if you could see in the dark.

"Phoebe?" Clint's voice outside the door.

I shoved the wet images into my back pocket. The boys shouldn't see these. Nobody should.

Out in the hallway, I rejoined them and a babbling Eleanor. She was the only one of us who wasn't terrified.

We went through a pair of double doors, the once-gilded trim now grayed with neglect. This must have been a ballroom or a vast master bedroom. Quite a place in its day.

Just inside, Clint tripped over something. It was large and curved, almost person-sized.

His hands searched inside the contraption, and it rocked back and forth, making almost an eerie whistling sound.

"A bassinet," Clint said. "Dawn must have made it for Eleanor."

Grinning, he placed Eleanor inside, and she cooed sweetly. But something strange tugged deep inside me. It couldn't be a bassinet. Why would the girls have a bassinet just waiting here? They didn't know we were coming. Whatever it was, it must be something else, but I didn't know what, so I said nothing. I kept moving, deeper into the dark. The floors were soft here. I leaned down and picked something up.

A blanket. It was just a regular blanket.

"What is this place?" one of the boys asked, and it gripped me all at once. *Their* bedroom. We were in their bedroom. And perhaps they didn't want to be disturbed.

"Maybe they've gone," Clint said, and at that, a chorus of steely voices giggled.

Then they were everywhere.

The flashlights vanished from our grasp, flung to the opposite side of the wall by hands we couldn't see. Bits of light remained, a beam here or there, but nothing to guide us. Nothing that could show us the way out.

How there could be only five girls in this room, I didn't understand. Something moved at my feet, whispering past. Something else overhead, clinging to the ceiling. The walls crawled, and shadows devoured us. There was movement everywhere, and whimpers that weren't their own. They belonged to the boys. Fear had gripped them, marrow-deep, as they intuitively understood it: that here in this place, we were the invaders. And now the girls were evicting us the only way they knew how.

"Clint, I think—" I started to say, but it didn't matter. The terror had already boiled over in the room, and the boys were running. In every direction, without purpose, without logic.

A body not made of metal, but of flesh and blood, rammed into me, knocking me to the floor. I reached up in the dark for a hand to guide me back up, but no one was there. Whoever had sent me toppling down had gone off, vanishing without a worry about what became of me.

Footfalls all around me in the shadows. Heavy boots—men's work boots with their thick, unforgiving tread—trampled my hands, my arms, my legs.

"Please," I tried to scream, but my voice was lost in the din of the boys' mewling fear.

But even as I got a heel to the jaw, I wasn't the one in the greatest danger.

The baby.

I had to get to Eleanor. Before those boots turned her tiny body to powder.

I crawled back to the thing that Clint called a bassinet, but it was empty. Desperate to find her, my hands followed the curves inside the contraption. The curves like a waist and hips. I was right. This wasn't a bassinet. It was part of a molted skin, an exuviae like the ones my butterflies discarded in the spring. But these were thicker. Tougher. The empty bodies of girls who no longer needed a shield to shelter them. They were their own protection now.

The girls had changed. Whatever they were meant to become, they already were.

I snapped back to this place. Eleanor. I still had to find Eleanor.

Back along the floor, I crawled on hands and knees, past Mr. Carter, who hadn't run with the rest. He stood his ground. He came for a fight, and that was what he was getting.

In the pale beam of the flashlights, limp and discarded on the floor, I caught glimpses of what came next. His sneering, hideous face, everything about him twisted and angry for no good reason. The hammer from his toolbelt lifted over his head, ready to strike whoever or whatever he found in the dark, even if it was his own daughter.

A shadow gliding back and forth, disorienting, until it was ready. Then a heavy metallic foot crushed the last of the flashlights, and darkness consumed the room. At once, the world was reduced to sounds, not images.

A wheeze like a sick rabbit caught in a trap.

The crack of bone. Fingers first, one by one, followed by something bigger. An arm, maybe. Or both arms.

The scream of a man who was broken and beaten and could no longer pretend he was anything else.

Mr. Carter ran now, faster than the boys, faster than anyone I'd ever known. Defeated by whatever was in the gloom, he ran and screamed and pissed himself on the way out the door, the stench of urine permeating everything.

A laugh now from inside the room, throaty and metallic and so jubilant it set my skin buzzing. It was the most joyous laugh I would ever hear in my life. Something beyond triumph. Something like freedom.

Her face was obscured, but I knew it was Lisa. There was no one else it could be.

More movement, more boys traipsing through the shadows, desperate to find their way out. Unconcerned when they trampled me.

I dragged myself along the floor, still searching for the baby, still coming back with my hands and heart empty.

In the corner, there was a door to another room. A smaller space, a closet maybe, a place that should be safe from the ruckus. I pulled myself in and closed the door behind me. It was just to catch a breath, anything to escape being crushed, anything to be alone for an instant.

Inside, bits of light were coming in through a window. Although this room had been mortared up with decay the same as the rest of the mansion, a tiny spot in the glass was left untouched. I peered through it. I could see Clint's house from here, situated right next door. I squinted harder at a first-floor window below, and realized I was looking directly down into Eleanor's nursery.

A babble behind me, and I whirled around. Someone else was here, and she was holding Eleanor. The baby's chubby hand was wrapped around a glassy finger.

"Hello, Dawn," I whispered. Of course this was her room. Even in her exile, she'd been keeping vigil over her child, watching her through this lonely window.

I moved closer, and while I couldn't see her face clearly, there were hints here and there in the moonlight. A glint of a pewter cheekbone. A few strands of long hair, thick and wet as seaweed. But even in the dark, Eleanor knew who this was. Every child could recognize her own mother.

"How are you?" I asked. "What's happened?"

Where's Jacqueline? is what I wanted to say. The only question that mattered to me, but I couldn't form the words.

Dawn couldn't form the words either. I wondered if the transformation had stolen all her speech from her, or if she simply didn't want to speak to me. I couldn't blame her for that.

Instead, she murmured something, a lullaby perhaps. The best she could do for the child she couldn't care for.

We crouched in the dark as Dawn held Eleanor in those gnarled, rusted arms. With every breath, she was careful not to move too quickly, or else she'd cut her own child.

But the two of them together like this couldn't last. The sun would soon sneak up over the lake, and the other parents would come looking for the baby. Dawn knew that. Thick tears seeped down what I could see of her face, and a strange sob trembled in the back of her throat. As much as she wanted to keep Eleanor, that was no longer possible.

With shaking hands, she passed the baby over to me.

She trusted me with her daughter. Never could I have imagined an infant to be such a heavy weight in my arms. I didn't want to steal her from her mother, but I couldn't deny Dawn either. Not if this was what she wanted.

She opened the door and nudged me back into the master bedroom. Her hand was cold and strange on my back, like an anchor pulled up from the dark depths of the lake. Then the door clicked closed behind me, and Dawn retreated back into the obscure corner she now called home.

I was alone with Eleanor. The flashlights had all gone dim, and there was no sound, not in the entire mansion. No more laughter. No more boys.

No more girls, either. If this was their bedroom, I expected them to be fluttering about, preparing for the coming daylight, preparing to sleep, but maybe they didn't rest during the day. Maybe they didn't rest at all.

With my arms wrapped around the baby, I moved along the wall, feeling for which direction to go. It didn't help. Almost instantly, we were hopelessly lost in the mazelike house. I started down a hallway but was quickly turned around, tracing and retracing footprints, always ending up back in the bedroom with no windows.

I breathed out and tried again. Searched for the staircase. It had to be here somewhere. I'd found it once before. That meant I could find it again. Even the darkroom would help. If I discovered that, I could follow the hall, reversing my steps from earlier. I could do this.

Eleanor fussed, and I held her closer.

"It's okay," I whispered, but she didn't believe me. I didn't believe me either.

We went down a corridor and around a corner. This had to be right. This had to be the way.

But something glinted in the dark. That grayed, once-gilded trim. Still in the bedroom. Still trapped.

I clutched Eleanor tighter and closed my eyes. We couldn't get out. I'd come here, and now we couldn't escape. I wanted to protect the girls, but I couldn't even protect myself.

A fluttering next to me. Everything in the world stood still.

"Hello?" My voice was thin and sounded far away. "Who's there?"

A hand on my arm, tugging gently, guiding me.

My breath caught in my throat. It was Jacqueline's hand, chilled and damp, yet still so familiar, so achingly familiar.

With elegant footsteps that never quite made a sound, she led me out to the long, winding hallway and down the elusive stairs. We were back in the kitchen, moonlight creeping in around the edges of the door, the same way we'd gotten in earlier. Almost out now. Almost safe.

But not safe, not unless Jacqueline came too.

"Don't stay here," I whispered. "We can still run away together.

It's not too late."

She moved closer to me, and for a moment, I could almost see her. The curves of her face were the same, even though all the flesh had withered away. Then she wrapped her fingers tighter around me, burying the sharp edges of herself into my skin, as if to remind me who she was now. How everything about her was dangerous.

"It doesn't matter," I said, my voice wavering as the pain of her touch seared through me. "You're still my best friend."

A moment of hesitation. One that might as well have lasted a lifetime.

But it didn't last a lifetime. It didn't last nearly long enough.

The back door opened, and Jacqueline pushed me through it, her hand tender but final too.

I blinked, half-dizzy on the porch. The moonlight was dim, but everything outside looked lit up and almost garish after the darkness of the mansion. No more than an hour had passed since we'd crossed into the place where we weren't welcome. As a group then, but now splintered, the boys scattered into the night like buckshot. Even the echoes of their screams were long gone. I had outlasted them. Of course I had. For all the good it had done.

The door slammed shut, and Jacqueline's serrated hand twisted the lock. But she did more than that. On the other side, I could hear her mortaring up the seams of the door like a bee at a honeycomb. She'd sealed me out. I couldn't reach her now, because she didn't want me to.

Eleanor fussed softly in my arms as I collapsed to my knees on the back porch and tried not to scream.

FOURTEEN

My bedroom is more cluttered than I remember it. Vinyl caked in dust, faded-out bell bottoms, and yellowed diaries with their locks and secrets rusted out. All of Violet's old Polaroids, and Jacqueline's notes too. Eighteen years of a life packed beneath a bed and bulging out of splintered dresser drawers, every crevice that should have been cleaned out long before I left. My mother had probably told me to clean it out that summer, but, of course, I didn't listen. None of us were very good at listening that year.

From the bottom of the stack, I pull out a picture of Jacqueline and hold her in my hand. This one was taken at her eighteenth birthday party, the last birthday we celebrated together. I wonder if they still celebrate where she is now. Are there cake and streamers and foil-wrapped gifts there? Does she ever think of me and wish I was at her side? Because I think of her all the time. Every day. Even when I tell myself not to.

I drop the picture on the hardwood floor and bury it beneath a sprawl of records. At the bottom of the drawer, there are other pictures, murky photographs developed in the dark. Nobody but me and the girls has ever seen those. There are too many things I've never talked about to anyone. Not my mother or my father or a string of boyfriends and therapists, all of whom failed due to no fault of their own. All because I won't remember. Because I can't let myself think of it. That last night.

A knock on the downstairs door. I leap toward the hallway, relieved to have any excuse to escape the past for another minute.

"I'm coming," I say. Maybe it's Quinn, or Eleanor. Someone who can help me unravel this.

I bound down the stairs and swing open the front door.

A gust of wind off the lake slaps me in the face, but that's the only thing that greets me. No one else is here, not on the porch anyhow. The construction crew is around, their hard hats glistening in the cold sun. A holler for safety, a creak of a crane, and down the block, another Denton Street house falls. It's Violet's this time. That strange triple moon sign in the plaster is only dust now. Every trace of the Rust Maidens will soon be scrubbed clean from this neighborhood.

I shiver in the December afternoon. Someone knocked on the door, but there's no one here. I should be surprised. I'm not. This is what I'm starting to expect. Each day since I've gotten back, I'm convinced I'll find someone—find *them*—only to realize I'm still alone.

My mother is out picking up a few more moving boxes. Only five days now. We'll be out before Christmas. Happy holidays to us.

No more house. No more Denton Street. No more Eleanor or Quinn. I could wait this out. I could run for good this time and not look back.

But I don't want to do that. I want to help them. These two girls, both of them as good as strangers to me, but that doesn't matter. I need to do something, so they don't end up the same

191

as me. Or the same as the Rust Maidens

There's still one person I haven't seen yet. Someone from that summer who might be able to help me, or at least might be able to help Eleanor.

I grab my coat just inside the living room before I return to the porch and lock the door behind me. It seems like a silly thing to do, sealing up a home that's almost empty, but I do it anyway. I do it because it feels right.

Then I start walking. Past the houses with expiration dates. Along a sidewalk that hasn't been repaired in years, maybe even since I still lived here.

At the end of the street, past the old corner store, I see the Presbyterian Church. There's a light on inside. Despite the cratered walls and the crack in the stained glass window, they haven't marked this place for demolition. Instead, there are girders holding it up and a brand-new sign. UNDER CONSTRUCTION.

I roll my eyes. How fitting. The church will stand longer than our homes, longer than the people who inhabited this neighborhood.

I should keep going. This isn't where I need to be. This has never been a place I've needed to be.

But this city is a tricky one. It never misses a chance to confound you. When I'm almost past, I hear it. A faraway giggle, sing-song and devious, and something else that sounds like a lullaby. I whirl around and gaze upwards at the steeple that never seemed so tall before.

Are they inside? If I walk through those double doors, will I discover the girls waiting there?

Another giggle, strained and distant and dancing away from me, and I can't help myself.

The pews stink of mouse droppings and failed righteousness. I expect a team of people working on repairs, but it's only one man. He looks up when I walk in without knocking.

"Hello," he says. "Can I help you?"

A new preacher. Young and bright-eyed and definitely not a local. Way too much hope in him for that.

"You're not from here?" I ask. It's probably a rude way to start a conversation, but he only smiles and shakes his head.

"I'm over from Indiana," he says. "They sent me here to fix this place up. With everything going on in the world today, people need guidance right now."

"People always need guidance," I say as I glance around. There are no giggles at the pulpit, no girls peeking out between the pews. I must have imagined them. I've been doing that a lot lately.

"Is there something you're looking for?" the preacher asks.

I hesitate before regarding him. "Did they tell you about the neighborhood's history?"

"You mean those girls back in the eighties?" He stiffens on instinct. "They mentioned something about that. Did you know them?"

Instantly, the question knocks the wind out of me.

"Yes," I say. One word. That's all I can manage.

"I'm sorry," he says, and at first, I think he's just being polite. But a sadness crosses his face, and I realize it's not lip service. It's honest-to-goodness empathy. I didn't think they made that model in Cleveland anymore. But then again, he did say he was an out-of-towner.

"You know, the lost are never really lost, not in the eyes of the Lord. They can always be found." He sucks in a heavy breath, and a pigeon flutters overhead in the rafters. "The Gospel of Luke talks about this in chapter fifteen."

No, not a sermon. Not *this* sermon. I bite my bottom lip until I wince at the pain. He's going to tell me the parable of the lost sheep. Is this guy for real? His solution to a cache of missing girls is to lecture me on some fucking biblical sheep?

The corners of my mouth twitch, and I want to scream. I want to hear how loud my voice will echo in this place where there's no congregation, no hope, no point in its miserable existence. Not that there was ever a compelling reason for this church to exist, not even thirty years ago when we all pretended to believe.

But as the preacher keeps speaking, earnest as only a fool

can be, I don't scream. I just wait here as he recites the whole damn passage. No reason to be rude again. Besides, none of this is his fault.

"Thank you," I say when he's done, and I almost mean it, because at least he was kind to me. It might be the first time a preacher stood inside this place and showed an ounce of genuine kindness to anybody.

I start to walk away, my chest tightening. Why did the girls lead me here? What did they want me to find?

Nothing. There's nothing they want me to find. They want me to remember. I've been trying for so long to forget what happened here, and maybe now I need to stop running.

I'm halfway to the door before I turn back to the preacher. "You know this neighborhood, right?"

One eyebrow arches up curiously, and he nods. Of course he knows the neighborhood. He knows the worst places, too. How else is he going to recruit the sheep?

"Any idea where the particularly lost hang out these days?'

He inspects me, slowly deciphering my meaning. "There's a place," he says, "four blocks over. It's called the Backdoor Bar."

I smile. "Thank you," I say, and this time, I mean it.

$$\text{)O(}$$

It doesn't have a neon sign. It doesn't have windows either. But the heap of cheap cigarettes piled outside the door and the stench of stale urine in the gutter make me sure this is where the preacher meant. I stand on the street, staring at the splintered white façade and the hand-scrawled letters on the awning. Now that I'm here, I realize this probably won't help. But I have to do something.

The door swings open, and a whiff of despair, heavier than all the heartache in the world, overwhelms me. I want to turn back. I won't turn back. Inside, empty peanut shells crunch beneath my boots, and an old-timer in a dirty booth leers at me, his lips curled back, revealing a cavernous mouth that might as well go on forever.

I shiver and keep walking, past a row of empty tables and a craggy bartender old enough to remember when this city was known for more than its failures. I see him now, who I came for, right where I expected him. In the corner, at the end of the counter, Clint sits on the barstool he calls home. I take the seat next to his, and he looks up lazily, his eyes filmed over.

"Phoebe," he says, as if he's been expecting me to show up in this woebegone watering hole for years.

I order a whiskey sour and try not to stare too hard at him. I hate to see what he's become. When I finally look close, it's what I figured. His face is yellowed from drink and lined with regret, gaze distant and swirling with all the things he could have done differently but didn't bother to. Every ugly thing about him has seeped out through his pores. He's a walking portrait of Dorian Gray.

"Your daughter needs you," I say and take a sip of my drink.

He grunts. "I don't have a daughter," he says. "That way it's better for me. Better for her, too."

Of course this is his answer. I grit my teeth and hate him a little bit more. I hate myself too—for caring about him once, for blaming Dawn, for thinking that if I ran, it would make a difference. This place is in me, the same as it's in him. I can't free myself by hiding or fleeing or pretending it didn't happen.

Bob Seger crackles on the worn-out jukebox behind me, and I swallow a breath of rank air.

"Eleanor isn't doing well," I say. "She needs a parent, Clint."

Another grunt. "She's probably too old now to go the way her mother did, right? Because that'd be my advice: get out any way you can. Do better than me. Better than you, too."

He turns to inspect me, and I squirm under the weight of his stare. His head tips slowly up and down, gaze sliding over my body as he surveys me like I'm a prime piece of real estate. As if there's any of that left in the whole city of Cleveland.

"You're looking good." He takes a swig of his beer and grimaces at the skunk flavor. Then he looks harder at me, remembering something. Or someone. "But then you were always the better choice."

Choice. Something Clint always got. Something the Rust Maidens never did.

"There was nothing wrong with Dawn," I say. "At least not until you got hold of her."

This hits him dead-center, and even harder than I expect. Maybe because he knows I'm right: he ruined her. All her dreams were crushed to ash the moment he climbed on top of her in the dark.

As always, Clint's pain wears off quickly and his lips curl into a grin. "You always did have a mouth on you," he says. "Learn how to do anything new with it lately?"

My whiskey sour is dripping down his face before I can stop myself. A pity, too. The booze was worth a hundred times what he is.

This is, as I should have known, a complete waste of time, and time is the one thing I've wasted enough of. A five tossed on the bar and I'm out the door, the chill of December wrapping around me, reminding me I'm alive. It's nice to remember that sometimes.

Why did I come here? Why did I ever bother with Clint?

My breath seizes up in my chest. It's because after all these years, I want to tell someone. Someone who knew them. I want to confess the truth.

That I know what happened to the Rust Maidens.

But it shouldn't be Clint. If I finally say it aloud, it should never be to him.

My head spun, I shortcut down an alley that's overflowing with discarded beer bottles and wadded-up fast food wrappers. I want to get back to the house, to be anywhere except right here.

But a hand's suddenly on my elbow, and I'm wheezing too hard to cry out.

Clint whirls me around to face him. "You can't run," he says. "You have to see."

Still gripping me close, he kneels to the asphalt and picks up a discarded beer bottle. His eyes wild, he tosses it against the building. The glass splinters in the air, and I scream, shielding my face with my free hand.

"Clint, stop," I say, breathless with fear, but he won't listen. His grasp tightens on my arm, but he seems more desperate than cruel. One bottle after another against the wall, some half filled with flat beer, some filled with old urine, all the liquid running down the building and onto our shoes.

Then he stops. I glare at him, ready to break his jaw or holler again or call the police. But he just points to the ground.

"Look," he says. "It's for you, Phoebe. It's from her."

I follow his accusing hand. The shattered glass has formed a pattern. Over and over, repeating up and down the alley. All the same shape.

A triple moon.

I inch away, but Clint pulls me into him.

"They're still here." His breath is wet and hot in my ear. "It doesn't matter what we do now, Phoebe. They'll never leave."

I wrench myself free and run. Faster than I knew I could. Away from the bar and Clint and the message that can't be from her.

I can't go back the way I came, the way in front of the bar, so I have to take a different route. Past the place I already visited my first night back. It rises up over me, a hulking behemoth that will never set us free. I blink up at the stacks and the rusted-out ladders and the spout where the flame used to be.

Nobody ever dismantled the old steel mill. They didn't bother to remove the coke oven or the pig-casting machine or the empty blast furnace. And outside, they never took down the chain-link fence. They left it to rot and remind us of everything we'd lost.

A real estate development company came in about fifteen years ago and surveyed the land and made all the preparations to dismantle the place. For a strip mall, my mother told me. But something happened—bankruptcy, or cold feet over ghosts, or maybe just plain old apathy—and the project went into limbo. Now the whole property is a specter of its own.

I edge past the red graffiti on the asphalt to get a better look at the mill. The only way in from this side of the factory is through a hole in the fence. I shouldn't do this, but I already know that I will.

This gap isn't very big, and it takes me a moment to contort my body to fit. I'm sure I'll make it through, but halfway in, my jacket gets caught. I twist my shoulders before starting to writhe and thrash, but it doesn't help. I can't break free, and I can't slip out either. I'm trapped here, in this place where I shouldn't be. Where no one will even know to look for me.

I turn my face to the fence, still trying to pry myself free. A piece of jagged metal from the chain-link passes across my cheek. Its touch like a single fingertip, cold but familiar. I close my eyes and tell myself I'm wrong. The rust didn't reach out for me. The rust isn't alive. There's no one else here.

When I look again, the metal is lifeless before me, and my jacket is unsnagged from the fence. Maybe I was never caught at all. Or maybe someone helped to set me free.

I won't linger here in the cold and try to figure out which it was. My chest tight, I pull myself inside the fence, and I don't look back. Instead, I turn to what's left of the mill. Rust drapes over every corner, coating all the stacks like luxurious velvet. This should be jarring somehow, seeing my past with-ered and peeling before me, but it almost looks like the decay has always belonged here. It's certainly more comfortable in Cleveland than I am. I inhale a sharp breath and catch a whiff of earth, but nothing else that we once expected in this place. No smoke from the never-ending fires that used to burn here, and no sweat of men at the end of their shifts, walking across this same crumbled asphalt, their tin lunchboxes in hand.

I move into the mill through a back door, hanging limply from its hinges. With the walls corroded around me, I wander through the tall, echoing space. Dust lilts in the air, and a vague smell of sulfur clogs my nose. Everything in here creaks accus-ingly at me as I pass, and I feel crowded, even though I'm alone.

This was never the biggest factory in the region, and time

has made it smaller still. I walk across the entire mill in less than five minutes, and then I circle back and try again, ducking beneath sagging conveyor belts and creeping past a pair of air heaters that long ago went cold. Searching for anything. Searching for them.

This is foolish. I don't belong here. There's nothing I can do with these dead things from the past. I don't know who I am, thinking I can rescue Quinn and Eleanor somehow. I couldn't save the girls before. I can't even save myself.

But I keep trying anyhow.

In the center of the plant, there's a blast furnace, its immense steel body at the heart of everything, towering over the rest of the equipment. When my dad took me on a tour of this place when I was a kid, I couldn't stop staring at it from across the mill.

"It looks like a giant lava lamp," I said, almost breathless.

He slapped his thigh and laughed. "You're not wrong," he said.

I place one palm on the chilled metal, rusted with time and neglect. I expect to find the girls in the decay, but all of them are long gone.

But they were here once. They were real. I have to remind myself of that sometimes. In my worst moments, I almost believe that I dreamed it all. I don't know if that would be better or worse.

From behind me, a shadow passes across the wall, and my heart quickens. Are they here? Have I finally found them?

I turn around and start to say her name, but it's all for nothing.

Bundled in a heavy jacket, Adrian nods at me. "Sorry to disappoint," he says.

I scowl at him, irritated at his very existence. "Why are you here?"

"Because I thought you might be." He takes a step closer to me. "What happened here, Phoebe?"

I hesitate, my lips moving silently with the truth.

"Nothing," I whisper instead.

Adrian sighs. He knew I'd say that. He knows I won't talk to him—*can't* talk to him—after everything that's happened between us. This still doesn't deter him. He offers me a ride home. I almost say no out of spite, but it's a mile back, and I'm so cold and so tired.

"Fine," I whisper, and together we head out the opposite side of the mill. Adrian's discovered a way in and out that doesn't involve the chain-link fence. That means he's probably been here before. He knows more than he lets on. That's how he's always been.

I climb in the passenger seat of his car, and we don't speak the whole trip back to Denton Street.

)O(

At my house, with Adrian trudging up the porch steps behind me, I knock on the front door, and my mother answers.

"Hello," she says, more to him than me.

He smiles. "I found her," he says.

I glance between the two of them. My mother must have sent him to look for me. To bring me home. Those phone calls about Adrian weren't random updates. After I left, my parents must have kept in touch with him. I imagine the three of them over Sunday suppers, my chair conspicuously empty. Maybe he even worked side-by-side with my father in the garage, tinkering with the Impala, keeping it running, keeping the past intact. Like it would make any difference.

My mother invites him inside. I get no welcome. She probably doesn't think I need one.

"Why are you here, Adrian?" I keep walking, past my crumpled-up sleeping bag and the musty old family Bible in the corner.

"Because I didn't like how we left things," he says.

I scoff and climb the steps. "It's a little late to worry about that."

"I'm trying to fix things. I think you can understand." He follows me upstairs and into my bedroom.

The top dresser drawer is halfway open, and an image of Jacqueline with her sad, strange smile is waiting to greet us.

Adrian stares at her. "What is all of this?"

"Nothing," I say, and stand in front of the dresser, blocking off as much of it as I can.

Adrian sways back and forth, trying to see around me, to get a glimpse of the diaries and the photo negatives and the other secrets tucked away. He wants to know what I've got here, and what he can use for the museum.

I roll my eyes. "You don't change, do you?"

He blushes at this, a caught child, and he starts to say something, an apology of sorts, but my mother's voice carries up from the living room.

"Get out. Now."

More words, furious ones that boil in your veins, and then heavy footsteps, two pairs. I hold my breath. Adrian does the same. Another holler, and Eleanor comes crashing through the door with my mother close behind her, swatting and cursing at the air.

"I told you to get out," my mother says, but Eleanor just ignores her, setting her sights on me instead.

"Phoebe," she says, a feral look in her eyes. "You're leaving soon, aren't you?"

I nod, my head drooping with shame.

"Then tell me," she says. "Before it's too late. Before Quinn goes the same way. What happened with the girls? What did you see?"

The three of them are all staring at me now, and I'm sure they know everything. I'm sure I'm wearing the truth on my skin, a tapestry of the past, etched in wrinkles around my eyes and the hundreds of gray hairs I've earned.

No one knows how the girls disappeared. No one except me.

But I can't remember. After all these years, I *won't* remember. If I have to admit how I've failed them, I fear I'll crumble to ash.

"Please leave me alone," I whisper before slipping through my bedroom door and heading outside.

This is a coward's move.

It's the only thing I can think to do.

In the backyard, I climb up one last time to what's left of the treehouse. This should be my chance for a proper goodbye, an overdue farewell to the specters of my insects, but I'm not alone. Quinn is already there, tucked against a limb where there used to be a corner.

"Hello," she says, and I do my best not to stare at her arm. The wound hasn't festered any more since yesterday. No bandages. Nothing. Maybe I'm wrong, and Eleanor and I both imagined this. Maybe Quinn won't be the same.

She runs her finger along a lonesome edge of the treehouse. "The butterflies come back here sometimes," she says. "It's like they remember this used to be for them."

"Not just for them." I yank a rusted nail from the floorboard, and it shivers in my hand. I recoil and let it fall below into the dirt. "This place was for us too."

The construction crew works late tonight. Quinn and I go down to the sidewalk to watch the next house fall. It's almost sunset when it crumbles. Lisa and Kathleen's house, the one that should have been taken apart years ago.

"It won't be long now," Quinn says, and the streetlight flashes off her arm. Something glistens there like polished metal, and all around the wound, her skin is already puckering. The same as old leather. The same as Jacqueline's.

I close my eyes. This cycle that none of us can break. God knows I've tried, but all I can do is make things worse. There was nothing I could do then, and there's nothing I can do now.

I need to stop pretending. I need to stop lying to myself that I can make a difference. This city evicted me once before, and it's time to let it evict me again.

"Take care of yourself," I say to Quinn, before turning away and walking home alone, sobbing silently all the way.

FIFTEEN

"Phoebe, you have to come down."

"You can't stay up there forever."

"It will only be worse the longer you don't listen to us."

This had been going on all morning. My parents and the other parents and every nosy person awake at this terrible hour had been having a one-sided argument with me. Ever since I left the mansion and climbed up the treehouse alone.

Only not quite alone. Eleanor fussed in my arms. That was the crux of the problem. I wouldn't let my parents or Clint or anybody else up to claim her. Apparently, the world would prefer you leave a baby alone in a mansion or in a milk crate on an empty porch than care enough to protect her.

According to them, keeping her up here wasn't kindness. It was kidnapping.

"I'm not a very good abductor if you know where she is," I

called down to the ground.

"Phoebe, please," my mother said, coaxing me the same way she did when I was a kindergartener who wouldn't brush my teeth. "Just come down and it will all be okay."

But nothing would be okay now. An hour before sunrise, somebody—probably Clint or one of his rubbish parents—had called the police. Now I counted no less than six uniforms milling about the backyard like aimless cockroaches. Nobody could figure out what to do next. It was all "maybe try this" or "no, definitely try that" or "just berate the girl until it's all too much and she gives the baby up out of mere exhaustion." Not that anything could exhaust me enough to let them have Eleanor. Dawn had asked me to care for her. I'd failed the Rust Maidens enough already. I couldn't fail them again.

Indistinct voices on the ground. I strained to hear what their next plan might be. Three times, so far, the fathers had wedged a Craftsman ladder up against the window, but whenever they started to climb up, I kicked it back down again and hollered at them to go away. There was talk of bringing a fire truck into the yard, as though Eleanor was a mewing, wide-eyed kitten stranded in a too-high branch, but it was decided that the houses on Denton Street were packed too close together to maneuver the vehicle in successfully.

"Too bad." I sneered down at them through the window before I ducked back inside. Part of me feared that if the police couldn't come up with any better strategy, they might just open fire, Bonnie and Clyde-style. That would solve the problem. That would solve me. Some people in this neighborhood would probably say that was the only way to solve me.

I curled in the corner, Eleanor in one arm and my tartan thermos tucked under the other. The adults downstairs weren't getting either one. The butterflies fluttered by, unfazed at the early morning hijinks.

"Phoebe?" My mother's voice, distant and strained. "What happened in the mansion?"

I poked just my eyes over the window. "I don't know," I said.

"What did Clint tell you?"

"Nothing." She pursed her lips and grimaced. "He won't talk to anyone."

I grunted. Typical. "How about Mr. Carter? Ask him what he saw."

My father hesitated. Nobody in the yard would look at me. "He's gone."

I squinted at them. "Gone?"

My mother waved one hand in the air like it was all too much for her.

"Kathleen says he packed up his pickup truck and left at dawn. Didn't even say goodbye." She sighed before adding, "Didn't change his soiled clothes, either."

I let out a cackle that ricocheted off the sky. This was the best news I could expect. That bitter old beast finally realized what he should have always known: that his youngest daughter was more powerful than he'd ever be.

Pack your bags, I wanted to say to everyone. *Make like Mr. Carter and leave. Because those girls deserve this town more than you do.*

"What luggage did he take with him? A crate of Mad Dog 20/20?" I laughed again. "I assume he left his regret piled up at the back door. That'd be too heavy to carry."

"Phoebe." My mother snapped her tongue and glared up at me. "You're not helping."

I smiled at her. I wasn't hurting anything either.

The government men were the next to arrive, dragged out of bed earlier than any of us liked. The three of them consulted with the police and parents on the ground and formulated a plan of attack, which basically just involved Adrian positioning the ladder for a fourth try and climbing up himself. Though I considered knocking it down when he was halfway up, I didn't. A clever scheme, to send him. Other than Jacqueline, he was the only one at this point that I would talk to. Though she would have been the most convincing of anyone.

He was in the treehouse before I could decide what to do

next, so I just crawled backwards against the wall.

"I won't give her to you," I said, and cradled Eleanor closer to me.

Adrian wavered in the doorway, bluish crescents rimming his bloodshot eyes. "They'll arrest you, Phoebe," he said, "and I won't be able to stop them."

"So?" My body stiffened, defiant to the last. "Let them try."

He shook his head. "You know they're going to take Eleanor one way or the other. You can't stop that."

He was right. Either I gave her up now and saved myself from the county jail, or they took down the treehouse piece by piece to get her. And I didn't know how to take care of a baby anyhow. Eleanor hadn't eaten or had her diaper changed or had any of the things that I should have known how to do. No matter what the choice, I made the wrong one. I was failing Eleanor just by being near her. Failing her, and failing Dawn too.

I squeezed Eleanor's tiny hand. She babbled softly at me. Then, with every fiber of my body fizzling with defeat, I passed her to Adrian and tried not to sob. She squirmed and cried out in his arms as he carried her down. The parents rejoiced, and somebody took her away. Far from me. Far from where she belonged.

I watched through the window, hating all of them. Even Adrian, who flashed his government badge at the police and worked his magic, sending them on their way, all of the officers mumbling and kicking the grass, disappointed they didn't get to lead me away in shackles.

When they were gone, I huddled in the corner and wished I didn't exist. Dawn had made one request, just one, and I couldn't even do that right.

By the time I came down to earth myself, it was after dark, and the yard was empty. Nobody cared much now that Eleanor was safely back at home with Clint. As safe as anything with Clint could ever be.

I stood frozen in the grass and stared at the house. In the yellow glow of the dining room, my parents drifted back and forth, clearing their plates after dinner, their mouths moving but not making a sound, at least not one I could hear. It was like watching a silent movie of your life, only without you in it. They didn't look happy in there without me, but they didn't look miserable either. I'd disturbed them enough today, so I just left them alone and sneaked between the houses to our driveway. The Impala was already unlocked, the key in the visor.

I turned on the radio, reclined in the driver's seat, and pretended I had somewhere to go.

WMMS buzzed through the speakers. Request hour. I rolled my eyes and almost flicked off the station. Listeners were always so terrible at picking good songs. I didn't know why the DJs let them choose to begin with.

Something whispered behind the car, strange and tinny, but when I looked back, it was gone. Or it was never there at all. I was seeing ghosts where there were only shadows.

The DJ came back on the air. "WMMS, what song would you like to request?"

A hushed voice crackled through, strange and soft but still so familiar. "Can you play "American Girl" by Tom Petty?"

Everything in the world stood still.

"Absolutely," the DJ said brightly. "Is this a dedication to anybody special?"

"Yes," the voice whispered. "For Phoebe."

Jacqueline. I turned up the radio like I would find her in the static, but it was only those opening guitar riffs and that nasally voice that always sounded as close as family. How did she call from the mansion? There was no phone. And how did she know I was listening?

Unless it was them that passed by a moment ago. Unless they weren't visible in the night anymore.

The payphone down the block. She called from the Ma Bell payphone, the same place I'd reached out to Kathleen from all those weeks ago.

I was out of the car and running before I could think it through or figure out what I would say to her. I should have taken the Impala, but somehow, it seemed that maybe I could make it faster on foot. That I was so determined I might fly. I didn't stop running, not until I got there where she wasn't.

Breathless, I stood in the empty darkness at the corner. My hand reached out and touched the receiver, but it was cold. Maybe I was wrong. Maybe she wasn't here.

But then headlights flashed on the payphone, and I saw it there, glinting. The shape of a triple moon, etched into the booth, made by a hand even stronger than glass. I looked to the street, hope surging through me. Somewhere, past these rows of crowded houses, a car backfired, and the smell of smoke and wet earth mingled in the air.

I stared into the murk of the evening. There was no one. Maybe I was too late. Then, as I turned away, back toward Denton Street, toward home, there they were in the corner of my eye, moving away from here. Away from me.

I slipped out of the phone booth and followed as best as I could. It wasn't easy. Their bodies were more shadow than human. Everything about them shifted constantly. The color of rust one moment, a senseless gray the next. Only when they stepped against a clearing could I see them, their figures in sharp relief against the blank of the night sky, a sky that had no rot or want. Otherwise, they blended into the decay of Cleveland, and there was plenty of that to go around.

At first, I could barely tell them apart. But the longer they moved and the more I followed, the better I could see them. They were one, but they were also still themselves. Jacqueline's steps always softer than a ghost's. Dawn cowering in on herself, ashamed at her mere existence. Helena and Violet, paired up together, eager to follow. And Lisa, leading them everywhere they went. Always so strange and unreachable, she was the first to change. That meant she knew the most about this, had felt the transformation stirring in her the longest. This was a role she'd been born to play, the de facto leader of girls who were now just like her. She was no longer alone. My heart swelled for an instant, that girl with no friends united at last with others that understood. But there had been a trade-off. Now I was the one who was alone. The world always balanced itself out like that.

We were half a mile away from home before I realized there was only one place they could be going. Straight for the steel mill.

I crept behind them, struggling to keep up. They glided through the rusted fence like it was water, but I wasn't so limber. I had to climb over, and I had to wait until they were out of earshot. Otherwise they'd catch me following, and might disappear altogether. Maybe forever.

This was such a strange place for them to go. But in a way, I understood. This mill had given us life. Food on the table, roofs over our head, a shape to our everyday existences. Now it was closed up, bound for rust, and soon to be forgotten. The girls were the same, and they understood that. They would take this place and repurpose it for themselves.

They moved into the heart of the machinery and gathered around the blast furnace, so still in the darkness. Everything here was corroded and old, except for the door that led to the inside of the furnace, the space that used to heat up the rest of the mill. It was so odd to see that one spot of newness in a sea of rust, and these girls shadowed against it.

Their voices were nails against glass as they whispered about what to do next.

Then, apparently, it was decided, because they turned together toward the snarls of metal. Their hands extended as one into the darkness, toward the blast furnace. Though I couldn't see their faces, I imagined them with a shared look of reverence. Worshippers at an altar, ready to give themselves over to a higher power.

But it wasn't to be. Unlike the chain-link fence, their fingers didn't go through the furnace. Instead, their bodies were solid and whole, like normal girls. At this, Lisa shook her head, and the others mimicked the movement. Something was wrong or not quite right, or not quite ready.

With their heads tipped down, they were gone as quickly as

they'd appeared, and I guessed where they were going. Back to the mansion. Back to their temporary home.

I turned, desperate to cut them off before they got there, to figure out a way to move faster than darkness, when a voice like a distant bell draped over me.

"Hello, Phoebe."

It took me a moment to realize that Jacqueline was standing right in front of me.

Her eyes were filmed with oil, and her skin—if you could even call it that now—was a tapestry of pewter-colored metal and broken glass and water that dripped thick and viscous from her body. There was almost nothing of her left. Unless this was who she really was, and the best friend I thought I'd known was the imposter.

"Hello," I said, my voice much steadier than I expected.

We walked together, out of the mill and down toward the lake. All the way, my guts roiled with fear that someone might spot us. What would they do if they saw Jacqueline like this? Would they steal her away from me? Or now that she was changed, would they just scream and flee, the same as Mr. Carter?

It didn't matter, because Cleveland was quiet tonight. We were alone. We were safe.

At the shoreline, we nestled in the sand. It wasn't our usual beach, but this was all part of one lake, wasn't it? The water was the same everywhere. Poisonous, but ours.

There was a small space between us, more than I usually left. I didn't know how close she wanted me.

"Are you afraid of me?" she asked.

"No," I said. "I think you're beautiful."

She laughed, and the sound like whirring machinery hummed on my skin. "You would say that."

"It's true." I tried to smile back at her, but couldn't. "What does it feel like?"

"Not as bad as you'd think." She traced a triple moon sign in the dirty sand between us. "It's painful sometimes. Change always is."

I hesitated before asking the same question she'd never had a chance to answer at the clinic. "Are you scared?"

She inhaled a heavy breath. "I'm not," she said.

There was a flash of hope in her dark eyes that had never been there before. Dread rose up inside me as I finally understood.

"Jacqueline," I whispered. "Do you *want* this?"

She wouldn't look at me. "I wouldn't have chosen it," she said. "This chose me."

But that wasn't the whole answer, and we both knew it.

"So you didn't choose it," I said, "but it doesn't bother you, does it?"

Jacqueline gazed at me, and everything in her looked lit from the inside. "It doesn't feel wrong, Phoebe. It feels like the only way."

Like fate, I thought, but couldn't bring myself to say it. This force of nature stronger than both of us, pulling Jacqueline away from me. And her, my best friend, willing to listen to its siren call. Maybe she'd been straining to hear it all her life. I couldn't give her a future she wanted, so something else did it for me.

We watched the waves ripple in the moonlight.

Then I peered at her in the dark, struggling to discern her from the shadows. "Would you like to go in?" I asked.

She shook her head. "I can't, Phoebe."

She didn't have to explain. I'd figured it out already. Lisa had vanished for a moment in the water. Maybe she did it on purpose, or maybe she didn't. All I knew was that the decay was hungry for the girls, and the girls, in their own way, were hungry to go to it. But it had to be the right time and place. It had to be what the Rust Maidens chose. They had a say in that much.

I wanted to tell her that it was all okay. That we could fix this. But I knew that wasn't true. Not anymore. It had gone too far.

So we just sat together quietly, the way that we used to. Back when we thought our lives would turn out differently. Back when we didn't know what to think.

Just before dawn, the boats started to come in, and we couldn't stay in the open any longer. Together, we clambered to our feet, and with her eyes uncertain, she reached out and took my hand. My fingers tingled with her touch. I expected it to hurt, but it didn't. Nothing about her was painful. Either that, or everything was, and I was too numb now to know the difference.

On Denton Street, the neighborhood was awakening, and we sneaked together through what was left of the dark to get her home before one of the mothers saw what she'd become. It was too early for a scream like that.

At the back of the mansion, Jacqueline untangled her hand from mine and moved toward the door. Her lithe fingers peeled up a splintered board, and though the space looked much too small to welcome her, she could fit into places I couldn't imagine. Her body contorted and she started vanishing into the darkness. When she was halfway in, I held my breath, thinking she wouldn't look back. But she did.

"It won't be long now," she said, and slipped the rest of the way into the house. Out of my reach.

The Rust Maidens were almost ready. It was almost time. For what, I couldn't comprehend, but I did know this: right now, she was still here. Maybe we couldn't ever reverse the transformation, but that didn't mean we couldn't figure out a way to live with this.

Underneath it all, she was still Jacqueline. She was still my best friend.

I walked home, resolve rising inside me. I was ready at last to talk to my parents. Ready to ask for their help. This wasn't over yet. It couldn't be over.

But everything in me stood still when I reached the front porch. My mother was waiting there for me, a splayed newspaper in her hand and tears in her eyes.

"What have you done, Phoebe?" She wilted against the doorway. "You foolish, foolish child."

When I was close enough, she shoved the paper into my

arms like a bomb. I unfolded the page and read the top story, first word to the last, without stopping.

It was Kathleen's work, and this was the article the first one should have been. No unbridled fear, no triteness so cloying it made your teeth ache. She took her time this round. There were quotes from doctors and nurses and family members, most off the record, but some on. There were charts and theories, better than anything the rest of us had invented. She'd done well. She'd told everything. This was the Kathleen I'd always admired, the one I wanted to be like.

The one I now hated.

Because I was there too, on the page, looking like the fool my mother accused me of being. It wasn't a picture, and it wasn't even my name, but anyone familiar with this neighborhood knew it was me.

Those on Denton Street have been mostly apathetic in gathering answers. A cousin of one of the girls had shown initial interest in assisting this investigation but later lost interest, perhaps too busy cavorting with her own government sources.

That was a low blow. Honest, but unnecessary. Still, I couldn't blame her for telling the truth, but I could loathe her for it. No one could stop me from doing that.

I kept reading. I kept going. All the way to the final line that stopped my heart.

By the end of next week, the government representatives intend to remove the girls to DC for further research.

Adrian. My lover the liar. The Judas I should have always known he would be.

With my head heavy, I leaned against my mother, but her arm was cold to me.

I deserved that. For what I'd done—to the neighborhood, to the girls, to myself—I deserved so much worse.

And that was exactly what we were going to get.

SIXTEEN

The house is empty now. Our lives retired to storage, or moved into my mother's one-bedroom apartment on Detroit Avenue. I've refused to visit there. I don't want to see what's left of her, how she'll reach the finish line of life, cramped and alone and in unfamiliar territory.

I wish I could do better by her. I wish I could do better by anyone.

She and I walk through the house together, one last time.

Into the dining room, where no one will ever have Sloppy Joes again. The kitchen where mothers will no longer gather for Virginia Slims and gossip. Up the steps and down the hallway and past my bedroom.

This is the only room that hasn't been hollowed out. The diaries and Polaroids still sprawl across the floor and in the dresser that I didn't empty.

My mother frowns. "You aren't taking any of your things with you?"

"No," I say, and close the door. Let the wreckers come and destroy the past like I should have years ago.

We're done here now. Nothing tethers us to this place anymore.

Back downstairs, that old Bible still sits in the corner of the living room. My mother picks it up.

"I'll wait outside," she says. There's no hint of sorrow in her voice, and although the temperature's holding steady at zero, she heads to the front porch. She's too tired to stand in here another instant. For the last twenty-eight years—ever since I left, ever since that summer—she's been saying her goodbyes to Denton Street. There's no room for sentimentality in her heart.

But all I am is a sack of sentimentality. It disgusts me, but it's true.

The red phone jacked into the kitchen wall glistens at me through the doorway. Utilities won't be turned off until tomorrow. That means it's not too late.

I creep toward the receiver, like I'm trying to sneak up on it, and I dial a number I memorized long ago. Then I stand here, wound tight inside, on the last phone call I'll ever make from home.

It only rings once before she picks up.

"Kathleen Carter, *Chicago Tribune*."

Though it's been almost three decades, her voice is the same. That catches me off-guard. I was expecting something different, something withered and aged. But she's as fresh and eager as that girl who fled Cleveland without remorse, without one glance over her shoulder. At least not until I called her that day from the payphone down the block.

"Hello?" she asks, impatience singeing her voice. "Is anyone there?"

I breathe in for courage.

"This is Phoebe Shaw." That's all I say. I don't have anything else for her. If she wants to talk, she can talk. If she doesn't, she can hang up.

I wait, wondering which choice she'll make.

"Hello, Phoebe," she says finally.

"Hi," I whisper.

After everything, life didn't turn out so bad for Kathleen. She went on to become the reporter I always knew she'd be. Promoted at the *Tribune*, nominated for awards, a six-figure book deal for her memoirs. Over the years, I'd kept up with her work, and for a while, I even clipped out her articles and taped them in a leather-bound scrapbook. Then it became too much, the pain of sliding the articles into place, taping them down, remembering. Over and over, like a record that would never stop skipping.

After more than thirty-five years on the job, she should probably be retired by now, but why would she bother? What's waiting on people like us? Retirement would be as empty as this room where I'm standing, a daily reminder of what was missing.

"What is it you need?" she asks, her voice even, the utmost professional.

"After I left," I say before changing course mid-sentence, "after you left, after *everything*."

I stammer out something even I can't recognize. Words, I guess, but not decipherable ones. This isn't going well. I grip the phone tighter, and the plastic bows in my hand.

Another breath. Try again.

"Did you ever figure out why?" I ask. "In all your research, did you determine what happened? Or if we could have prevented it?"

It's a fool's question, but it's the only thing I want to know. If we could have stopped it then, maybe I can stop it now. Maybe it's not too late to help Quinn, and help myself too.

Kathleen hesitates, and I'm sure that she knows the real reason I'm calling. That it's happening all over again. That I need her help.

"Phoebe," she says at last, her voice soft and sad. "If I knew any more now than I did then, don't you think I'd be back there? Still trying to find her? Trying to save her?"

Sorrow stitches up my chest and holds me so tight I feel I'll never move or breathe again. There it is. The answer I knew she'd give me. That it's all useless posturing. You can't stop the sun from rising or the tides from coming in. You can't stop the girls from becoming what they became.

I nod once to myself, as satisfied as I can be. "Thanks for talking with me."

"Anytime," she says, and hangs up without saying goodbye.

I stand frozen, still holding the receiver, listening to the melody of static on the other end. I already knew this was what she would say.

Even now, after all these years, part of me swells with happiness for Kathleen. At least she got out and stayed out. She didn't watch her life swirl down the drain like last night's flat beer. I still hate her a little, but I still admire her too.

I set the phone back in its cradle and turn away from the wall. That's it. That's all I've got. She has no ideas. Neither do I.

I cross through the living room and close the front door, not looking back once.

Outside, my mother lingers in the yard. She looks up at me and smiles.

"Do you want to get lunch before you head out? We could go downtown to Tower City."

This is so pitiful, the warble in her voice, the desperation setting in. We both know this is it. Goodbye, maybe forever this time.

"I'm not hungry," I say.

She nods. This was the response she expected from me. I'm nothing if not predictable.

I'm ready to leave, but I can't. Not yet. There's one question I've been wanting to ask her. Not that it matters after all these years, but I ask anyhow.

"Why didn't you move before now? Why stay here?"

She sighs, and her breath fogs all around us. "Why did any of us stay?" She shakes her head. "It's the only place we thought we belonged, and I always felt like I owed it to them. That if we left, and others moved in who didn't know the girls, it would be like forgetting them."

Forgetting them. Like I've tried to forget.

"Believe me," I say, "leaving wouldn't help."

Yet that's exactly what I'm going to do. Run from this city all over again. I turn toward the Impala in the driveway, but my mother grabs my arm.

"Wait," she says. "There's something I want to give you."

She passes me the Bible. I start to ask her why I would need this, if she's still trying to convert me. But then I see it. An old envelope, yellowed and crushed at the edges.

I take it out, instantly knowing what's inside.

My college bond money. This was the envelope Jacqueline and I searched for. Now I've finally found it, almost thirty years too late.

"It was worth ten thousand then," my mother says. "It's about three times that now."

I gaze at her, convinced it's a strange trick.

"Take this back." I dangle the envelope out to her, the withered paper quivering between the tips of two fingers, not wanting to touch it, not wanting to claim it as my own. "You need it more than I do."

"No, baby, I don't." She looks at me in a way only a mother can, her eyes soft and sweet and impatient. "It's yours. I always promised myself if you came back, I'd give it to you. And you did come back. Thank you."

"Thank you for having me," I say, and the words ache in my mouth. I sound more like a dinner guest than a daughter.

My mother takes a step forward before she kisses my forehead. "Goodbye, Phoebe."

And that's it. She climbs into her own car, parked on the street, and heads off to visit my father. To say her long goodbyes there, too.

I'm alone now.

My gaze slides down the street to the still-standing houses. There aren't many of them left. Our house. Clint's and Eleanor's house.

Quinn's house. She knows I'm leaving today, but she hasn't

come to see me off. Down the block, there's a light on inside, and I wonder if she's still there. I wonder if she's still *her*.

Eleanor isn't one for goodbyes either, but she has shown up to see me off. She watches me from the sidewalk on the other side of the street, her eyes heavy and accusing.

We could still talk. It's not too late for that.

I step forward and start to say her name, but she just shakes her head, tears already staining her cheeks, and turns away. This has been too much for her. I've had my chance to explain things, but I didn't bother, and now she's lost to me. Everything here is lost to me. Jacqueline's house looms down the block, an upstairs curtain fluttering. There's somebody there, moving just out of sight. Watching me, waiting for me.

They can wait a whole lot longer. They can wait forever, as far as I'm concerned.

With my lone duffel bag tucked in the trunk, I climb behind the wheel of the Impala and drive off. Not into any sunset. Not into anything. For all I know, this car will sputter out a mile from here, or ten miles, or a hundred. I probably won't make it far, but I'll go as far as I can.

On the highway, I take one last detour.

Adrian is in his office, door open, his shoulders hunched over pages of blueprints. When I'm standing close enough, I recognize the drawings. It's for the monument he's building outside. The one for the girls.

He looks up at me and smiles. "I didn't think I'd see you again," he says.

"You won't after this. I'm just here to say goodbye."

This is it. I've done what I came for. Everything I need to do in Cleveland is finished, yet I don't move from this spot. I just stand here at the desk, my fingertips balancing me, considering what to do next.

Adrian senses this in me, my indecision, and he seizes instantly on it. "Don't leave," he says. "Work on this project with me. Nobody would be better for this than you."

A crack forms inside me, and I want to stay. Adrian, always

the persuasive one. Always the heartbreaker. If I remained here, it would all be the same. But not the same. Not without her.

I shake my head. "I can't."

Adrian hesitates, and something sparks in his eyes as he measures his next words carefully.

"Jacqueline wouldn't want this," he says. "She wouldn't want you to be running after all these years."

Her name on his lips. It's all wrong.

"You don't get to talk about her," I say. "You don't get to talk about any of them. Not to me. Not like you knew them."

"I'm sorry," he says, and honestly sounds like he means it.

But I won't let him have this. I won't give him an inch.

"You betrayed them," I say. "You betrayed *us*."

What I want to say is, *You betrayed me*. Because even now, standing face to face with him after almost thirty years, I feel like the same jilted teenager. The one who trusted him. But I don't say it. I just turn and walk away, down the long hallway and out into the cold.

I shouldn't have come here. I should never have returned to Cleveland, and I should never have bothered to speak to Adrian again.

Back on the road, tears blurring my vision, I rev the Impala through traffic, escaping University Circle. Escaping these places that were supposed to be mine.

It's not quite rush hour yet, which means the highway is mostly open. By the time my vision clears again, tears dried, focus restored, I'm on I-90 heading east. To where, I don't know. New York? Philadelphia? Some random town on the Atlantic where the water doesn't catch fire? It doesn't matter. So long as it's any place that isn't here.

But Cleveland isn't ready to let me go yet. Before I cross the county line, the knob on the car stereo twists, and the speakers crackle to life.

Karen Carpenter's voice pours into every crevice of the car. Jacqueline's favorite song: "Close to You."

"No," I say, and punch it off, but the radio fights me. It moves again, controlled by an invisible hand, and the song returns. It won't let me forget, no matter how much I'm desperate to do just that.

I want to scream. Maybe I do, I'm not sure. Or maybe it's just the scream of the bald tires against the asphalt as I twist the wheel hard, my hands cold and unforgiving. The Impala slides over ice and salt and two lanes into the median, where it's all frozen earth and stiff grass. A feeling of motion and then a feeling of suspension, of not going anywhere. The car's stopped here, halfway between two sides.

The radio keeps crackling, more saccharine guitars and sweet lyrics. All of it too much. All of it from her.

I hold my head in my hands, the whir of the road around me, those cars with places to go, drivers who know what they're doing, zipping past. But I can't move. Here on the slick of the leather seats, I'm trapped. Not in the future, but not exactly in the past either. I'm nowhere and everywhere at once, suspended in between. Desperate to choose.

A choice. That was what they always needed. To decide for themselves.

I can make a choice too. I can stop running away.

With a steadiness budding inside me, I guide the Impala back the way I came.

Back toward Cleveland. Back toward Denton Street.

It's only ten minutes. It's the longest trip of my life.

I park on the street where I used to live, and I walk, unshaking and unafraid, to the split-level with the slate roof.

No knock. No polite make-believe. I move up the front steps and cross the threshold into the past I've avoided all these years. With my head high, I climb the familiar staircase to the second floor and march down the hall until I reach the end. Then, with all the strength in me, I throw open the door to Jacqueline's bedroom.

On the other side, she's waiting there to greet me.

SEVENTEEN

The newspaper with Kathleen's article slipped through my fingers and fluttered across the welcome mat. I couldn't move from the doorway or from this moment. The day was new, the sun low in the sky, but the swelter of late July had settled in for the long haul, draping over me like bolts of burlap.

I was alone, more alone than I'd ever been. But here I was, on the street where I lived, where I'd always lived, the only place I could call home. And my mother stood next to me, the one person I should be able to trust, but she couldn't shift her gaze from her slippered feet. Not wanting to look at me, not wanting to see the thing she'd raised. The entire neighborhood could see nothing in me but a traitor. I'd turned against them, in favor of the girls and their insurrection from within; in favor of Adrian, an invader in our midst. But I'd done what I'd always promised to do: I protected my best friend, even if she didn't want my help anymore.

My vision pinwheeled at the edges, and I realized I wasn't

breathing. I choked in a mouthful of air, but it almost didn't help. It didn't change anything. I was still here where I didn't belong.

My mother moved away from me, a thousand miles it seemed, and she was back in the house before I could say a word, the screen door slamming shut like a goodbye.

I couldn't go back inside. Not to where no one welcomed me.

My feet heavy, I started down the stairs, but there was a figure up ahead in my path.

Adrian. Standing right in my way.

"Phoebe," he said, my name sounding all wrong. He said it almost as a question.

I hesitated, my body seizing up at the sight of him. For an instant, a familiar longing ached inside me, left over from that night. His skin against mine, scents mingled together. An escape.

He took a step toward me, slowly, unsure of himself.

"Don't," I said. Everything in me quivered with rage, and I was convinced if he reached out to touch me, I would take his hand and never let it go, not until I'd crushed every bone in his fingers to dust.

He sensed this in me. He was smart enough to know this much.

"It wasn't my plan," he said.

I scoffed. "But you didn't argue, did you?"

"It's not my job to argue."

It wasn't his job to be decent, either.

"How do you even expect them to get them out?" I asked. "It's not like they'll come to the door if you knock."

He wouldn't look at me. "We're bringing in equipment," he said. "They'll dismantle the house if needed."

"Like what? A wrecking ball? Bulldozers?" I stared at him, half-dizzy with fear. "You don't know where they're hiding. You take apart the house, and you could kill them."

He said nothing. Because he knew I was right. We stood in silence, as I gathered the courage to ask.

"When?"

He gulped down a breath. "First thing Monday."

Tomorrow. This was all going to happen tomorrow. Less than twenty-four hours until Jacqueline was lost to me, maybe forever. Probably forever.

"It might be better this way," Adrian said, his voice insistent, like he was trying to convince himself. "There are better facilities outside of Cleveland, Phoebe. The doctors elsewhere might be able to help the girls."

Or they might be better able to dissect them and stuff the leftovers in glass jars on a shelf.

Adrian kept talking, but I couldn't listen. So I ran. Like a child, I turned away and fled. As if that was enough. As if that was an answer.

And I didn't stop. Down the sidewalk, past the sagging ROOMS FOR RENT signs and the always-gawking faces peering out through Venetian blinds. Everyone readying themselves for Sunday sermon, but never too busy to watch.

But they weren't the ones I wanted. I needed to warn the girls.

Around the back of the mansion, at the porch I left only minutes ago, I pounded on the door.

"Jacqueline!" My voice split in two. "Dawn, Lisa! Anyone!"

I seized up, hopeful I would hear something on the other side. But there was nothing. That couldn't stop me, though.

"They're coming," I said. "They'll be here tomorrow. You have to get out. Before it's too late."

I listened and waited. A flutter inside, but not enough to be sure they'd heard, or if anyone was there at all.

This was probably for nothing, just like everything else I'd tried. I drooped against the door, pretending I could stay here forever, but that was my problem. I never wanted to admit defeat or accept change. I thought I could hold my breath, and everything would be okay.

Finally, I cobbled myself together enough to drag my body home. But not home. I wouldn't go inside and disturb my parents. They'd had enough of me to last a lifetime.

Up in the treehouse, the butterflies danced around me. I

cooed at them and called out the names I'd given them. I told them I loved them too. They probably didn't understand, but that was okay. Then I peeled the plastic off the windows. This late in the season, they no longer needed to stay, so they didn't. One by one, they ventured out of the treehouse and into the sunlight.

"Goodbye," I whispered.

There they went, a ballet of insects fluttering away. My whole life, vanishing.

"Phoebe?" My mother's voice. "Could you come here?"

"Yes," I said, and climbed down the rope ladder.

My mother stood beside me, and for the first time that whole summer, she looked right in my eyes, not flinching away at the sight of me. "We're going to church together," she said. "As a family. Just for today."

She was asking me for something. A request, not a demand. After everything, I couldn't bear to disappoint her again. Besides, where else was I needed?

My father was waiting for us in the living room.

"Ready?" he asked, and I nodded.

We didn't take a car. Instead, my parents and I walked like defeated soldiers to the church. We didn't speak. We didn't look at each other. We went because it was expected of us.

Everyone had become good at doing what was expected. We stood in line outside and watched as the other worshippers went in ahead of us without a complaint: the doctor and his wife, Aunt Betty with her pursed lips, Kathleen just a few paces in front of us, her head down.

A babble to my left, and I turned in time to see Eleanor spirited inside, cradled in the arms of Clint. The arms of the enemy. As though we weren't all enemies now.

And there, greeting the parishioners inside the door, was perhaps the best pretender of all. The preacher, smiling as though everything was normal, his face frozen in faux cheer, never belying the truth: that his only daughter was lost to him, and it was all his fault. This was all our fault, a neighborhood of fools.

His wife stood next to him, no smile, her hair grayer than I remembered it.

The sermon started at nine on the dot, and today was all about tolerance and kindness and every other maudlin topic. We were going to keep on as if nothing had changed. The girls got sick, the girls transformed, the girls were liable to evaporate into rust at midnight, our own grotesque Cinderellas, and we would just keep showing up on Sunday morning and praying and pretending nothing ever happened. But something *had* happened. Our lives had been ripped away from us, and we were too craven to admit it.

The sermon droned on, all eyes set on the pulpit. Set on nothing at all.

"But the fruit of the Spirit is love, joy—"

The preacher's voice, so inconsequential.

"—peace, patience, kindness—"

He'd never stop speaking, and they'd never stop listening. His even tenor glided over the final words. "—goodness, faithfulness, gentleness, and self-control."

Then my own voice, echoing to the steeple. "Hypocrites."

I was out of the pew and in the aisle now. I didn't remember taking the steps to get here, but the weight of my fury must have forced me forward, out of my seat and into the open. The organist leaned against a key in surprise before the instrument tinkled abruptly to silence, and the choir seized up, their mouths twisted in a ludicrous hymn that no one could hear.

"How could you?" I asked no one in particular. Or perhaps asked myself. "They need us. They've always needed us. But we didn't hear them."

All around me, heads drooped in shame. They knew I was right, these parents who loved their daughters, even if they did it all wrong.

I did have one unlikely ally, however. Across the room, someone else was standing up too. Adrian, trying to join me in my protest, trying to pretend he could make it right.

I shot him a glare that forced him back a step. Good. I didn't need him on my side. Not now, not when it was clear that his allegiances were as soft and useless as an undercooked egg.

The faces around me, once familiar, were all slack-jawed and twisted now.

"We have to help them," I said, and a thorn twisted deep inside me.

Them. The girls. The Rust Maidens. This was what we did. We stripped them of who they were. Everything about them, from the very start of this, was always impersonal. A snarl of generic files from the government. A mess of inoperable figures from the doctors' office. A curse on the lips of our fathers. All of us lumping the five of them together, because it was easier that way.

No. Not right now. Not to me. Not ever again.

My gaze searched the pews until I found Doctor Ross. Then I moved toward him. Just one step, just enough.

"Violet," I said, and though her father turned away at the sound of her name, it didn't matter. He heard me. He heard *her*.

A babble toward the back. Clint holding Eleanor, his face impassive, even bored. I glared at him until I caught his eye, and he sat frozen under my stare.

"Dawn," I said, and this one almost made me sob. This girl I'd hated. This girl I'd helped to condemn with the rest of the neighborhood.

Kathleen, so near that I could almost touch her. Her jaw set, she knew who was next.

"Lisa," I said, remembering that first night. The way Jacqueline and I had turned away because we didn't know what else to do. Maybe it was too late to stop this even then, but I'd never know that for sure. That choice had slipped away from me without my ever knowing it.

The preacher was straight in front of me, wanting to stop me, wanting to do something other than be the useless dupe he always was. I moved toward him and had to hold myself back from hurting him. But I did hurt him, with just one word.

"Helena."

She wouldn't be forgotten, even if he wanted to.

And Aunt Betty, next to my father. Always so close to me,

227

yet a world away. Her eyes swirled with rage, acrylic nails digging into the pew. But I wouldn't stop, not until I said it.

"Jacqueline."

My eyes blurred, but I couldn't let the congregation see it. I couldn't let them witness me fall to pieces.

With my heart in my throat, I turned and marched away, toward the double doors in the back. Toward the closest thing to freedom I could come by these days—someplace away from here.

In this, I expected to be alone. I wasn't. The rush of movement behind me was a whirlwind, the brush of Sunday lace against the slick of the pews, and the squeaks of newly shined shoes on the hardwood floors. Everything was moving at once. My knees weak, I bit down hard and didn't look back. All the resolve in me would melt to nothing if I didn't keep going.

When I was on the lawn, the grass wet with humidity, I finally glanced over my shoulder. Adrian had followed me, as had Kathleen. My parents came as well, and other parents too. Helena's mother, and behind her, half the congregation was leaving the church.

I wasn't the only one on the girls' side. I was just the only one brave enough to say it aloud. The one who said it first.

We could still help them. If we were together in this, we could prove to the girls that they didn't have to hide. Jacqueline might not be lost to me yet.

I started toward the mansion, but Adrian caught up with me first.

"We have until tomorrow," he said. "If you could reach them before then, I can request an extension."

I nodded and wondered if it wasn't too late.

But then Kathleen was suddenly standing with us too, pink-faced and breathless. "They're coming."

I stared at her. "Who is?"

She shuddered. "The rest of the neighbors. The ones who didn't walk out with us. They blame the girls."

"For what?" I asked, my hands twisted into fists.

"For everything," she said. "Especially the mill closing. And they aren't waiting any longer. They're getting them out of the mansion today. By any means necessary."

I choked down a breath. "Who's saying this?"

"Your aunt." Kathleen looked at me, so much sorrier than I even knew she could be. "It's Betty, Phoebe. She's the one leading them."

Of course she was. I turned back toward the end of the street. Here she came, commanding a horde right down the middle of the road, not caring if traffic needed to pass. What they wanted was all that mattered now. These concerned neighbors, and the last of the tourists, too. Jeffers and Godfrey at the tail end, their dark glasses obscuring their eyes, the same as when they'd arrived.

I held my breath and watched them in their chevron formation.

One that was moving straight for the mansion.

EIGHTEEN

The two factions had formed. The neighbors who were with us, and those who were against us, the ones who wanted to extract the girls against their will, as though it would be easy, no different than peeling worms off the asphalt. We met at the end of Denton Street, in front of the mansion the girls called home. Along with Adrian and Kathleen, I huddled with my parents and Helena's mother, who did her best to comfort the half of the congregation that had followed her. But that wasn't easy, especially when her own husband was against us.

Flanked by the smattering of followers he had left, the preacher parted the crowd and went after his wife, seizing her gruffly by the arm.

"Go home, Rachel," he said to her, almost cooing the words as he tightened his grip on her. "Take your pill and sleep it off."

She jerked away from him and laughed in his face. "I warned

you it would come to this," she said. "I told you I'd choose her."

The preacher's wife, lonely and missing Helena, all the while quietly crafting her own rebellion. I imagined her hand at midnight, holding a bottle of red spray paint at the abandoned mill. After all, who else would expect us to pray for the girls?

Nearby, Betty was pleading with my father.

"You can't do this," she said. "You can't think it's okay to leave them in there."

"And *you* can't honestly think it's okay to go after them like this." My father shook his head and pulled my mother and me closer to him. "Betty, this isn't the right way."

She fell back a step, and her face went gray. That was it, the thing that injured her worst of all. My father finally choosing sides, and not choosing her.

Something in her eyes went wild, and Aunt Betty sneered at me. "Whatever happens now," she seethed, "it's on you, Phoebe. You're the one who led them here. Now you'll watch as we get them out."

She turned away and marched toward the mansion. At least a dozen parents followed her. They traced the front of the property, kicking at the mortared stone, testing it for weaknesses, convinced their collective willpower was enough to bring it down. And they were probably right. This place was as decayed as the girls, and given the shape it was in, it wasn't safe to be standing even this close.

"Please don't," I said, and rushed at them, flailing and shoving and doing my best to break through their blockade, to stop them from whatever they were planning. But there were too many of them. They just pushed me back toward the street.

"We have to do something," I said to Adrian.

He shook his head. "I don't know what will help at this point."

"Please try," I said. "We don't have much time."

He nodded and slipped away from me, his body cutting through the crowd like a knife. Toward the front of the mansion. Toward where Jeffers and Godfrey had joined the others, still clad in those dark glasses.

I moved closer too, straining to hear their voices.

"This is getting out of hand," Adrian said. "We have to stop them."

But Jeffers and Godfrey shook their heads.

"We need to get the girls out," one of them said. "If their parents do that part for us, all the better."

Adrian moved forward another step. "The crowd could kill them."

Jeffers or Godfrey—or maybe it was both—shrugged. "For all we know, they might already be dead. We've got our orders. Take them back to DC in the morning, whatever condition they're in."

Adrian's shoulders broadened. "I don't care about orders. I won't risk hurting them."

Jeffers and Godfrey smiled, their faces sharpening with shadows. "Then you won't be an agent anymore."

It was a flurry of movement now, words lobbed back and forth, and a fist thrown this way and that. Adrian struck one of them—probably Jeffers—in the face, and Godfrey retaliated. Only he shoved Adrian farther into the crowd, knocking a tourist over. Cursing and spitting, the tourist scrambled to his feet and returned the favor, throwing a punch at whoever was nearest. A father, it looked like. Maybe Doctor Ross, I couldn't tell. Whoever it was, he heaved the tourist out of his path and into a circle of housewives.

Then it all tore loose. Thrashing arms and high-pitched screams and everyone fighting each other. Mothers who'd always agreed, or at least mostly agreed, now spitting and clawing and punching the same as their husbands. Tourists with no grudges, who didn't even know each other, coming away with bloodied knuckles and bruised eyes.

Nearby, a stranger grabbed a fistful of my hair, and my mother pried the man off me, only for someone to grab hold of her and pull her away. My father went after her, and yanked the person off my mother, but the two of them had already crashed away from me like a lifeboat in the fog.

"Phoebe," my mother called, but she was too far across the dozens of empty faces for me to reach.

In the middle of it all, Jeffers and Godfrey had Adrian pinned on the cement and were trying to handcuff him. They'd already taken his badge. He was nothing to them now. But too many bodies crashed together around them, and they couldn't quite keep hold of him.

When the preacher smashed into them, kicking Jeffers just for the fun of it, Adrian broke away. In the uproar, they didn't chase him down. There was enough else to keep them occupied. They tried to pull the tourists and fathers and mothers off each other, but they were only two agents, and not very good ones at that.

His face bruised, Adrian pushed his way through the throng to me, as I fought off another tourist.

"I'm sorry, Phoebe," Adrian said, and meant it, the best he could mean anything right now. But this had all gotten away from us. The parents were at every window, every door. I tried to push my way across the lawn, but their bodies were wild and flailing and I fell backward into the dirt. Some wanted to hurt the girls, some wanted to save the girls, but none of it was good.

"Lisa, where are you?" Kathleen wept. "Baby!"

"Violet, please!" Doctor Ross's voice. "You can take your pictures. Whatever damn pictures you want."

And then someone else, though it was hard to make out who it was. A mother, perhaps. Clint's mother. "We'll get those girls. We'll show them how a real parent punishes."

I started to say something to Adrian, something that could get us out of this, some way to keep this crowd from tearing that house open and crushing the girls.

But then everything in the world was blotted out by the sound of the roaring ocean.

Not an ocean, though. It was water all right, but it came from the ground. Somebody had twisted open the fire hydrant, and it was pointed directly at the mansion.

"Drown 'em out," a voice called, a voice that sounded like Betty's. "Those girls will come to us on their own."

The resultant streams cascaded down the front of the mansion like thick tears. Glass cracked under the power of the water, so heavy and unforgiving. Weighing down the walls and the hidden rust inside. Weighing down everything. Bit by bit, the mansion bowed under the water. The walls had already been buckling from the decay the girls had honeycombed over all the windows. The parents didn't know this. They didn't know this mansion was halfway to collapse already. Now the water would bring it down the rest of the way.

"I have to get them out," I said, and I was suddenly running—across the sidewalk, through the people, and straight to the house. Adrian was yelling behind me, but I didn't listen.

The crowd parted this time, mostly because no one wanted to get too close to the water. It was so heavy, pelting the façade like fists.

I kept going, away from the water, around to the back, and in through the door that had already given way.

Inside, it was no longer hopelessly dark. Through fissures in the cracking walls, bits of daylight poured in. The water came too, seeping in at every turn, through the collapsing roof and the broken-out windows.

"Dawn? Lisa? Helena?" My voice, not sounding like mine. Too manic, too strained, as if it was about to collapse as well. "Violet? *Jacqueline?*"

I searched everywhere I could, even as the house moaned. It seemed to be following me, the plaster and wallpaper peeling off like flesh. It was coming down, and I couldn't stop it, but still I searched, trying to find the girls. But there was no one here, at least no one visible.

Upstairs, the master bedroom was empty too, as was the darkroom, where there were no more pictures. Just hollow bins where Kathleen's chemicals used to be.

I scrambled back downstairs to search again, but this time, the staircase couldn't take my weight. It splintered and collapsed under me. I screamed out and fell the rest of the way down.

When I lifted my head, I was on the floor, my bare legs bloodied, red pinstripes running down my calves. Pain seared through me as I struggled to get to my feet.

Then, a hand in the shadows, trying to help me up. Adrian's hand, I assumed at first, but then the fingers went right through mine. Like they weren't there at all.

"Hello?" I said, but my voice was lost in the symphony of water.

I waited, still half-dazed from the fall. Out of the corner of my eye, I caught movement at the back door.

"Jacqueline?" I couldn't breathe. "Where are you?"

But there was nothing. Not until I heard Adrian's voice.

"Phoebe?"

"Here," I almost whispered.

Breathless, Adrian found me, his eyes wild. "Are you okay?" He took my arm to steady me. "Can you walk?"

I leaned on him until I regained my balance. It wasn't like I had a choice. Overhead, the roof lurched, and the sound like a restless child moaning set my skin on edge. From every crack-ing corner, daylight poured into the house, pushing its way into this place where it didn't belong. The outside world was getting in, and all I wanted was to get out. But only if I found Jacque-line and the other girls. I wouldn't leave them behind.

"I can't go," I said. "Not yet."

"We can't stay here, Phoebe." Adrian held my hand tight and guided me toward the door. But we were too late, because it no longer existed. Where the back entrance used to be, plaster, piled waist-high, was now blocking the way. We had to go out the front or not at all.

"Come on," Adrian said, and pulled me away as the kitchen walls caved toward us.

Down the hallway and into the foyer, we tried the front door, but it wouldn't budge.

"Back up," Adrian said, as he reached for something on the floor and tossed it toward the window. It wasn't until the object was halfway through that I recognized what it was. One of the girls' carapaces. We were tossing the remnants of them out the window. This seemed all wrong, but it gave us a way out. I didn't think they'd deny us that.

The house swayed, almost too late. But I didn't want to leave. I didn't want to abandon them. They might still be inside.

I turned back, my gaze lifted toward the ceiling. "If we could just search once more—"

I moved toward the dining hall, but Adrian was faster than me. He grabbed me around the waist and yanked me outside, just as the whole place gave way. Floorboards and drywall and an opulent chandelier that was always too gaudy for its own good. One piece after another, cascaded into the basement, into the darkness. To somewhere that might as well have been another world.

Wheezing, we collapsed in the front yard, the water still spilling down from the sky, saturating our clothes and choking us at the same time.

Behind us, the mansion was nothing but a mountain of rubble. Pieces of it had collapsed into the lawn and onto the street. Hundreds of shingles and splinters of wooden siding had tumbled against Clint's house next door, breaking out windows, dust caking everything.

All at once, Denton Street went suddenly quiet. The water continued streaming from the fire hydrant, but I could no longer hear it. All I could do was stare at everyone's faces. The parents stood there on the sidewalk, the ones who had been for the girls, and the ones against. They were united in something now, their cheeks colorless and drooping mouths twisted in horror. Even among the worst of them, this wasn't in their plans. They didn't mind the notion of hurting the Rust Maidens, slapping their wayward faces or yanking them out of the mansion by the hair they no longer had. They were okay with their daughters screaming in protest, coming home tired and angry and bruised. But this—the utter decimation of it—wasn't what they had in mind. They wanted girls they could punish, not girls they would bury. Or, in this case, ones that had been buried for them.

Aunt Betty took a step forward, her whole body quivering. Then with all the power left in her lungs, she cried out Jacqueline's name. At the last moment, she understood.

As I limped across the lawn, no one would look at me. They could barely look at each other after what they'd done. Somewhere in the crowd, my parents called my name, but when I gazed out into the mass of sobbing faces, I couldn't find them. Maybe they were lost in the din. Or maybe I was staring right at the both of them, but I simply didn't recognize them now. Nothing here made sense anymore.

Adrian had broken away from me to argue more with Jeffers and Godfrey, to insist this was all their fault. Not that fault mattered at this point. The girls were gone, either way.

Panting, I dragged myself onto the sidewalk, everything in me shivering and so sorry that I could barely stand.

My feet moved slowly, and I watched them, part of me convinced I was no longer real, no longer in this moment. It wasn't until I reached the other side of the crumbled mansion that I saw it. Something that should have been erased by the water, but hadn't been. A shape traced into the mud by that invisible hand.

A triple moon.

My throat tightened with a strange kind of hope. They'd gotten out in time. The girls had gotten out.

And I already knew right where they were headed.

But I couldn't leave for the mill, not yet, not when I looked up, the only one in the uproar who saw it. The stream from the fire hydrant wasn't pointing at what was left of the mansion anymore. Someone must have tried to twist it off again, but gave up when they couldn't quite manage it alone. They didn't notice that the water was now spewing against the house next door. Clint's house. A first-floor window had shattered, maybe from the water, maybe from the debris of the collapsing mansion. Either way, I heard her inside. Those strangled cries.

Eleanor. She was abandoned in there, where the water kept coming, unforgiving and uninvited.

The crowd, still arguing, still dangerous and confused, closed in around me, but I slithered between them, even as they pulsed closer, doing their best to suffocate everything on the street. Some of the parents hollered like fools, others sobbed, inconsolable at what they'd done. What we'd all done.

I left them behind. Up the porch stairs and past that milk crate where Eleanor had babbled only weeks ago. Somehow, the baby was safer then.

With all my weight, I shoved the front door open and searched the house. Inside, there were no more cries, no sound at all except that water, still flowing in where it didn't belong.

The nursery waited at the end of the hall. The door was closed, but liquid leaked under it. All this water, drowning everything. Drowning her. I threw open the door. The room was filled with bits of fallen debris from the mansion, everything wet and gray. All the larger pieces had missed Eleanor, but not the water. It had saturated her cradle. With my hands shielding my face, I rushed in and lifted her from the unlikely grave. This baby, this troublesome little baby who wasn't going to cause anyone trouble anymore.

Falling back into the hallway, my own weight too much, her weight too much, all of it too much. Eleanor's face was blue, and she wasn't breathing. This tiny thing in my arms was no different than a paper bag of groceries, or a pile of garbage destined for the curb. Nothing in her living. She was lost to me.

On the hardwood floor, I placed her on her back, my hands wet and useless. I didn't know what to do next. I didn't know how to fix her, or if she even could be fixed.

"Eleanor." I pressed on her small chest, again and again, convinced I'd crush every one of her ribs, but not knowing any other way. "It's okay. Come back. Please come back."

But she wouldn't come back. She stayed gone, just like her mother, just like all of the Rust Maidens. We'd lose everything tonight, and there was nothing I could do about it.

"Eleanor," I whispered and lifted her again, this time draping her over my shoulder, and patting her soft back, over and over, each time a little bit harder until I was sure I'd shake everything in her loose.

But it worked. She choked in my arms, her pale lips in the shape of an O, gasping like the last dying fish in Lake Erie.

"That's it," I said and pulled her so close to me that I thought we both might suffocate.

The water leaked further into the hall, threatening to destroy us yet. I had to get us out of here. I had to get us to the girls.

Back on the street, there was no Clint to take his only child. I couldn't trust him, anyhow. I couldn't trust any of them to care for her in the ruckus. I wouldn't have had to rescue her in the first place if they were up to protecting her.

I crossed my arms over Eleanor so they couldn't see that I had her. She'd come with me, to find her mother and the other girls.

Through the crowd, my head down, I rushed off with her, past faces both familiar and unfamiliar.

"Phoebe!" Adrian somewhere nearby, already sensing I knew something. That I knew where to go. His gaze followed me, followed my direction as I ran across the backyards. Toward the steel mill.

He called my name again, but I didn't look back. I ran, Eleanor nuzzling against me. Quiet, as if she understood. As if she knew the only way we could reach her mother was if we were both smart and silent.

The rusted chain-link fence was peeled back at the corner. They were already inside. My throat went dry, and I feared I was too late. They could be gone. This could all be for nothing.

But I had to try.

They were in the center of the mill when I found them. The five of them, their misshapen silhouettes stark against the daylight. Their backs were to me, blending into the rot of this town, and it was a struggle to keep them straight, which one was which. It shouldn't be hard to recognize my best friend, but it was, and that made my chest ache with a sorrow I couldn't comprehend.

What I did know for certain: they were ready. The transformation was complete. Nothing could change that, and nothing could change that they had to be here. The cold furnace in the center of the factory awaited the girls, this place that had given our lives form all these years. It had given our fathers purpose. Now it gave the girls purpose too. The blooming decay was like them, and they understood that. They belonged here. They belonged in these spaces that others wanted to discard. Spaces they wouldn't forget.

"Don't go," I said, and together, they turned toward me. Even looking straight at them, their forms were obscure, shifting like an illusion. I kept looking, kept trying to understand what they'd become. Scraps of rusted metal jutted out from their knees and elbows and shoulder blades, and the glitter of glass shimmered across their naked bodies. But somehow, past the gray pewter of their cheekbones and their long hair slick with crude oil and seaweed, their faces still had the shape of them, as though the same girls we knew were hidden somewhere in there. Eyes wide and dark and unblinking, they saw me now. Jacqueline saw me.

Dawn saw me too, and saw Eleanor. At the sight of the baby, she brightened for a moment. It was so strange to see it, the way for an instant she just looked like a girl, too young to be a mother, but one nonetheless.

When we were close enough, Eleanor reached out for Dawn's finger, the same way she had in the mansion, but there was nothing for her to grab. The girls were no longer flesh and blood. They were made of things too insubstantial to hold, water and rust and shadow.

Dawn shook her head sadly and tried to coo to her baby, but Eleanor just bleated out a cry that could cut a heart in two.

It didn't matter. Dawn couldn't stay. She turned away, tears of gray water running down what was left of her face.

The girls joined hands. They couldn't hold us, but they could hold each other. This was the way it had to be.

I wanted to go with them. I wanted to be one of them. But I wasn't. This summer had taught me that much. My arms quivering, I held Eleanor tighter to me, her eyes wet and red and desperate, an infant who knew beyond reason that she was about to lose her mother.

The girls looked at the door to the blast furnace, and then Jacqueline looked back at me.

"Phoebe," she whispered, her voice a gentle whir like a distant forge. Like she was already too far away to reach. "Could you help us?"

"How?" I asked, staring at her, and then at last, I understood.

This door. It was new, not rotted out like the rest of the mill. They couldn't touch the things that weren't like them. If they wanted to go into the heart of the factory, they'd need someone to help them.

I heaved out a sob. "You can't possibly ask me for this."

"But you're the only one I can ask, Phoebe," Jacqueline said. "You're the only one who would do this for us."

I stood there, staring at her, staring at my best friend. I could say no. I could deny them this. But all they wanted—all I wanted for them—was to be able to choose. And this was their choice. The one thing I could give them.

With Eleanor held tight across my chest with one arm, I cried out with everything in me as I swung open the door. Rot and rust and the future waited within.

"Thank you," Jacqueline said.

The girls went toward the darkness, and already I could see it was eager to devour them. Or maybe the girls were eager to devour it.

As the rest of them wavered between this moment and whatever came next, Jacqueline turned and watched me quietly.

"Goodbye, Phoebe," she whispered.

With the weight of my whole life bearing down, I gritted my teeth and turned my face away.

I wouldn't say it back. I wouldn't bid her farewell.

But it didn't stop her, either. Nothing could do that now.

Together, as one, the Rust Maidens moved toward the darkness and decay. I watched them go, desperate to invent the right words to stop them. But there were no words. There was nothing that could change this. It was as fated as the sunrise.

Sirens blared in the distance, and a shivering Eleanor sobbed helplessly in my arms, her body so small and heavy.

One by one, starting with Lisa, the girls fused into the rust that made them. Their bodies contorted into the shadows and metal, popping and writhing in ways that made my own bones ache. But the girls didn't cry out. Instead, they smiled. Their fingers and arms went first, the glass cracking through the steel, and then their legs and torsos twisted into the dark until only their faces remained. Even once their lips and ears and cheeks melded into the furnace, I swore I could still see those eyes looking out at me, dark and strange and somewhere too distant to fathom.

Jacqueline was last. I wanted to call her name, but I couldn't. I couldn't say anything at all.

At the heart of the blast furnace, she looked back once. As the darkness consumed her, she smiled at me and, in spite of myself, I smiled back. It was the most beautiful and horrible thing I'd ever seen, watching her become all that she was meant to be.

I blinked into the shadows, and she was gone. Away from the mill. Away from this city. Away from me.

And for the first time in my life, I was truly alone.

NINETEEN

All of the girls are here in Jacqueline's bedroom, a never-ending slumber party. In the peeling paint, I catch a glimpse of Dawn, eyes lonely no more, her body her own at last. A leak in the roof *plink-plunks* in the corner, and Lisa grins out of every droplet. If I squint hard enough at the blades of the overhead fan, sagging and yellowed and crumbling with time, Violet and Helena are there, hand in hand.

They're everywhere and nowhere. As big as a shadow draping the wall, or as small as an antique thimble. Their faces flash in and out on the trim, the plaster, the cobwebs.

It's no wonder they can live in this house. There isn't a clean spot in the whole place, everything peeling and warped and long past its prime. On the wall hangs a brass swing lamp, corroded and limp on its hinges. Next to a disintegrating mattress is the vanity table, cracked and gray and covered with rotting emery boards and rusted cuticle scissors and bent tweezers like the ones I used while trying and failing to save Jacqueline from herself. Shattered eye shadows and smears of lipstick and a dark puddle of old perfume, still vaguely sticky, array the shag carpet. Deterioration anywhere and everywhere it can find a space to live.

Behind me, in the hallway, a figure wavers back and forth. Not a Rust Maiden this time. It's my aunt, her face gray and her body so much smaller than I remember. In a half-mad state, she's let the entire house devolve. This is a form of bewitchery, of conjuring decay like she's calling to the dead. Her way of saying she's sorry. It's also her way of trying to reach her daughter. The one she lost. The one she betrayed.

And she's done a good job. Her daughter is here, after all.

She comes to me last, as though it's a game. But I can feel her, swirling in every crevice. Jacqueline. She smiles out at me, though it's almost difficult to call it that. How does the dust from a shadow smile? But that's what she's doing. It's what all of them are doing.

I drop to the floor next to her, and here I am, sitting with my best friend. We're together again. With melancholy half-choking me, I tell her all about my life, how I ran from this place after she vanished. How for the past thirty years, I've never stopped running, even when I was standing still, doing nothing, being nothing.

I tell her that I hate her and love her and miss her with every iota of my heart.

That I hope she forgives me.

That I hope she doesn't think I need to be forgiven. That I did my best, even if I failed to keep her here with me.

Jacqueline listens and laughs and tells me it's all okay. Her voice is a rhapsody of everything I left behind—an industrial lullaby, the waves at midnight, a city that's forgotten but never forgets.

This is what I need. What I've always needed. And it's what she needs too, one more moment together.

Then I ask her for something. A request she doesn't have to grant.

"Let Quinn go," I say. "Give her the chance that you didn't

have. That *we* didn't have."

All five girls materialize before me, their shapes more de-
fined now in the decay, and it's a dizzying sight. Helena and
Violet giggling together. Dawn singing her lullabies, the ones
she still hums in secret to her daughter. Lisa twirling in the
shadows, babbling nonsense. And Jacqueline, gazing at me and
seeing me in a way no one else ever can.

They hear me, and somehow, beyond words, I'm sure they
say yes. They're a force of nature, but not a cruel one. And every
cycle needs to be broken. Even they know that.

"Thank you," I whisper.

Nearby, Aunt Betty moves like a ghost through the shadows.
She passes me, undisturbed at the invader in her space, the one
she used to chase out every chance she got. I wonder if she remembers me. I wonder if she remembers anything.

I asked the girls to save Quinn, and now I have to try to save
someone too. I clamber to my feet and follow my aunt down
the hall. With her body hunched and weak, she barely looks up
at me, but I look at her.

"Come with me," I whisper. "Don't stay here like this."

Even after everything, she deserves better. She deserves to
extract herself from this withered house, to cobble together
what's left of her life.

But she shakes her head.

"You go," she says, and clasps my hands in hers. "I stay."

A long moment passes, an eternity that aches deep in my
bones.

Then a glimmer in her face shifts, and Aunt Betty looks into
my eyes and gives me a smile that might as well be a sob.

"I'm sorry, Phoebe," she says. "You know that, right?"

Everything twists inside me, a jumble of what was and what
won't ever be, and I nod, my eyes blurred. Before I can say a
word, she untangles her hands from mine and drifts back into
the shadow, back into the decay of her life. She disappears before my eyes, a Rust Maiden, one that's lost and living and all
her own.

I hesitate and wait, until I know it for sure: that I'm done here. Part of me wishes I wasn't, that I could stay forever, but that's not the way this works.

I move away from the dark and toward the stairs. At the last moment, I seize up. There's one more thing. The word blossoms in my throat, and I say what I should have said to Jacqueline twenty-eight years ago.

"Goodbye."

It's so simple, but it's right too. The whole house quivers in reply, a giggle in the walls that sounds like the flow of a river, and the sparks from steel heat, and the strange and lonely pang of freedom.

Jacqueline ripples in the shadows, and I watch her quietly. Her face is arcane to me now, but somehow, she looks like herself. A girl, the one I remember. Finally, with a grin, she disappears. Back to where she belongs and where I can't follow. Exactly the way it has to be.

I smile at the places she's been. Then I walk down the steps to the front door and back out into the world.

Another house down the block tumbles, and the foreman yells commands back and forth. I glance back at the notices tacked on the door. Some are from the construction crew. Some are from the city. They know Aunt Betty is inside. Someone will come for her soon. Then they'll take down this house along with all the rest, and among the decay, this will be the girls' neighborhood again. They'll belong more than we do. They always did.

A gust off the lake cuts down the block, and I pull up my collar. What I'd always believed was wrong. I didn't fail Jacqueline. I let her go. That's what she wanted, and in the last moments all those years ago, I helped her do that.

I need to help someone else do that too.

Quinn's house waits at the end of the street. I knock on the front door, and she answers. Her eyes are brighter than last night, and though a ragged bandage is still on her arm, the wound is no longer weeping or glinting or doing anything at all. It just looks like a scratch, plain and simple.

"This is for you." I pass her the withered envelope my mother gave me this morning. "If you have any trouble cashing it in, let me know."

She stares at me, confused that I'm back and that I'm giving something to her, a girl who's been given nothing in life. Her fingers fumble with the envelope, and with her lips pursed, she peeks inside.

"Phoebe," she whispers. "This is too much."

I smile. She doesn't know yet that it's worth triple that amount, but I don't tell her. Let it be a surprise.

"Get out of here," I say. "Before it's too late."

Quinn looks up at me. "Where will I go?"

"Anywhere you want." I breathe deeply to steady myself. "You can come back, too. Cleveland will be waiting for you."

It has a tendency to do that. To wait for those of us who left to find it again.

"Thank you," she whispers, and I squeeze her hand before turning away.

That bond money won't last her forever, and it's certainly not all the answers in the world. But it's a chance. It's a choice. That's what the girls needed back then, and it's what Quinn needs now.

Down the street, I look up at my old bedroom window. A shadow moves past the moth-eaten curtains. Someone's in my house. Not a ghost, though. For the first time, I'm sure of that.

The front door is still unlocked, and I go inside and climb the stairs. I find him there. Adrian, sorting through the pictures and diaries I abandoned in this room that's no longer mine. My mother must have phoned and told him that I left all my artifacts behind, things he could use for the museum.

When I walk in, he glances up at me, his face wan. "Hello," he says.

I crouch next to him, and my fingers graze the edge of a Polaroid. Jacqueline smiles up at me, and I smile back. Then I turn to Adrian.

"I'm not working for you," I say. "But I'll work *with* you. On the monument for the girls."

He stares at me a moment. "Okay," he says finally. "Do you have an idea for it?"

"I do." I turn to the last page in my never-finished diary, and with an old, mostly dull pencil, I sketch it out for him. A crude drawing, but it works.

"It's a butterfly house," I say as he examines it quietly. "That's what should go there."

One in the shape of a triple moon. Jacqueline's sign to me. This is what she and I should have always had. A sanctuary for us and for others like us, all those things that frighten everyone else.

Adrian traces over the drawing with his fingertips. "This will work," he says, and smiles.

And that's it. It's that simple. Me with a job in Cleveland, working at Case Western all these years after I should have been a graduate.

I'll stay here in this city. For now. Once the monument is done, I don't know what will happen. Maybe I'll leave again, or maybe I'll stick around and tend to the butterflies. They'll need someone. I'll need someone too.

This afternoon, I'll go to Sweet Evergreen, to find my mother and tell her what comes next. I hope she didn't expect our farewell this morning to last too long. If so, she'll be disappointed.

But first, I make one more stop.

Bayton Beach is colder than I remember it. A little cleaner, too. Not sparkling, of course, but not as terrible as when I came here with Jacqueline. The girls are still here in the city, but they haven't poisoned this place. None of this decay is their fault. If anything, they're the ones fighting it, the ones who want to see it all turned around. That means the transformations won't repeat themselves. That others won't fall to the same fortune. Those five girls will be here no matter what. That's their fate, and their choice.

I sit back on the shore and watch the waves come in. No

algae is blooming. The lake is quiet and blue and ours.

A shuffling in the sand, and then someone's standing over me.

"Thought I'd find you here." Eleanor plops down next to me, her breath fogging in front of her like smoke. I smile and shake my head. She knows me better than I give her credit for. This was a place I used to go, somewhere that reminds me of Jacqueline. She wanted to find me, and this is where she knew to come. This kicked-aside girl, more astute than anyone realizes.

"Quinn told me what you did for her," Eleanor says. "Do you think it will help?"

"I hope so," I say.

Eleanor plucks a piece of broken glass from the sand. "I hope so too."

We gaze together at the skyline. Far off, the clouds swirl with a storm that might come in. Or it might not. We'll have to wait and find out.

Only I can't wait anymore. I'm suddenly saying something, the words tumbling out of me.

"I helped them," I say. "The girls. That last night, I helped them leave us."

This confession I've ached to make. Here it is, spoken to the only person left who was there too.

Eleanor is quiet for a long time, and I'm sure she hates me. I'm sure she'll always hate me now.

"Is it what they wanted?" she asks at last.

"Yes," I whisper.

She nods. "Then it's not your fault, Phoebe," she says, and I finally believe it.

"Your mother loved you," I say. "She still loves you, Eleanor."

Despite the cold, her face reddens. "I know." She pulls her legs tight into her chest. "I mean, I figured that."

She won't look at me. She won't admit how much she wanted to hear it. How much that's all she's needed all these years. Now I've given it to her, that first kernel of truth, and I'll give her so much more. I'll tell her anything. Whatever she wants to know will be hers. What her mother was like before the transformation. What her father was like, fool that he is. How the Rust Maidens became what they were and are and will always be. I'll tell her more about that last day too, with her blue in the cradle, and the girls vanishing from us. But Eleanor doesn't ask, not right now. We have all the time for it, and she understands that. So we sit together, boots buried in the dirty sand, watching the end of the day settle over Cleveland.

A faraway loneliness tightens in my chest, and I want to tell her I'm sorry. For leaving this city and the girls behind. For abandoning her that summer when I knew she'd need someone.

But I don't say that. I say something else instead.

"I'll race you to the sun."

She turns to me, her eyebrows twisted, and I almost start to explain what I mean, how this is what Jacqueline and I used to do, the way we'd run and pretend we would never stop.

But then she exhales a sly laugh, and she's off, already ten leaps ahead of me. I'm up on my feet too. We're both running, sand kicking up, broken glass shattering beneath us. Headed down the beach into whatever lies ahead.

And we don't look back.

Gwendolyn Kiste is the author of the Bram Stoker Award-
nominated *And Her Smile Will Untether the Universe*, her
debut fiction collection available from JournalStone, as
well as the dark fantasy novella, *Pretty Marys All in a Row*,
from Broken Eye Books. Her short fiction has appeared
in *Nightmare Magazine, Shimmer, Black Static, Daily
Science Fiction, Interzone*, and *LampLight*, among other
publications. A native of Ohio, she resides on an abandoned
horse farm outside of Pittsburgh with her husband, two
cats, and not nearly enough ghosts. You can find her online
at gwendolynkiste.com.

Printed in November 2022
by Rotomail Italia S.p.A., Vignate (MI) - Italy